LIEUTENANT STANLEY DINKLE, UNITED STATES CAVALRY, GAPED IN AMAZEMENT....

He saw two Model T touring cars, obviously new. The wheel spokes, headlamps and radiators twinkled in the sun.

The tops were down, and each Ford carried a complement of three soldiers, two in front and one in the tonneau, the latter almost lost in a mound of baggage.

To the right-hand upright of each windshield, a white polo mallet was lashed like a flag standard. To its end was tied, in lieu of a guidon, a pair of lady's bloomers.

"Thunder and damnation," said Stanley Dinkle.

THE TIN LIZZIE TROOP
was originally published by
Doubleday & Company, Inc.

Books by Glendon Swarthout

Willow Run
They Came to Cordura
Where the Boys Are
Welcome to Thebes
The Cadillac Cowboys
The Eagle and the Iron Cross
Loveland*
Bless the Beasts and Children*
The Tin Lizzie Troop*

*Published by POCKET BOOKS

GLENDON SWARTHOUT

The Tin Lizzie Troop

PUBLISHED BY POCKET BOOKS NEW YORK

THE TIN LIZZIE TROOP

Doubleday edition published June, 1972

POCKET BOOK edition published August, 1973

This POCKET BOOK edition includes every word contained in the original, higher-priced edition. It is printed from brand-new plates made from completely reset, clear, easy-to-read type. POCKET BOOK editions are published by POCKET BOOKS, a division of Simon & Schuster, Inc., 630 Fifth Avenue, New York, N.Y. 10020.

L

Standard Book Number: 671-78302-5.
Library of Congress Catalog Card Number: 71-184918.

This POCKET BOOK edition is published by arrangement with Doubleday & Company, Inc.

Printed in the U.S.A. Cover art by Robert Schulz.

for JOHN MCGREEVEY: *we ride together*

Author's Note

John O'Hara has observed that "The 1916 Mexican Border campaign was the nearest thing we ever had to a gentlemen's war." So it was. Between the Villa raid upon Columbus, New Mexico, in March, and the attack at Glenn Springs, Texas, in May, almost 100,000 National Guardsmen were mobilized to defend us, including a few blue-blood, fancy-Dan detachments from the effete East. It was upon the society of these young gents that bandits intruded at Glenn Springs. Their response to such bad manners deserves to be recorded. Rambunctious and damnfool, it was also mechanized, hence historic—it mounted the American Mars on wheels.

The Tin Lizzie Troop *is fiction cut out of* Cavalry Journal *leather and the microfilms of faded newspapers. The names of real persons and units have been pruned to spare still-sturdy family trees. If the reader finds it incredible, as I do, he is advised to cross the border into the state of Coahuila, to the town of Caballo del Dios, as I did, and see for himself what is in the plaza. There he will gape at something which, on display today, fifty-six years later, is even more incredible.*

HENRY FORD: *"History is bunk."*

Contents

The Tin Lizzie Troop

1

The Philadelphia Light Horse Report to Fort Dinkle

"Damnation," said Stanley Dinkle.

It had taken him half an hour to compose the sentence, and he had just read it aloud. He read it again, listening. " 'The perfect service mount must possess good teeth, good digestion, a good appetite, soundness, size, and strength to carry his burden easily, legs long enough to maintain regulation gaits without overexertion, and good proportions.' " He heard the word "good" four times and the derision of the Rio Grande and laughter in the leaves of the pecan trees.

Oiling the tip of his pencil stub with his tongue, he changed "good proportions" to "beautiful proportions" and read the sentence again.

"Damnation," he said. He could never get away with an adjective as flowery as "beautiful." He groaned, and after some cogitation, and after scratching a mosquito bite on a shoulder with the pencil stub and one on an ankle with a big toe, and after twisting in his chair to the right oblique, then to the left oblique, by changing "beautiful proportions" to "fine proportions" he gave the entire sentence a more manly, even a military in his opinion, ring. Now he had a definition, a base of operations, and could continue. First things first.

Instead, he thumbed the pages of the April 1916 issue of the *Cavalry Journal,* the service quarterly published in Leavenworth, Kansas. There were articles on various subjects of interest to cavalrymen, including the first field notes from majors and captains chasing Villa with Pershing and the Punitive Expedition, plus advertisements for Blickensderfer typewriters, Capewell nails, Moet and Chandon champagne, Whittemore shoe polish, and Gurley engineering instruments. Champagne ha, he thought. Although he had never attempted anything more literary than a letter home, Stanley Dinkle was engaged in composing an article for submission to the *Journal* entitled "Selecting the Service Mount," a subject which, while not perhaps as engrossing as tactics and equitation, ought to be recognized by the editors as fundamental. Besides, it was the only theme upon which he dared to write. Horseflesh was his meat and mistress. And besides that, he had been a second lieutenant for eight years, and it had recently occurred to him that a contribution to the *Journal* bearing his name might suggest promotion to his superiors.

He put down the magazine. Resolutely he bent to task and table. If he could get another sentence, he would have two, and two, he assumed, would breed a third. It should be as simple as bringing a mare to a stallion—lock 'em up and let 'em go. He started a second, disapproved it, wadded the sheet of YMCA stationery, poked it into a hole in the screen, scribbled a few words, and repeated the process. Most of the holes in the screen were already stuffed with socks too darned to salvage and handkerchiefs too infirm for the nose. In breeches, bare feet, and BVD top he sat on the porch of a one-room adobe house painted by the previous tenants, unknown to him and long departed, a noble purple. It had been his home and depot for a month. It stored this bachelor inventory: chair, table, cot, cardboard suitcase, weapons, ammunition, clothing, rations, kerosene stove and lamp, a pot, a pan, and his immortal soul. Fifty yards below the door ran the Rio Grande, glazed by the sun. Since the river was thirty yards wide at this point, and the middle of the stream marked the international boundary, according to his calculations he was situated sixty-five yards inside the United States of America and sixty-five yards and any fraction of an inch from revolutionary Mexico. He was on the brink.

His problem, he decided, was that he didn't know what

in hoot he wanted to say. So he commenced a list under the heading "How to Tell a Plug," enumerating both the physical and temperamental defects of animals not up to service snuff. "Narrow chest; molars wearing," he jotted down. "Blind in left eye; loins long and weak; tucked up; rough trotter; parrot mouth; stumbler; cribber, chews picket line constantly; teeth and digestion not good as evidenced by amount of corn passing through whole."

I am off my trolley, thought Stanley Dinkle.

I wish they'd show up.

I hope Flossie Grebs don't.

I have got to quit thinking about sex.

Locating clean socks, he tugged on his boots and banged out the screen door and strode through the May heat into the cool of the grove to the picket line and fed his horse, Hassan, a handful of oats and tickled his ears and leaned against a pecan tree. His command of six men from the Keystone Lancers had decamped that morning for El Paso, their month's tour of duty ended. Good riddance to bad rubbish. He hoped the new batch, due any minute on assignment for another month, would be a better lot, men for a change, not boys, and from an ordinary, dirty-neck National Guard outfit.

I am lonesome. I am lonesomer, admitted Stanley Dinkle, than Woodrow Wilson in a whorehouse.

I am thirty-two years old and not getting any younger.

Returning to the porch, emplacing himself once more at his table, and finding his plug list dull as dishwater, he addressed himself to one headed "How Contractors Will Hornswoggle You If You Let Them," which registered the deceptions practiced by horse sharps attempting to foist inferior stock upon the government. "Blowing up a sweeneyed shoulder," he began, "doping with arsenic or lobelia to prevent detection of the heaves; doping with cocaine or gasoline for bone spavin; filling cavities above eyes with air because such cavities are very evident in old horses; freezing a bad joint with chloroform; pulling a rag wet with ammonia between the hind legs to force an animal to go wide if he is a brusher."

Rising, he put down the pencil, picked up the *Cavalry Journal,* and banged out the screen door. The bowels might be a bother at certain times, but at others they were a blessing. Striding round the house and down the slope towards the Rio Grande, he disappeared at its edge into a thick stand of river cane, the reeds green and ten feet high. Here, entering an outhouse painted pink, he disposed himself comfortably, and in this verdant bower passed a few minutes in perusal of his favorite magazine. One article in particular fascinated him. It was a short defense of the saber authored by a second lieutenant named George S. Patton, Jr. "Truly," wrote Patton, "a saberless cavalry in the face of the foe would be like a body without a soul. It is the saber, and the hope of some day fleshing it in an aggressive enemy, which gives to cavalry the dash and initiative which has made history on many a field, and has inscribed so many historic names on the scroll of fame. Can infantry produce such men as Murat, Seidlitz, Sheridan or Stuart? No!"

He thrilled. What he would give to pen a style as peppy as that, to roll out periods as balanced and sonorous as the cannonading of the sea. With the sentiment, however, he disagreed, albeit regretfully. Patton was right about cavalry "dash and initiative," wrong about the saber. If there was one thing an officer must be, it was up-to-date. He was. He prided himself on keeping up with the times, militarily speaking, on staying abreast of every new-fangled weapon and drill. And if there was one thing the U. S. Cavalry must soon face, it was the obsolescence of the saber as an instrument of warfare. The day of the automatic pistol had come, and he was ready for it. There were no flies on Lt. Stanley Dinkle. He remarked a note to the effect that Patton, whoever he might be, was at present on duty with the expeditionary forces in Mexico—lucky devil. Some men could have their cake and eat it, too, could turn out articles and be published and at the same time tear around Mexico mounted on gallant steeds doing gallant deeds, while others, equally meritorious, equally brave, were held prisoner with their pants down in a pink privy, their "scroll of fame" a Sears, Roebuck & Co. catalogue.

He couldn't imagine what he'd done to deserve this fate. In the two months since Villa's attack on Columbus, New Mexico, the War Department had mobilized 75,000 men and railroaded them to the border, and more thousands were on the way. From Vermont to California, from Oregon to Florida they had been called up, from forty-seven of the states, and now, by National Guard division and brigade and regiment they were camped from Dryden, Texas, to Yuma, Arizona, cussing and discussing and learning one end of a rifle from the other and marching up and down and comparing blisters and writing mournful letters home and whistling for a war to happen along, any war, to give them something useful to do. Only the cavalry units among them were functional. These had been cut up into six-man squads and stationed along the border at twenty-mile intervals to patrol it, a chore for which they were obviously better suited than infantry. And where was the real, the regular U. S. Cavalry while this semi-civilian fandango was being danced? It was in Chihuahua with Blackjack Pershing where it belonged, every splendid regiment of it but two, the 6th at Fort Riley, Kansas, his own, and the 8th, at Fort Bliss, acting as a "home guard," to which he'd been attached on temporary duty. And it was these unfortunate regiments which had been stripped of junior officers to tend and motherhen and spank into fighting trim the squads of National Guard pony boys at the patrol posts. Instead of being where Patton was, therefore, where most of the career men were, south of the border, he, Stanley Dinkle, sat twiddling his thumbs, sat quite literally on its lip. For the last month he had wet-nursed six of the Keystone Lancers, charming lads and dandy polo players. He waited now upon a second month's allotment and in the same breath cursed its coming. He despaired.

Emerging from his pagoda, he kicked the door shut and climbed to his house, his table, his one sentence and two lists. He reread them. The first list seemed to fit him to a T. His loins were weak. He was tucked up. He was a stumbler and a cribber, he chewed constantly at the picket lines of life.

I am a plug, thought Stanley Dinkle, slipping pleasantly into melancholia. I will never be a thoroughbred.

I remember a girl in Zamboanga had eyes like Smith Brothers cough drops and bubs like ice cream cones and made those bedsprings clang like a gong.

I ought to pull a rag wet with ammonia between my hind legs to cool me off.

He heard something. To ears which delighted only in the sweet harmony of hooves, the sound was an affront. It was a chugging, not a clop. It advanced from the direction of Edhogg, and as it neared, and grew in volume, it became absolutely identifiable. It was the racket of internal combustion engines.

That was impossible. No vehicles passed this way except an occasional wagon or, once in three weeks, the Jeffrey Quad truck sent out from Fort Bliss with a load of hay and grain and rations. The truck was not due for two weeks.

He came to his feet, peering. Whatever the conveyances might be, they were obscured by the grove. And then they cleared the trees and chugged into raw, appalling sight. Even then it took him a minute to see what he saw.

He saw two Model T tourers. Though dusty, they were obviously new. The wheel spokes twinkled. Sunlight glanced from brass headlamps and radiators.

Each auto trailed a string of three horses of beautiful proportions.

The tops were down, and each Ford carried a complement of three soldiers, two in front and one in the tonneau, the latter almost lost in a mound of baggage.

Hanging from the radiator cap of each vehicle was a feed bag, from the mouth of which protruded the neck of a whiskey bottle.

To the right-hand upright of each windshield, a white polo mallet was lashed like a flag standard. To its end was tied, in lieu of a guidon, a pair of lady's bloomers.

"Thunder and damnation," said Stanley Dinkle.

2

Ivory, Apes, and Peacocks

Ducking from the porch into the room, he yanked on a clean shirt, shoved in the tail, looped on a necktie and tied it, tucked the ends between the second and third button of the shirt, pinned a gold bar on his collar, dusted his boots with a dirty shirt, clapped on his peaked campaign hat, adjusted it, returned to the porch, opened the door, and marched, box-shouldered and iron-spined, to welcome his new command.

They had pulled the Fords up and shut off the engines. As he approached, one trooper dismounted and pranced to report, smiling and extending a hand.

"I'm Corporal Phipps. A pleasure to meet you."

Dinkle ignored the hand. From the pulpit of his eyes he surveyed the automobiles as though they were scarlet women plying their trade while the plate was being passed. "You the ranking non-com?"

"The only striper. That's right."

"That's. Right. Sir."

Phipps blinked. He withdrew the hand and came to indolent attention. "Sir," he said.

"Then you get those men out of those Tin Lizzies and into formation and you do it chop-chop," said the officer evenly, "or I'll take you over my knee and nail a shoe onto your rear end and every time you sit down you'll sound like a blacksmith shop."

Phipps's cheeks reddened. He about-faced and barked. In nothing flat he had the other five hopping over the sides of the autos and all six of them in line and at attention. They were cramped from the long ride, Dinkle knew, but he let them stand there, little lead soldiers in a row, while the high sun sweat them and the muscles of their legs twanged like Jews' harps. Up and down the sulky line he inspected them, hoof to mouth, hocks to cruppers. Had their transport and animals not given them away, their finery would have. The uniforms were olive drab, like his, but they were also togged out in gilt hat cords and custom-tailored shirts and breeches. They sported sand goggles. Round the corporal's neck were slung expensive binoculars. Disdaining the web leggins generally issued, they had splurged on leather puttees with buckle straps. To Beau Brummels such as these, a private's pay of fifteen dollars a month would be small change.

He confronted them. In the side-mirrors of their stares, officer and enlisted men sought the truth about each other. They were men in their early twenties, every one taller than he. He stood only five feet eight inches off the ground, and it was difficult to exert authority when he must look up at troopers rather than down. At their age, one of his nicknames had been "Stub." Their skin was made of rare roast beef, their bones and teeth of vegetables, their blood of vintage wines. So chock-full of vim and vigor were they that it erupted on their upper lips in healthy foliage. He was built like a beer keg, with a deep chest, a sinewy behind, and thick legs as bowed as staves, legs which even boots could not become. They appeared to favor two styles in mustaches: the warlike, those waxed into fierce Turkish hookahs, or the romantic, the vines allowed to laurel the corners of their mouths in Edgar Allan Poetry. His hands were paws, the fingers blunt. Except for a powdering of dust, they were perfectly groomed. They were the sort to brush and trim and bathe and shave with scrupulosity. His hair he cut himself, short on the sides and Prussian on top, and it was red. His other sobriquet had once been "Carrots." They were toilet-water types. His body was a barrack. They were silver spoons. He was a mug.

"Ahem." Dinkle cleared his throat. "Orders?"

"Here, sir." Phipps took a folded sheet from his shirt pocket and handed it over.

Dinkle unfolded it. They were from the Philadelphia Light Horse, officially a National Guard troop but actually, like the Keystone Lancers, a hoity-toity military men's club to which only the most well-born and wealthy scions of the most well-born and wealthy were elected. "I will call the roll," he said. "Alexander M. Phipps."

"Here, sir."

"H. Horace Biddle."

"Here."

"Sir."

"Sir."

"Stewart H. Darlington."

"Here, sir."

"Frederick R. Den Uyl."

"Here, sir."

"William A. Pugh III."

"Here, sir."

"Lucien T. D. Thayer."

"Here, sir."

He folded the orders. "Very well. You're to be here for a month. My name is Lieutenant Dinkle and I'll be your CO. Our duty is to patrol twenty miles of the border and to train. Training will start in the morning." He paused, wondered whether or not to be merciful and put them at ease, decided against it. "I suppose you met the Keystone Lancers coming down from Marathon." There was no response. "Well?"

"Yes, sir," said Phipps.

"And they told you all about me," he said. "What I expect of men in the way of discipline and effort." Since he hadn't put these as questions, he let an answer go. "Did they refer to this place as Fort Dinkle?" They looked guilty as sin. "Well?" he pressed.

"Yes, sir," said Phipps.

"Well, it isn't. According to Headquarters, Department of the Southwest, at Fort Bliss, this is Patrol Post Number Two, and that's what I want it called." He swept the line. "All right, follow me and I'll show you around."

He led them first across a snaketrack sand road to the parade ground, an area approximately the size of a football field which the Lancers had cleared of rocks and cactus. At the far end, six crooked mesquite limbs were set in the sand at intervals. "We drill and shoot here," he said, "every day."

Across the road again he indicated the purple house. "BOQ." He pointed at a pyramidal tent of yellow canvas, erected a hundred yards west of the house. "That's your Sibley," he said, adding a witticism he regretted immediately, "Home sweet home."

He started for the river, but stopped by the jungle of cane and parted some stalks to expose a wooden box, a two-holer. "Enlisted men's latrine," he said. "Officers on the other side."

They trooped after him down to the river. "This is where we run out of United States," he said. "In case you haven't seen it yet, that's the Rio Grande."

They looked at it as if to say, so that's the border, that's what we were shanghaied two thousand miles to guard, and shrugged. Then they looked at him hopefully, confident he must have something more to show them, something more interesting than a patch of sand, a house, a tent, a latrine, and a river. Instead, he turned and headed for the pecan grove. Slowly they scuffed along after him. He could almost hear ebullient air hoosh out of their balloons at the prospect of thirty days in a place as desolate as this, and had no sympathy. It would never occur to them that he had already served a month here and faced a second and only the good Lord knew how many after that. In the grove he avoided the autos like the plague, pointed out the picket line strung from tree to tree, and paused a moment to check the condition of their animals. They were Morgans, better mounts than he would ever own, and shipped, probably, from the East in private Pullman cars with velvet upholstery. The longer he admired them, tied to the Fords like cows, the greater grew his ire. "You pulled good stock all the way from El Paso behind those corn poppers?" he demanded.

"No, sir," said Phipps. "We put them on a train and met

them in Marathon, then drove down here. Only one flat tire, too."

"What gave you the notion to drive here in the first place?"

"Well, sir, we bought the cars for runabouts. You know, to toot in to El Paso from Camp Stewart. Then we thought it might be bully to have them here."

"It won't be."

"Sir?"

"This is a cavalry post and you're cavalrymen—or will be. I want you to park these contraptions out of sight and I won't want them started again till the day you leave. That's an order."

"Yes, sir."

"And get those feed bags off them, and polo sticks, and those damned bloomers."

"Yes, sir."

"Then care for your animals."

"Yes, sir."

"Then you may unload. I suppose the Lancers also told you about the strikers across the river. Well, you may hire 'em if you wish, but you're to see to your own mounts. We will have no stableboys here."

"Yes, sir."

Dinkle was halfway to his house when he heard them whistle, and by the time he reached it, six dirty urchins in ragged shirts and pants materialized out of Mexico, splashed across the river, and scampered past him into the grove. These were muchachos hired originally by the Keystone Lancers to act as strikers, or personal orderlies. They had evidently been awaiting an invitation to come over and sign on for another month, to cook, wash, and clean for, and probably pilfer from, the young lords of the Main Line.

He sat in solitary state on his porch and tried to concentrate again on his article, but as the afternoon waned, what transpired outside was too distracting. The autos, referred to in loud but affectionate terms as "Henrietta" and "Olivia," were urged snorting out of sight in the grove. Rest in peace, he prayed. But there was no peace. The unloading commenced. He had to watch it. For out of the tonneaus and luggage racks of the autos came everything but ivory, apes, and peacocks. He itemized trunks and rifles and suitcases and footlockers and bric-a-brac and a case of champagne and saddles and a case of whiskey and reserve gasoline in ten-gallon milk cans and bedding and tinned goods and polo equipment and a ukulele and a hall tree and cans of crankcase oil before he broke the lead of his pencil stub and had to whittle a new one and gave up, fuming. The Philadelphia Heavy Horse, he fumed, packing up for war as though they were going on a picnic. He had drawn another lot like the last, only worse, because these were apparently even richer specimens, and spoiled rotten.

I am in for a Godawful month.

I wish I had a lewd woman here. I would wallow in her like a hog.

Corporal Phipps knocked.

"What is it?"

"Five o'clock, sir. Time for Retreat."

"Retreat? Oh, well, we don't stand it out here, Phipps. No bugler."

"We have one, sir. We always stand it."

"You have. You do." Dinkle gritted his teeth. Of course the bon ton would bring along a bugle, one made of solid gold, no doubt. Of course the upper crust would dote on ritual. "Very well. Form your men on the parade ground."

"Thank you, sir."

Dinkle waited three minutes, then left the house and crossed the road and there they were, five of them lined up and wearing sabers, yes, sabers. And here came Phipps, carrying not a bugle but a table-sized Victrola, yes, a Victrola. He set it on the sand, wound it up, angled the horn, poised the needle, found the groove, and taking his place, called the line to attention. And as the recorded notes of a bugle pierced the ears and scratched the vacuous Texas sky, the officer, mouth open, unsure whether he were being made the butt of a colossal joke or presiding over a lunatic asylum, ordered "Present sabers!" Six bright blades flashed.

They will drive me bug, thought Stanley Dinkle.

3

Over the River, Perfumed and Passionate

Rations were issued by the lieutenant from the stores in his house: hardtack, canned beef and beans and tomatoes and jam and coffee and sugar and milk.

While these were toted by their muchachos to the Sibley tent, the Philadelphia Light Horse, as ordered, struck bloomers and polo sticks and feed bags and attended to their animals, freeing them from the Fords and tying them to the picket line in the grove and currying, watering, and feeding grain, after which they hauled tops up on the autos, snapped on isinglass side curtains, and bade "Henrietta" and "Olivia" fond adieu for a month.

Fatigued by the long trek by train and motor from El Paso, they reclined then on their cots, sipped whiskey and water, played several of the latest hits on the Vic, including "I Ain't Got Nobody" and "Where Did Robinson Crusoe Go With Friday on Saturday Night?", and while the muchachos cooked supper outside, evaluated their new CO. He was even worse, even more brasshat, they decided, than they'd been warned. The consensus was that he resembled a tarantula, that tiger of the desert which had terrorized National Guard camps from Laredo to Nogales. Although none of them had ever seen one, a tarantula, so the rumors flew, was naturally mean, would jump thirty feet when in the mood to sting, and would stranglehold, toe-hold, and gouge in order to inject its venom into a hapless victim. Such a description fit Dinkle like a glove. Small he might be, but he had nippers as incontestable as ice tongs.

After supper all six of them—"Lex" Phipps, "Bid" Biddle, "Stew" Darlington, "Freddy" Den Uyl, "Phew" Pugh, and "Luce" Thayer—strolled down to the river, removed puttees and shoes and socks, and stood side by side in the cool water. They were silent. The evening hushed them, and the purling of the Rio Grande, telling over and over the pebbles of its bottom like beads, and thoughts of home. It had never seemed as far away, and yet, curiously, as near. Even more curiously, all six seemed to recall, with only minor differences, the same house. It was a country place, a half hour's rattle westward from the city on the Paoli Local. Duplicate of a Victorian mansion, stocked with English or Irish servants, it was made of stone and steep gables and dormer windows and proud porticoes, and it was set in spacious lawns studded with beeches or surrounded by formal gardens with Italian statuary. In such sibling houses all of them had been born and raised. But as intimately as they shared the stream with their feet now, they had shared in the past, besides an environment, a heredity as well, and a tradition. The fact was, they were like as peas in a pod, in speech and education and taste and bias and pedigree. They were the end products of old Philadelphia families which, by means of incessant, almost incestuous, intermarriage had contrived to hold on to old wealth. They were society. Episcopalians every one, preparatory to college they were sent to St. Paul's, their sisters to Miss Wright's School. They played cricket, tennis, and polo, they rode to hounds with the Radnor Hunt Club. They shopped only at Wanamaker's, Strawbridge & Clothier's, Jacob Reed's, and occasionally at Caldwell's, the jewelers. Except for the formal announcement of weddings, debuts, and funerals, neither the *Public Ledger* nor the *Evening Bulletin* had the temerity to mention their names. When they came of age, and their fathers were portly enough to retire from it, they selected a mount from their private stable, drilled every Monday night in their private armory, and after a recruit period, were elected to membership in the Philadelphia Light Horse.

The young men gazed. Over the river, perfumed and

passionate, Mexico sprawled. Her breasts were stony hills. Dark ranges in the distance were her thighs. The evening sky was silk of violet and coral. They sniffed. The air was spiced with cooking smoke. They cocked ears. They heard the tinkle of goat bells, and from the mesquite trees the moan of doves.

Mexico excited them. The mystery of her, the sights and sounds and odors of her, the otherness of her flesh—these caused a subtle agitation in the groin. Between their toes the river ran like lust. Toward exotic Mexico they tilted, drawn by her as down the decades adventurous young men before them had been drawn, seekers after gold and truth and death.

On the opposite shore, by the same magic which had produced the muchachos, a girl appeared. She was bronze and comely. She wore a white blouse. She smiled at them. They groaned at her.

"Luce" Thayer throbbed a chord upon his ukulele. In chorus they sang to the maiden, serenading her with the most popular ballad on the border then:

When we get back from Mexico,
When we get back from war,
The National Guard can go to hell,
We won't enlist no more.
We'll take a bath and change our clothes,
And swear before the Lord,
To emigrate to Michigan,
And vote for Henry Ford.

She smiled again, complimented by what she believed must be an expression of amorous intent, and clasped hands at her bosom.

"Freddy" Den Uyl knew as much Spanish as the rest, which was next to nothing. *"Coma say lamba,* Senorita?" he lisped. "What's your name, kiddo?"

"Conchita," answered she.

"Conchita!" they sighed.

An urge got the better of "Freddy" Den Uyl, as did all his urges. He waded toward the dusky princess. His chums followed, putting bare feet boldly one before the other, since the stream was only knee-deep.

To their detriment, they often followed "Freddy." He was their most reckless cardshark, their best toper, their most single-minded chaser of skirts. Youths of his origin seldom strayed from the straight and narrow, but when one did, it was difficult to beat the Dutch. Every asset bequeathed him by his forebears, rectitude and thrift and piety and temporance and a banking fortune, "Freddy" seemed resolved to dissipate as rapidly as possible. Having inherited while still a minor, his legal guardian was a drunkard uncle whose only function was to funnel to his ward whatever money and bad advice "Freddy" required, and he required a great deal of one and little of the other. Falling into fast company, he was expelled from Cornell, where he was a Psi U, for reasons academic and extracurricular. He was next expelled from Penn. He was next expelled from Virginia. At twenty-two, Private Den Uyl was rich, a loafer, and an undeniably decadent influence. He was worth millions, give or take a million. Unless seen to by a barber, his mustache soon became a cabbage. Unless attended by a manservant, he lived like a pig. Yet there was a kind of harum-scarum charm about his lisp, the affectation of his gestures, the vagrancy of his mind and morals.

"Conchita, girlie!" he panted like a tugboat, spattering water, leading the pack.

"Soldier, where in hell d'you think you're going!"

The roar stopped "Freddy" in his tracks. They turned. It was the tarantula, his nippers unsheathed and quivering. He had spotted them from his porch while meditating upon the nuisance of Flossie Grebs, which only stoked his ire. He bowlegged it on a beeline down to the river's edge and fired an index finger at them.

"You are now out of the United States!" he rasped. "Not only that, you're AWOL. Not only that, when you cross this river one inch over halfway you're invading a foreign country. You thumb your nose at the War Department and the White House. You could hang. We have orders from God on down to stay on our side unless attacked. Now, I want to see how damned fast you can get your tootsies out of the state of Coahuila and back into Texas!"

Hangdogging it, the culprits sloshed toward him. By the time they reached the sand and stood about wiggling discomfited toes, he had cooled off and could address them in a style almost befitting four stars.

"Never let me catch you crossing the Rio Grande again," he said. "Boys will be boys, I know, but I don't think you've got it through your heads why we're here. This is no overnight weenie roast and songfest. Maybe it isn't a war, either, but it might be, any minute."

He had a thoughtful gander over their heads at the far shore. They looked, too, and were surprised. It was another Mexico. The land lay darkening and ominous. The doves were stilled. The girl had gone.

"One more thing," he said. "You're in the Army now, on active duty, not the National Guard. And I'll prove it. You start pulling guard tonight. Private Den Uyl will walk first post. With rifle. Loaded."

He could have knocked them over with a feather. "Guard, sir?" asked Phipps.

"Every night. If you challenge and get no response, shoot. The password is 'Conchita.'" He managed a grim smile.

"But sir," Phipps protested, indicating the peace and quiet across the river, "guard against what?"

Stanley Dinkle stared at "Lex" Phipps. The question was snot-nose and insubordinate, and his impulse was to dress the whole baby-face bunch down one side and up the other. But he had been hard enough on them for one day, particularly the first. Besides, they were really very vulnerable. Their faces gave them away, they hadn't yet learned to wear the mask of maturity. They were colts, and if they could be led to water by a girl, they could be by an officer who practiced the right psychology, and made to drink. And so he spared them, and scratched instead for an answer to the question. Didn't they realize, he might have demanded, that there'd been a revolution going on over there for the last six years and still was?

That a man's life on that side of the river wasn't worth a plugged nickel? That there were more bandidos to the square mile over there than there were cucarachas? That if they could get valets for a whistle and a hot tamale in a white blouse for a song, they could also get fire and rape and robbery and murder from Mexico any fine night for free?

He let it go. Obviously they didn't realize. One day they might. Pray to God they'd survive it. Annoyance drained from him, to be replaced by a slow wash of sadness. Surely he had never been as young. Or as dumb.

"Guard against what?" he repeated, turning. "In case you're interested," he informed them over his shoulder, off to his house through the twilight, "that's what the Thirteenth Cavalry said at Columbus."

4

A Good Morning's Work

The Philadelphia Light Horse were mustered on the parade ground, mounted, at seven o'clock the next morning.

Privates Darlington and Pugh were assigned patrol. Darlington was to ride the U.S. side of the river ten miles east, Pugh ten miles west, armed and at a walk, to fire only if fired upon, to keep eyes peeled, noses clean, breeches buttoned, and report back to Patrol Post 2 by noon any sign of suspicious activity. This would be standard procedure henceforth, two men riding in rotation and hooking up with the patrols from Posts #3 and #1, twenty miles to the east and west. By this means, the Army contented itself, the entire Tex-Mex border could be kept under daily surveillance.

Then the CO noticed that his troopers had reported for duty wearing sabers. "Before you start," he said, "you may take off those can openers and store them. And that goes for everybody."

"Can openers, sir?"

"Sabers. The cavalry is a modern arm, and the saber is dead as the dodo bird."

Their mouths opened and closed. Then they scowled. It was as though he'd profaned the purity of their sisters.

"Not with the Light Horse it isn't, sir." It was Private Biddle speaking up.

"Sorry, it is here."

"But, sir, we're accustomed to wearing them," argued Private Thayer.

"Then you can get unaccustomed."

"You mean, sir, we can't even wear them for Retreat?" whimpered Corporal Phipps.

. He hesitated, which was always dangerous. "If you want to clank around in them at Retreat, that's your privilege," he conceded.

"And if we take the field?" asked Biddle.

"This is the field," the officer snapped. Biddle would be the one, he knew it in his bones. Biddle was going to give him trouble. "Let's have no more lip," he said. "I want them off now. That's an order."

They obeyed him, grudgingly, and while they put away the cutlery, Dinkle had several long thoughts and a good disgusted spit. In addition to everything else, they were clearly chronic "beefers," and you could never talk beefers into amenable enlisted men. You had to train the starch out of them, which he intended to do, starting now if not sooner.

Darlington and Pugh went their opposite directions and he told the remaining four to mount up, the first subject this morning would be equitation. Having observed them operating Detroit junk, he wanted to see how they handled horseflesh.

First he tested how they "gathered" the animals and how they followed commands to march, slow trot, trot, and gallop. These they must have learned at Mount Gretna, Pennsylvania, the two-week camp and revel in which the Light Horse indulged each summer.

Next, for two monotonous hours, he had them ride individual exercises on command: broken lines, the circle, the half-turn, the figure 8, the serpentine. These were riding hall exercises they must have practiced many a Monday night in their private armory at home.

Next, he let them rest the animals while he prepared to critique. Dinkle found himself at a loss. They rode well, he would have to admit, though he hated like sin to. To the inexpert eye, they seemed born to the saddle. He appeared grafted. They danced. He wrestled. To the trained eye, however, they were show riders, not cavalrymen. He recognized at once the Guy V. Henry Method. It was a seat more ceremonial than military, ideal for prancing down Broad Street or Walnut Street on parade or escorting dignitaries being honored by the city of Philadelphia—duties which constituted, so far as he was concerned, the only reason for the existence of the Light Horse in the first place. But it was an unnatural seat. It separated rider from horse, and the real cavalryman had to be one with his mount. On a long march, the Henry Method would tire both of them excessively.

He told them so. He said they rode well, but on campaign it was better to be comfortable than pretty, better for both man and beast. He wanted them to be less "bouncy," to get closer to their transportation, to drive the saddle throat deeper into the crotch. "And one other thing. Your hands are too active. You keep too much tension on the reins, and this makes for nervous animals. They can't relax, they have to be ready at all times for a rein command. That's as bad as having too passive hands, so that commands come without warning. Contact between a rider's hands and a horse's mouth should be gentle and steady. So watch the joints of your shoulders and elbows and wrists and fingers—keep them relaxed."

They didn't believe a word he said, but they were insulted anyway. No one in the City of Brotherly Love would dare cast aspersion upon their horsemanship. They were the military flower of the metropolis.

"If you don't mind my asking, sir," said Biddle, "where did you learn to ride?"

Dinkle did, but he was ready. "For the last two years," he said, slipping the ace from his sleeve, "I have been Instructor in Equitation at the Mounted Service School at Fort Riley."

Next, he ran them through the Manual of the Rifle, Mounted. They performed it perfectly, sweeping the Springfields in and out of the near-side scabbards with vaudeville dexterity. They would. He asked if they had shot for the record at Camp Stewart and they said yes, and also at summer camp, and had scored high. They would. He asked if they had also used the pistol, which raised their eyebrows. "The .45 caliber automatic. Don't tell me you don't have them."

"Yes, sir. They were issued at Stewart."

"But you didn't think you'd need them this morning." He

shook his head. "Well, go get 'em. Wear them from now on. You're going to be married to pistols for the next month."

While they were gone he moseyed into the grove, shelled himself a pecan, and munched gloomily. A border crawling like flies with thousands of simple, patriotic chumps and he, Stanley Dinkle, a simple, patriotic career officer, had drawn these humdingers. It was more than mere mischance. It was a fate as mean and cuckoo as Champion T. Grebs, her father. Which reminded him—Flossie was overdue. She hadn't been by the post for a week. With his luck, she'd probably show up about this time some morning, while he was drilling the troops, and he'd have nowhere to hide. They'd split their sides. He could never look them in the eye again.

His pupils returned fully equipped: new web belts with ammunition pouches and new snap-flap holsters and new pistols carried low on the right thigh in the best Billy the Kid tradition. He first had them raise the holsters hip-high, with the comment that they were likely to encounter few fast-draw artists out here, then checked to see if the weapons were loaded. They were and he thanked his stars he'd checked. It might have been a massacre.

Next, after removing magazines and unloading chambers personally, he gave them a full hour's instruction in the Manual of the Pistol, Revised, Dismounted, barking commands till he was hoarse:

"Raise . . . pistol. Lower . . . pistol. Withdraw . . . magazine. Open . . . chamber. Close . . . chamber. Insert . . . magazine. Return . . . pistol."

They were clumsier than cub bears and knew it and blamed him instead of their own ignorance and he knew they did and didn't give a pinch of dried owl dung. "This is called a pistol, automatic, caliber .45," he said, "but what it really is is a pocket cannon. It will blow a hole in you the size of a silver dollar. So until I'm dead sure you know one end from the other, I'm not letting you load with live ammunition."

Next, he ordered them to mount up again, and when they were on the Morgans, had them repeat the Manual of the Pistol, Revised, Mounted, through each of the four gaits, march, slow trot, trot, and gallop, up and down the parade ground, then gathered them again.

"Now," said he, "what I'm easing you into is the latest tactic. The new cavalry cut-'em down. The Mounted Pistol Attack. We were talking a while back about the saber being obsolete. We agreed it is. It has been since the Charge of the Light Brigade. This has replaced it." He thumped his holster. "While you're slicing off an arm here and a leg there with a saber, I can kill seven men with this. Use it in formation, add the weight and power and speed of the horse, and you have cavalry at its best. You have a branch of service no country can ever do without."

He paused and pointed. "See those six mesquite limbs down there? I had the Lancers put them up for just this purpose, the Mounted Pistol Attack. What I want us to do is all aboard again—I'll ride with you—and on my commands march, draw pistols, lean forward, rest the rein hand on your animal's neck, extend the right hand with pistol as far as you can over his head between his ears—don't touch him—and aim. Watch me, do as I do. After we pass between the limbs, on my commands lean back, haul on the reins, stop and rear and turn on haunches the way you would on a cow horse or a polo pony, then march back and aim again and pass between the limbs. That way we hit the enemy front and rear within seconds. Then, after we walk through it we'll step up the gait—slow trot, trot, maybe even the gallop. Let's go."

They were wilting now, like lilies, but after he fetched Hassan they dragged themselves on top and awaited his commands from the end of the line. Down the parade ground they marched, drawing pistols, leaning, aiming, pretending to fire, between the limbs, stop and rear and turn, lean and aim, pretend to fire, and marched back, then repeated the maneuver slow trotting and trotting, twice each. Finally, for dessert, he led them into the Mounted Pistol Attack at a gallop, the horses snorting and breaking Napoleonic wind, his shouts spurring the line through hosts of dust:

"Squad to the Pistol Attack!

"Draw pistols!
"Forward, charge!
"Troopers, about!
"Forward, charge!"

That put the frosting on the cake. The Morgans were cross-eyed and pigeon-toed. Phipps, Den Uyl, Biddle, and Thayer had to assist each other from the saddle. It was two o'clock in the afternoon.

"A good morning's work," said Lieutenant Dinkle.

5

The Commandant Is Honored by a Visit from a Lady

He congratulated himself. That was the system: don't argue with 'em, don't hobnob with 'em, and train 'em to a frazzle. If it had saved his skin with the Keystone Lancers, it must also, he was convinced, with these young lords of the Main Line.

To get his mind off sex, that evening he skirmished with mosquitoes and tried to add to the list of horse defects for his *Cavalry Journal* article. His last item had been "Teeth and digestion not good as evidenced by amount of corn passing through whole."

Life is passing through me whole, thought Stanley Dinkle. My teeth and digestion are good, but I ain't getting any nourishment.

He lowered the wick, blew out the lamp, went to bed, and slept for an hour before catapulting from his cot.

"Stanleeeee! Yoo-hooooo!"

It was enough to wake the dead. He knew that loud, gravelly bray only too well. His first stricken thought was, oh my God. His second was, she's never come by at night before, she's sneaked away from the old man and if he finds out there'll be hell to pay.

"Stanleeeee!"

His third was, it's Phipps's turn on guard, he'll stop her.

To his dismay, there was no challenge. He couldn't see her, the night was pitch-dark, but he could hear the clomp, clomp of her rubber boots around the grove as Flossie Grebs bore down upon the house.

"Yoor ladylove's callin' on you, Stanleeeee!" she hollered. "You get outa that bed an' get dressed!"

It was too late, no guard could stop her now. Everyone in the Sibley must be awake and listening. This would be the ruination of his system and of him.

"You don't wanta get dressed you don't have too, Stanleeeee! You can crush me in yoor nakedy arms ha-ha-ha!"

Out the door he banged in BVD's and panic, down the slope he flew toward the cover of cane and the safety of his pagoda. He was conscious of horses nickering on the picket line, of sleepy exclamations from the tent. The Light Horse were roused and amused and bumbling about. The screen door banged again. She had dared to enter his house.

"Yoo-hoo, where are you, Stanley sweetie?"

He reached the outhouse and flung open the door, intending to barricade himself within. Instead, someone within burst out and upon him, and the shock of collision cast them both into the cane, where they tumbled amid the stalks, locked in hand-to-hand combat.

"Who're you?" hissed one, his hands about the other's throat.

"Who're you?" the other choked, crushing his antagonist in a bear hug.

"Dinkle—"

"Phipps—"

They released each other. "Phipps!" cried Dinkle, his anger heightened by embarrassment. "What in hell are you doing in the officers' latrine?"

"Answering a call of nature, sir," responded Phipps, assisting his superior to his feet.

"God damn it, you're on guard!" the lieutenant shouted. "Get up there and escort 'er off this post!"

"Is that you, Stanleeeee?"

"Oh, Lord, she's heard us," groaned Dinkle, "she's coming! Vamoose!" And he rushed up the path and out of the cane, Phipps after him.

"I love you, Stanleeeee!" she brayed, advancing from the house. "An' you love me, you know you do, you little bowlegged darlin'!"

"Who is it, sir?" Phipps panted.

Stanley Dinkle cursed the day he was born, the day she was dropped, and the day he had walked into a recruiting office. "That," he puffed, "is none of your damned business!"

It was the explosion of a shotgun which sobered up the situation, as well as the bull bellow. "Where be you, Dinkle, you bastid? You get inta my poor gel's pants I'll blow yer ass off!"

For the shotgun brought the Philadelphia Light Horse charging in undress out of the Sibley to repel what they believed to be some sort of armed invasion. Running headlong into two men they could not identify, they grappled courageously with Dinkle and Phipps.

"Floss, you whoor, you git on home or I'll shoot yer tits t'San Antone!"

It was not this fatherly admonition but the trumpeting of a mule which terrorized the horses and caused them to break the picket line and hightail it out of the grove and through the chaos of Fort Dinkle.

Champion T. Grebs let go the other barrel. Fending off various belligerents and attempting to avoid being run down by stampeding animals, by the light of the muzzle blast the Commandant had one horrifying glimpse of a mouth, mounted on a mule, a red cave of wind dug deep in hair, entirely toothless.

6

An Officer and Gent by Act of Congress

In the morning he maintained a stiff upper lip. To his troops he explained merely that the intruders had been a woman and her father who worked a cinnabar mine a mile down the road and who were both, due to isolation and hardship, a bit batty. He intended to forget the episode, and he advised them to do likewise.

The Mounted Shotgun Attack by mule, old man, and daughter was in fact the only interruption of what became, in another day or two, a routine. At night the Light Horse stood guard, walking the perimeters of the post, rifles on shoulders. To keep them on their toes, and to defend the officers' latrine, at least once a night the indefatigable Dinkle challenged the guard unexpectedly, bellowing at him from behind a tree or a creosote bush, scaring him half out of his wits.

In the mornings two men were told off to patrol the Rio Grande ten miles east and west. No suspicious activity, in a military sense, was observed, although "Luce" Thayer reported two women doing laundry on the Mexican side and "Freddy" Den Uyl's mount, an urban horse of taste and refinement, one day met a rattlesnake, whereupon it hurled its rider into a cactus. His wounds, while painful, and suffered in the line of duty, did not, opined the CO during the dethorning, qualify him for the Purple Heart. The four in garrison fired weapons for scores at paper targets tacked to the mesquite limbs, were tutored in equitation and squad formations and the Manual of the Pistol, Revised, were taught how to exchange pistol magazines and rifle clips at the several gaits, and always, always, dashed up and down the parade ground in the

Mounted Pistol Attack till both men and beasts were casualty to the staggers.

Afternoons were devoted to the care and cleaning of equipment. Dinkle turned out to be, in addition to everything else, a fussbudget. He required that every scrap of leather, from stirrups to bridoons, be cleaned and soaped daily, and that saddle blankets be brushed as well as hung to air. And he was adamant that they do these things themselves, besides tending the animals. Denied the services of their muchachos, who crossed the river at daybreak to cook and wash and tote and housekeep the tent and return to their native land at sundown, they doubted they could survive so strenuous a regiment. Dinkle distrusted the muchachos. Small businessmen they might be, but they might also, he insinuated, be spies, taking back over the river information as well as gringo pesos.

At five o'clock the Philadelphians formed for Retreat, with Victrola, with sabers. Before supper was served them, they drank enough to alleviate dull care. They got, if truth were known, a trifle tiddly. After supper, as darkness descended and another night of guard duty loomed, they harmonized on "Roses of Picardy" to uke accompaniment or played records calculated to lift the spirits, snappy numbers such as "Twelfth Street Rag" and "Oh, How She Could Yacki, Hacki, Wicki, Wacki Woo."

Gradually it dawned on the Light Horse that they were stuck. Fort Dinkle, Patrol Post #2, call it what you would, they were marooned here for a month as surely as castaways upon a desert isle. Here they must exist, half a continent away from home, in as desolate a place as they could conceive of, a pimple on the rump of Texas, a place so lonely that when you talked to yourself there was no one to listen. They commenced to count days.

Sometimes they sneaked into the pecan grove and mooned over the Fords, the sweet chariots which would eventually deliver them again to Camp Stewart and their comrades, to bright lights and the belles of El Paso. Identical twins, the only way to tell the touring cars apart was by the garish stickers on their doors—"Danger, 100,000 Jolts!" on "Henrietta," "C'mon, Baby, Here's Your Rattle!" on "Olivia." They were dusted daily and stored with high-speed clutches engaged. They seemed ready, even eager, to go, and the compulsion to crank up was well-nigh irresistible. The tarantula, however, had given strict orders. The Light Horse were spoiled, of course. They chafed under what to them were the privations of service in the field and the indignities of service under an officer their superior only in rank. And they were homesick. They longed to return to the station in life to which wealth and breeding entitled them. And they were full of beans. They spent every emotion to the last penny. In short, they were young. And so, in lieu of laying hands on the crank, the six stood in worshipful silence about the autos, caressing brass and steel and rubber. Their eyes misted.

There were small consolations. After several days of pretending, the CO gave them magazines of live ammunition, and they charged the mesquite limbs yelling, leaning forward, heavy automatics thrust between the horses' ears, and fired five fast rounds at cardboard bull's-eyes, passed between, reared, turned on haunches, spurred, fired two more rounds, and yelling, galloped off and left the decimated foe behind. When they pulled up, legs weak, hearts bumping, the snuff of powder sharp in their nostrils, hands clenched and trembling about the butts of their weapons, something, they knew not what, had happened to them, something elemental. They were speechless and shy. Even a pretend Mounted Pistol Attack, they discovered, was more exciting than polo. It frightened them a little. It bared them before their Maker.

And the Jeffrey Quad truck grunted in from Bliss with hay, grain, rations, and packets of mail, plus two weeks' editions of the Philadelphia papers. H.M.S. *Russell,* a British battleship, had been sunk in the Mediterranean. General Hugh L. Scott, Army Chief of Staff, had met General Alvaro Obregón, Minister of War of the de facto government of Mexico, on the International Bridge in El Paso to discuss an agreement by which the tensions along the border might be eased. Secretary of State Lansing had informed the imperial German Government that so long as the new instructions to U-boat commanders relative to the neutrality of American shipping remained in effect, normal diplomatic relations between the two nations would continue. It was not remarked that Lieutenant Dinkle received no mail.

And one afternoon he let them ride into Edhogg for a bottle of soda pop.

When they were safely out of sight, he skulked into the grove to feed one of his pet prejudices. He'd seen many a Model T on the road, he'd even taken a spin in one owned by a fellow officer at Forty Riley—but Stanley Dinkle hated the critters. Put into harness on the farm, as many of them were, to pull plows or supply power for threshing and cutting wood, they might have a certain utility, he would grant, but they were in general a nuisance, even an abomination. They symbolized to him an age increasingly flaccid and corrupt, an age putt-putting its merry way down the road to perdition in a parade of flivvers. Could you expect chivalry of a knight if you sold his fiery steed for soap and mounted him on a rattletrap? Should a virtuous female be expected to hang onto her virtue at forty miles per hour?

Warily he circled "Henrietta" and "Olivia." Their canvas tops towered over him. They were brand new and black of course. "They can have any color they want," Mr. Ford was reputed to have said of his customers, "so long as it's black." On the windshields were factory stickers: "Notice to User. To obtain best results this car should not be driven faster than 20 miles per hour for the first 500 miles." And they were dolled up with the latest accessories. Standard acetylene gas headlamps had been replaced by electric, the bulb horns by brass-belled, hand-operated Klaxons. They had nickel-plated hubcaps and rubber-cushioned foot pedals and cradle carriers at the rear for two extra spare tires and Handy-Pandy luggage racks bracketed to the right-hand running boards and Stewart speedometers attached to the dashboards. And really slick, instead of regular caps, the radiators were crowned with winged brass Boyce Motometers, glass-faced and inset with a red-level temperature gauge scaled from "Good Average" to "Higher Efficiency" to "Danger-Steaming!"

Stanley Dinkle sighed. No doubt about it, "Henrietta" and "Olivia" were lulus. He had an unholy impulse to crank one up, but compromised by sliding behind "Olivia's" wooden steering wheel and sniffing her leatherette upholstery and fiddling with her spark and gas levers as though he knew what they were. He coveted her. One like her, however, even without the doodads, would cost him $360, and to squander almost half his savings on a damned automobubble would be an act of which a man of his horse sense was incapable. He got out, slammed the door, and gave her tire a good swift kick. To think that mere whippersnappers could pool their pin money and buy two for toys—it was a shame and a crime.

He sat that night in his pink pagoda down by the river, meditating upon the nocturnal visit of Flossie Grebs and her father. Just as he feared, it had done him considerable harm. He detected a new laxity among the men, a slight indisposition to swallow his orders. And from their tent last night had issued a new war cry: "I love you, Stanleeeee!" From such small acorns, mighty mutinies grew. He could hear their laughter now, at his expense.

He could indeed, from the box latrine on the other side of the cane. He couldn't assign the voices, or pick up every word, but he got the gist. His ears burned. He caught the terms "tarantula" and "slave driver" and "bowlegged little darlin'." Then they hooted. One of them had coined a new name for the CO: "Stanley Steamer."

Later, in a mirror, by the light of the kerosene lamp, he introduced himself to Stanley Steamer. If only those brown, Barney Google eyes could be an impenetrable blue. If only he could cut lines, the insignia of command, into that baby face. If only he were ten years older, with a tongue that would skin men like mules and shrivel their stones into BB's. If only I could take myself apart, he thought, and put myself together again, I could do a whale of a lot better job. Anybody could. So if I can't make cavalrymen out of summertime soldiers in a month, it isn't my fault. I'm doing the best I can, considering my liabilities. I read the *Journal* on "How to Train National Guard Units" until I'm blue in the face, but it's no help.

The Guard they're talking about ain't the Philadelphia Light Horse. So I will go on as I am, doing my duty, but I will not take any folderol from them. Anytime they want to have a showdown we will have it, and when we do, they'll learn a Stanley Steamer will beat a flivver any Sunday in the week.

It came the next afternoon. He was a stickler about inspection. He followed the rules prescribed in paragraph 190, Cavalry Drill Regulations, 1902, corrected to 1911, and having explained them in detail, expected strict adherence. When each soldier's gear was ready, everything carried on the off side of the horse was to be displayed for inspection on the off side of a bed blanket, and conversely, everything carried on the near side was to be laid out on the near blanket side. But this afternoon, while each man stood at attention under a broiling sun beside blanket and gear, Dinkle noted that Thayer had reversed the display order, and called him on it.

"I'm sorry, sir," said Thayer.

"Put them right," Dinkle ordered.

"It's beastly hot, sir."

"Now," said Dinkle.

"Can't he make it right the next time, sir?" Darlington stuck in his two cents worth.

"Now," said Dinkle stubbornly.

"Begging your pardon, sir, but isn't the matter rather picayune?" This was Biddle.

"Picayune?" Dinkle gave him the withering stare he wished he had.

"Yes, sir," said Pugh. "They don't have inspection every day with Pershing, I'll bet."

"Or the armies in France either," added Den Uyl.

Here we go, thought Stanley Dinkle. That damned old madman and his daughter have undermined me. But if these pipsqueaks think they can get my goat they have another think coming. "This isn't France," he snapped, "and we're not with Pershing."

"But it is the field, you said so yourself," argued Phipps, "sir."

Dinkle faced Thayer. "I gave you an order."

"I believe you also said the cavalry's a modern arm, sir. Would you call this inspection modern?" Biddle was back again.

The officer stepped down the line to him. Biddle would be the one, he'd known it in his bones. "I would," he said.

"I wouldn't," said Biddle, omitting the "sir." "If the saber's obsolete, as you claim, so is this rigmarole."

"In your opinion."

"In my opinion."

Pvt. H. Horace Biddle smiled, spreading his scimitar mustache and displaying white teeth for inspection. Ten years the officer's junior, even at attention he was at ease. The world might be composed in the main of slag, but his family owned most of the anthracite, and the most aristocratic name, in eastern Pennsylvania. A member of the Ivy Club at Princeton, from whence he had been scheduled to graduate next month, he was handsome, he was a six-goal polo player, he moved with grace and decision, he had the dynamism of the natural leader. But there was something lethal about "Bid" Biddle, a blue-steel indifference which warned he would be dangerous to mishandle. Like a .45 automatic, he was loaded and cocked but never locked. He smiled, but never laughed. He smoked thin cigars. He would never die in bed.

"In your opinion." Dinkle bit his lip at the repetition. It was his second mistake. His first had been letting them distract him from Thayer. Too late, he recalled point two of his system: never fall into the trap of argument.

"In my opinion," smiled Biddle. "And furthermore, Lieutenant, if the saber's obsolete, isn't the horse?"

It was the ultimate blasphemy. Stanley Dinkle lost his temper, his third mistake. But they were insolent, pampered young pups, and it was time he tied a tin can to their tails.

"How in holy hell would you know!" he cried, his dander irretrievably up. He enfiladed the line. "How'd any of you know what gives cavalry dash and initiative? You're not cavalrymen! You may be when I'm done with you, but you by God aren't yet!"

Biddle could be as long-winded as a Philadelphia lawyer. "Dash and initiative, Lieutenant?" he inquired. "I'd say cavalry's on its last legs. I'll give you odds in five years it's entirely mechanized."

"Mechanized!" Stanley Dinkle tore off his campaign hat and waved it at the pecan trees. "If we're ever attacked here, you chase after them in those mechanical cockroaches and see how far you get!" He marched up and down for a minute, as furious with himself as he was with them, glaring into each sly, sweaty face, then returned to his tormentor. "I'll be damned if I'll debate with you, Biddle. It's a waste of my time. I'll tell you the difference between us. I'm a professional soldier and you're not. I know my business and you don't."

But the other had the last word. "There's another difference, Lieutenant," said he. "You're an officer and a gent by act of Congress. We were born gentlemen."

7

A Tender Scene at the Dryass Mine

Lieutenant Dinkle saddled Hassan the next day and poked a mile down the sand road westward. His mission was to inform the Grebses in no uncertain terms that Patrol Post #2 was a military area and any trespass by civilians, whether by day or night, was prohibited.

The road meandered away from the Rio Grande. The terrain drifted into a drear series of ledges layered with black ash. No birds defied it. No trees tried. The ledges overhung veins of ocher earth. There had been much mining activity hereabouts at one time, the officer understood, but the profitable ore bodies were long since played out and only two or three scratch-as-scratch-can operations were still extant. It was just as well. It was an inhuman place for humans. Even the cactus had pulled up stakes.

He came to the signs.

DRYASS MINE the first proclaimed; CHAMPION T. GREBS ONER, the second. GIT TO HELL OWT OF HEER THIS MEENS U GODAM U counseled the third. ONLESS U GOT $10000 CAPITTLE amended the fourth.

Dinkle hooked a knee around the pommel and considered them. They were a synopsis of Champ Grebs's personality. To put it as kindly as possible, he was a sour-livered, trigger-tempered, dung-tongued, crack-brained old bastard with two obsessions: that his claim held vast quantities of cinnabar which would make him a rich man had he the capital to develop it, and that his daughter, Flossie, was young, beautiful, innocent, and the object of intended rape by every man who set eyes on her. Only two men had, in years: Harley Offus, the general store keeper in Edhogg, who was married, and the bachelor second lieutenant who had the misfortune to be stationed in her vicinity. Once she set lustful eyes upon the latter, it was he, not she, who became the object.

Dismounting, he tied Hassan to a sign, removed his ammunition belt and pistol, laid them over the saddle, took two steps, and stopped. Turning, he buckled on belt and pistol again. Speak softly and carry a big stick.

The first time Flossie Grebs came by his post on her way into Edhogg for supplies and put her peepers on him, she proposed matrimony, pleading a raucous case in the presence of the Keystone Lancers.

Changing his mind, he removed pistol and belt and laid them over the saddle again. If he were to be gunned down unarmed, he'd have the satisfaction of knowing Grebs would go to trial for it.

On the second occasion she was accompanied by her sire, who offered her hand and charms to him in return for $10,000 "capittle," a bargain too magnanimous, in the miner's opinion, to turn down. Dinkle declined with thanks, and Grebs took instant umbrage. He swore marvelously. He hawked up and spat toads of phlegm. He embellished his remarks with prodigious farts. "He's fearful windy," explained his daughter during a brief intermission. "He tightened up an' helt in, though, he'd sail off like a hot air b'loon." When the officer resumed drill, the old reprobate snatched a shotgun from the wagon bed preparatory to murder, upon which Dinkle took to his heels and the sanctuary of the pecan trees while his troopers doubled up.

He started along the wagon tracks which must lead to the mine, his boots billowing ash.

Flossie Grebs would not take a gentlemanly no for an answer. She continued to court and harass him, to the limits of his pride and patience, but her descent upon his post night before last, and her father's, exceeded those limits. They had no legitimate business in a military area. They had no right to mortify him before his men. Another such shivaree and Stanley Steamer could kiss discipline good-by. The Light Horse would have him over a hilarious barrel. Distasteful as the errand might be, therefore, dangerous even, he had to draw a line, personally and officially, and forbid them to cross it.

He climbed a ledge. In the depression below, in an ashpit the size of his drill field, was the objective, the dark O of the Dryass Mine in an opposite ledge, and nearby were scattered its appurtenances—a coal pile, a wagon, two tethered mules, a shack, a tar paper convenience, and a figure, moving. It was a frightful place to work, much less to live. God had not forgotten such a place. He hated it Himself.

The officer summoned up his blood. He marched the wagon tracks downward.

As he neared, the mine machinery made sense to him. For a smelter, Grebs used a Civil War cannon barrel, firing it with coal freighted in from the railroad at Marathon. After the coarse cinnabar ore had been wheelbarrowed from the shaft and crushed and mixed with coal and fired in the cannon furnace, he cleaned out the soot and worked it with lime to extract the free quicksilver. Dinkle located the retort table where this was done, and the trough which inclined from the table to a covered pot buried in the ground. From this pot the mercury was dipped and poured into iron flasks and sealed for hauling and sale. The officer wondered that an operation as primitive as this would fill enough flasks each year to fill four bellies, two mules' and two Grebses'.

Evidently it did, but only by dint of a terrible labor, morning to night. As he approached, Dinkle saw that the figure was Flossie's. Her back to him, she was using a sledgehammer to crush the larger chunks of ore before shoveling them into the furnace. She swung the hammer like a section hand, and Dinkle was reminded of the poet's line, "The smith a mighty man is he." She was certainly more male than female, and certainly mightier than he. She wore rubber boots with apertures cut for her toes and patched long pants and galluses and a dirty shirt with no sleeves. She was six feet tall and she could dandle him like a baby if she pleased and he could smell her ten feet off.

He tightened the knot of his necktie. This was a formal call.

She sensed someone. Dropping the hammer and whirling into a John L. Sullivan stance, she clenched her knuckles into clubs. Then her expression altered to one of joy and teeth. Expressions on Flossie's face were as subtle as Bull Durham advertisements on the side of a barn. Her next was apprehensive. After a look at the mouth of the horizontal shaft, she strode to Dinkle, clapped a hand over his mouth, wrapped one muscular arm about his waist and half walked, half carried him toward the Grebs domicile. He kicked and gurgled but was helpless, and so resigned himself to studying his destination. It was a fortress rather than a shack. It was constructed entirely of railroad ties and ice molds, oblong boxes of iron flattened out. Even the windows, which lacked glass, were shuttered with iron. From a military point of view it was more defensible than the Alamo. Hustling him round the corner and through the only door, she pitched him inside, and joining him, slammed the door and bolted it, then shuttered both windows with iron clangs.

"There," she said. "Now hush," she said in a tone dulcet enough to crush ore and loud enough to be heard in Mexico City. "He ain't due outa the shaft for a spell. He'd of strung you up by the nuts we was t'stay out there. Pa's a corker."

I am in the soup, thought Stanley Dinkle. This is the Wild Woman of Borneo.

"Miss Grebs," he began.

"Set down, Stanley," she said, assisting him with a left hook to the ribs. "Make yoorself t'home."

"Miss Grebs," he began. The place was hot as Hades and stank to high heaven.

"Floss t'you, sweetie."

"Miss Grebs," he began, "I have come as a representative of the United States Army to tell you."

"You changed yoor mind! You wanta marry me!"

His eyes adjusted. Enough light seeped between the

railroad ties and around the iron shutters to permit limited vision. He had been deposited on a heap of gunnysacking under which, he assumed, was a bed. "To tell you," he continued, "that my post is a military area and I cannot allow unauthorized civilians on it."

"You mean the other night? That was a ruckus!" she enthused. "Nearly had you where the hair's short, huh, Stanley?"

"At any time, day or night." The shack's interior was almost as sumptuous as its facade. He made out another bed, a table, two chairs, one of them under his hostess, and a cone of empty tin cans garnished with flies. "What I'm saying is, Miss Grebs," he continued.

"You love me!"

"What I'm attempting to say is, it is off limits to you and your father."

"Yoor cuckoo for me, goddammit," she said.

"No, I'm not," he said. "I am not."

"Well, I am for you!"

"No, you're not," he said. "You are not."

During this impasse they squinted at each other through the gloom. Flossie Grebs wore her hair in a bun tied with a piece of twine. It was streaked with cinnabar dust. Her big hands were red with same. She had a mole on her chin. The bridge of her nose went east, the tip west. Her eyes were undecided.

I have seen a face like that before, thought Stanley Dinkle. It was on a horse at Fort Riley.

He rose. "I'll be going."

"I'll call Pa," she said.

He sat down and took off his hat. "Miss Grebs," he said, "how many men do you know?"

"You," she said. "Pa. Mister Offus."

"No others?"

"I seen some in Marathon. We go up there twicet a year."

"El Paso?"

"I never been."

"Aha," he said. "There you are. It isn't me. You don't

know anybody else. You'd be attracted to any man hereabouts."

"I never had a chancet!" she cried. Belligerently she blew her nose on the tail of her shirt. Had he not lent her an ear, she might have taken it. "We come down here from Colorada ten years back, livin' in the mountains. Nary man around. Pa had him a silver claim he worked an' then the shaf' flooded. That's how come he calls this the Dryass. He had him a wet one alltimes in Colorada, caught the rheumatiz an' catarrh. He's a tough ol' shitepoke, though. Ma run away with some tinhorn drummer from Kansas City when I was nine an' a year later she come back ruint. Oh, didn' she weep an' didn' she wail! You know what Pa done? Beat hell out of 'er, druv 'er off, never did see 'er again. So anyways, we hitched up the mules an' come down t'Texas for the climate. Been here ever since," she concluded, "two birds in the goddam wilderness. Break yoor back for two, three flasks a year. Two, three hunderd dollars cash money's all we eat an' buy coal on. An' nobody t'talk to but each damn other. So yoor a sight for sore eyes, Stanley."

He twiddled the brim of his hat. "Why don't you leave?"

"Pa'd die," she said.

"Die?"

"Ain't you see 'im? How he shakes? How he's got no teeth? That's from what they call 'ex-cess sal-i-va-tion.' You breathe in them mercury fumes workin' the soot with lime an' you get the shakes an' yoor teeth fall out. An' without choppers he can't eat hard food, just sof.' So he goes around fartin' up a storm. Sof' food'll do it. Gasses up yoor guts like you wouldn' guess."

"I see," said Dinkle politely.

"He wouldn't pass away of that, though. I was t'leave 'im, it'd hammer his heart."

"I'm sure," said Dinkle.

"I'm all he's got but for two mules an' two guns an' the mine."

"Is there actually much ore in there?"

"Hell, no," she said honestly. "There's naught in the Dryass Mine but beans an' dreams."

"Oh," said Dinkle, rising. "Well, Miss Grebs, I'll be going now."

"I'll call Pa," she said.

He sat down and put on his hat and tried to appear nonchalant, as though staying were his idea. But sweat bubbled under his collar and the stench of the place made him slightly sick at his stomach.

She may be the plug-ugliest woman I have ever met, thought Stanley Dinkle, but she is not going to play on my sympathy. I am not a fiddle.

Flossie Grebs crossed her legs, demurely, hoisted a rubber boot, and through the cut hole counted her toes. Suddenly she dropped the boot with a thud. He jumped. "I ain't good enough for you!" she cried.

"My dear Miss Grebs," he said.

"I can write my name an' I can cipher some—you wanta see me?"

"No, thank you," he said.

"An' I can read! Here—" She leaped up and pulled a leather-covered tome from beneath a bed. "*Ivanhoe* by Sir Walter Scott. You wanta hear a page?"

"No, thank you."

She flung the book at the cone of tin cans, irritating the flies and producing a dreadful clatter, then clomped to stand over him, hands on hips. "Yoor makin' me mad, Stanley," she warned. "I love you but I might bust you one."

That rankled him. He'd had a bellyful of being bullied. He set a military jaw, determined to restate once more the purpose of his call and take his leave. "Miss Grebs," he began.

"An' I ain't fancy enough for you, am I? Don't you have no 'magination? Can't you 'magine me I was t'gussy up?" She stooped over him. "Goddammit, give me a chancet! I love you!"

"You do not," he protested. "I'm just here. Miss Grebs, I insist."

She inclined over him like a retort trough over an open

pot. Then her voice melted. "Don't you know, darlin'? In this vale of tears you make do with what you got."

"You're just lonely," he argued, turning his head to escape the downpour of her passion.

"So're you," she said. "Yoor a lorn man, Stanley Dinkle. Terrible lorn."

"Damnation, Miss Grebs. I am not."

She put powerful hands on his shoulders. "How old're you?"

He struggled. Had she been a man—although he had doubts about her gender—he'd have kneed her in the crotch. "Old enough," he grunted.

"You'll never see thirty again, noor will I." Her chin descended on his chin. "We ain't got much time, the neither of us." In the center of the mole on her chin bloomed one wistful, spinster hair. "I think of you nights, down the road, lyin' in yoor bed an' wishin' for a woman, an' me here, wishin' for a man. It's a pity."

Back, backward into the gunnysacks he was coerced. "Miss Grebs, there are limits!" he panted.

"I'm scairt, Stanley," she whispered. "So're you. We're scairt we won't find somebody."

His hat brim impacted with the wall behind him. The hat itself crushed forward over his eyes. "I'm an officer!" he expostulated. "In the United!"

"We ain't youngsters, we can't be choosy. Maybe I ain't fit for the Zigfield Follies," she conceded, "but look at you. A banty rooster with red hair."

Her breathing fired his nostrils. Now it was as though he were being smeltered, reduced by her ardor to his irreducible elements.

"But I'll have you if you'll have me," she cooed. "Two's company, Stanley. Look at me."

She lifted his lid.

He looked, but not at her. Something behind her mesmerized him.

Through an opening between the railroad ties, directly across the shack from them and on a level with his head, something resembling a mean, obscene penis was being stealthily inserted, inch by inch. It was the single barrel of a 12-gauge shotgun.

"Oh, my God," groaned Stanley Dinkle.

She sprang from him at the roar outside: "Floss! Floss! I'm locked out! Who's in there?"

Dinkle, too, was on his feet in a flash. He skipped to the left, beyond the table, but the barrel tracked him.

"I'm all right, Pa! It's the lootenant!"

"Dinkle, you bastid!"

The officer skipped to the right, hopped over the other bed, and took refuge behind the stove, but the barrel moved with him like a divining rod. "I'm on official business!" he yelped.

"I'll blow yoor business off!"

Flossie Grebs was also active, trying simultaneously to elude the muzzle of the gun, which wavered to and fro and waggled up and down, and to unbolt the door. That done, in two lioness leaps she reached her guest and pounced, crashing with him to the floor and screaming, "Rape! Rape! Shoot, Pa, shoot!"

The room exploded. Within the stalwart walls, the effect was similar to that of an artillery piece. Amid a hail of pellets Flossie Grebs set Dinkle on his boots and made for the door with him. Dizzied by the blast, however, he was not yet capable of locomotion. Roller-skating on a tin can or tripping over Sir Walter Scott he fell again, and she was forced to drag him by the necktie. Outdoors, she propped him vertical and provided him with momentum by means of a shove. But the delay had been fatal to her plans.

Champion T. Grebs rounded the corner. Raising his reloaded weapon, he would have filled the officer with lead had not his daughter interposed her body between him and his prey. "Outa the way, gel!" bellowed the miner. "He's my turkey!"

"No, he ain't, Pa, he's my rooster!" she cried. "Shoot him an' you shoot me!"

Dinkle accepted her protection rapturously. Throwing his arms about her from the rear, he clung to her torso as he might have to a tree trunk. The sight of Champion

Grebs would have been enough to palpitate the stoutest heart. "Excess salivation" had indeed wrought awful havoc. In the red maw of the mouth, every tooth was conspicuous by its absence, while the hands, even the shotgun, trembled like leaves. And his beard, horrid with cinnabar dust, was sufficiently long to offer accommodation to "two Owls and a Hen, four Larks and a Wren." Before such a spectacle any man might have quailed, but in the last half hour Stanley Dinkle had also endured personal abuse, sexual assault, and cerebral concussion. What overcame him now was a discovery irrelevant to all of these. He hung on for dear life to a feature of Flossie Grebs's anatomy the existence of which he had not suspected. His arms circumnavigated an incredible bosom. He introduced himself to a brace of breasts more copious than any in his acquaintance of fantasy. He squeezed. He smiled.

Hot dog, thought Stanley Dinkle.

I have read of the Seven Wonders of the World. I would rate these below the Pyramids but above the Hanging Gardens of Babylon.

"Danger, 100,000 Jolts!" he said to no one in particular.

"Take yoor dirty hands off'n her tits!" howled Champ Grebs, breaking outraged wind and advancing on the pair, weapon at shoulder level.

"Thanks for the hospitality, Mr. Grebs," the officer smiled.

"Leave 'er be 'less you brung the capittle!" added the old panderer.

"Don't shoot, Pa!" Flossie cried, beginning a withdrawal. "He's bughouse about me!"

"I was raised on a farm," Dinkle reminisced, apropos of nothing. "Milked many a cow in my day."

Her withdrawal necessitated his. In unison, along the wagon tracks and away from the shack they retreated in a unique dance step, a combination of the bunny hug and cakewalk.

"Floss, you whoor, let loose of 'im!"

"Don't kill my lover, Pa!" begged the distraught Flossie. "Kill me!"

" 'The monkeys have no tails in Samboanga,' " Dinkle informed them.

"You bitch, I'll dynamite the both of you!" resolved the ancient miner. "I'm countin'—one, two!"

At this juncture he was taken with a catarrhal fit, requiring him to cough and then to expectorate at some length, a respite which Flossie Grebs turned to her own advantage. Starting her hero with a violent push, she hurled herself upon her father.

"Run, Stanleeeee, run!" she shrieked.

"Three!"

Stanley Dinkle ran. Through the black ash he galloped, across the depression and up the ledge, his course rapid but erratic. When the 12-gauge was discharged, he was safely out of range, although a spice of buckshot on his backside sped him on his way.

8

The Battle of Mount Bagsak

Corporal Phipps knocked at the door of the purple house late that afternoon. "Sir?"

"Yes?"

"Sir, I'm here to express our regrets."

"For what?"

"For the fracas over inspection, sir. And for what Biddle said about officers and gentlemen. He's sorry and we're sorry."

"Oh. Well. Regrets accepted."

"And to ask you, Lieutenant, if you'll have dinner with us tonight."

"Oh? Well." Dinkle scratched a mosquito bite. To his sorrow, he had already broken rule number one: don't argue with 'em. To accept the invitation would be to break number two: don't hobnob with 'em. But he was enormously pleased. And if there was anything he had need of after his ordeal at the Dryass Mine, it was civilized companionship. "Ahem," he said. "You may inform the Philadelphia Light Horse that I'll be happy to put on the nose bag."

Phipps grinned. "Thank you, sir. We'll see you at six."

Light my bulb, thought Stanley Dinkle, and call me Edison. They are decent lads after all.

I shall dine off gold plate and wiggle my little finger and be a friend to man.

Passing the muchachos, who were preparing the repast, the CO presented himself promptly at six o'clock in polished boots, combed carrot hair, tucked tie, and gold bar on the collar. Since their arrival he had not been inside the Sibley, a new-fangled pyramidal affair of yellow canvas sixteen feet square with roll-up sides for ventilation, but the Light Horse, even a first glance told him, had contrived to improve the quarters of their predecessors, the Keystone Lancers. A swanky walnut washstand stood outside the door, while the interior was furnished with a wooden floor, cots with let-down mosquito nettings, a poster picture of Theda Bara, "The Vamp," in a black negligee, several lamps and comfortable chairs, a large table, a poster picture of Mary Pickford, "America's Sweetheart," in curls and a white dress, a rifle rack, clothes trees, and a poster picture of Pearl White in a perilous situation, all of which were neat as a pin—another responsibility, he assumed, of their small strikers. It was scarcely field conditions. It was the lap of luxury.

"Lex" Phipps seated the honored guest.

"Phew" Pugh welcomed him with a cup of champagne from a bottle chilled in the Rio Grande.

"Freddy" Den Uyl regaled him with a record on the Vic, "There's a Little bit of Bad in Every Good Little Girl."

"Stew" Darlington filled his cup.

"Bid" Biddle played another ragtime tune, "He May Be Old, But He's Got Young Ideas."

"Luce" Thayer filled his cup.

Every man had been assigned his task and timing. It was going swimmingly.

Between records, and encouraged by the champagne, to which his lips were total strangers, the officer got something off his chest. "I know this duty isn't quite what you expected when you were called up," he said. "It's a pretty rotten post, I'll admit. But in this vale of tears you make do with what you've got."

His hosts nodded agreement.

"You'd rather be with Pershing, of course, chasing Villa over in Chihuahua. Well, in case you're interested, so would I. I'd give my eyeteeth to be. So whenever you get the notion I thrive on this life, just remember, I hate it here as much as you do."

There was a lull.

"I'd rather be in Europe, fighting with the Brits," said "Stew" Darlington.

"Me for the French," said "Luce" Thayer. "And the mademoiselles. Ooh-la-la!"

"Now, that's an authentic war," averred "Freddy" Den Uyl. "Gads if I know what kind of cotillion this is."

"We'll be over there soon enough," said the CO darkly, studying his bubbles. "In any case, they also serve who only stand and wait. And drink champagne," he added in a stab at humor.

Dinner was served by the muchachos. Even by officers' standards, it was a banquet. They had tinned terrapin shipped from the East by indulgent families, and a roast of pork garnished with fresh vegetables and hot rolls purchased or pilfered by the little Mexicanos across the river. Seated at the head of the groaning board, it seemed to Dinkle that his table manners were a subject of inordinate curiosity, and to divert attention from his knife and fork, he inquired politely into the history of the Light Horse. The young men were delighted to oblige. They were as packed with tradition as with pork. A group of lawyers, bankers, and merchants organized in 1774 as self-supporting volunteers to protect the Continental Congress, the troop had acted as personal bodyguard to General Washington, not incidentally doing the Revolution yeoman service at Trenton, Brandywine, and Valley Forge. When Lee had the temerity to invade Pennsylvania, it dropped its briefs, chattels, and receipts and drove him out at Gettysburg. It sailed the bounding main to Cuba in '98. It held a glorious guidon high, it paid its own patrician way, and to this day, almost a century and a half after its first call to arms, it was still the official military unit of the city of Philadelphia, heading its parades and escorting its visiting dignitaries.

Coffee was served.

"Hell on hooves, sir," said Phipps. "That's the Light Horse!"

"Really?" asked Dinkle.

"You should see us in our dress uniforms," said Pugh. "Blue coats and white breeches!"

"High black boots!" said Darlington.

"Black helmets and a beartail plume!" chirped Thayer. "The berries!"

"Really?" asked Dinkle. "Like the Horse Guards. Over the Big Pond, in London."

"Someone said that to Daddy once," lisped Den Uyl. "He was furious. 'Only the tails,' he said. 'That's all we ever saw of the British.' "

The table was cleared by the chief cooks and bottle washers. The guest of honor accepted a whiskey and water from Pugh, a cheroot from Biddle, and a match from Thayer. Biddle nodded at Phipps.

"Tell us, sir," said Phipps. "How long have you been in the Army?"

"Eleven years."

The pause was pregnant.

"You mean, sir—if you don't mind my asking, sir—you mean you've been—" Phipps stopped.

The officer completed the query. "A shavetail for eleven years? No. I was an enlisted man for three."

"Oh," said Darlington. "Then you went to the Point."

"No." Dinkle drained his cup. Pugh hopped to the flowing bowl for another. "I was commissioned in the field."

"In the field?" they chorused.

"In the Philippines."

"In the Philippines?" they chorused.

He tested the new libation and found it good. He puffed on the cigar and found it likewise. "Yes," he said. "In ought-five. With the Fourteenth Cavalry, under Colonel Scott. That's General Hugh Scott now, Army Chief of Staff."

They were properly impressed. He didn't notice that they abstained from after-dinner drinking, or that the other five glanced meaningfully at Thayer.

"Sir," asked Thayer, "can you tell us a little something about service in the Philippines?"

He was delighted to oblige. Army HQ had been at Zamboanga, under General Leonard Wood, but in '05 he himself was stationed on the isles of Sulu, with HQ at Jolo, and engaged, along with his outfit, the 14th, in pacifying the islands. They were equipped with Colt .45's and Krag rifles and having a devil of a time with the Moros, the natives, whom the Americans called "goo-goos" and who were well armed with Remingtons and Snyders and barongs, big razor-edged cleavers which would cut a man's body in two with one stroke. In addition, the Moros used spears and blowguns with poisoned arrows, and when they went into battle they beat on copper war gongs.

"Amazing, by George." Den Uyl spoke for all, then added, almost on cue, "Sir, exactly how does an enlisted man get a commission in the field?"

"Well, you have to do somethin', I mean be mixed up in somethin', out-of-the-ordinary. I was. I mean, I happened to be." The officer was embarrassed. He was having difficulty enunciating. His tongue tangled with his teeth. "Then afterward, Colonel Scott says, 'Dinkle, I like your style.' An' asked me if I'd care to attend Mounted Service School, an' be an officer, an' I said I would. Then he was transferred to Washington an' I figured he'd forgotten, but nope, he didn'. Comes a letter through channels an' away I went. Got the good ol' gold bar in ought-eight." He tipped his cup in self-congratulation. "So you see, actually I wasn't commissioned in the field. Got it for somethin' happened in the field three years b'fore."

A brief intermission followed. It was darkening in the Sibley. Someone lit a single lamp. The officer's cup was empty. Pugh replenished. The six young men drew chairs or sat on cots close to their commander, surrounding him on three sides. The entire evening had been but prologue to this moment. Now the stage was set, the lights were up, a rapt audience was assembled. If champagne and whiskey and good fellowship had done their proper work, the Light Horse could be sure of their man, and hence, their entertainment. There remained only one crucial question to ask, and since "Bid" Biddle had conceived and directed the comedy in the first place, he had reserved that pleasure unto himself.

"We don't mean to pry, Lieutenant, but we're honestly interested. Could you tell us what it was you were involved in? That is, what brought you to the attention of General Scott?"

Stanley Dinkle planted his elbows firmly on the table. He felt fine and dandy. If an army marched on its stomach, so did an officer, and a woman was only a woman but a good cigar was a smoke. He looked about the table, basking in the warmth of each fresh, innocent face. Good fellows every one, like bubbles they had risen in his esteem. And if the bill for the banquet was a story, he'd pay up gladly, for he had a crackerjack, and true to boot. He'd had the Keystone Lancers on the edge of their seats with it in this very tent not a month ago. He drew on the cheroot. He smiled a friendly, terrapin smile.

"Ahem," he said. "Well, here goes then. Don' really like t'talk about it. Soun's like tootin' my own horn. But it'll give you an idea what war's all about. You don' know, b'lieve me, you don' know. So here goes. How I got t'be an officer. Battle of Mount Bagsak."

The Moro chieftain giving them the most trouble on Sulu in '05, he said, was Panglima Hassan. He was a juramentado, as were his warriors, a fanatical follower of the Prophet sworn to kill Christians in the belief that if he did, he'd be taken at once to paradise on a white horse with a green mane. So the Army had no choice—if Sulu was to be pacified, Panglima Hassan had to be permanently disposed of. Once he was proven to be mortal, and thus a liar, resistance would collapse. Then word came one day that the chief was hiding out in a nipa hut in the crater of Mount Bagsak, an extinct volcano, and Colonel Scott immediately led K Troop, sixty men including Private Dinkle, on an overnight march through jungle and cogon grass. As dawn came, the troop lay prone around the lip of the crater, scarcely breathing, weapons at the ready.

Stanley Dinkle reached for a phonograph record and placed it on the table before him. "Here. Here's the crater, round." Heads craned closer. He read the label. " 'There's a Broken Heart for Every Light on Broadway.' Well, well. Anyway, here's the crater. We're lyin' aroun' the edge, lookin' down in. Here, this hole in the middle, that's the hut. Interperter hollers in Moro t'surrender. No answer. He hollers again. Not a peep. Colonel commands fire. Say, boys, we shot that hut t'smithereens. Then a squad of six men goes down t'mop up."

He paused for suspense. "But it's a trap. Here—" He ran a finger across one side of the record. "Here's a ravine, jungle, thicker'n a raspberry patch. Suddenly some Snyders let loose out of it. Four of the six men cut down. Terrible. We start plungin' fire into the ravine. They shoot back up an' bang on gongs an' holler 'Bismillah! Bismillah!' "

The Light Horse jumped.

"Terr'ble racket. Then silence. Whatsa matter? Is ol' Hassan dead? Juramentados wiped out? How we gonna find out? Colonel Scott, he doesn' know."

Stanley Dinkle had a last deep draw on his cheroot and pitched it out the tent door. "Well, don' know what got into me, but I start down. All by my lonesome. Carryin' a Krag carbine. Well, I slide down an' head for the ravine. Can't see in for the vines. I'm about ten feet off when oh-oh, here he comes."

In the lamp the wick sputtered, but there was no other sound. The young men were spellbound.

"Hassan. Crazy as a bedbug. Swingin' a barong, whoosh, whoosh. I fire three times an' hit 'im three times. But a Moro takes lead like a grizzly bear an' he keeps on comin'. The Krag's empty an' say, I tell you, boys, I was sayin' my prayers. He swings at me with the barong, I swing at him with the Krag. Bam! They connec' an' away goes the barong an' away goes the carbine! We jump for 'em! He grabs the Krag an' aims an' pulls the trigger—click! I grab the barong an' swing like Ty Cobb at a curve ball—whoosh! Guess what!"

As one man, the Light Horse leaped to their feet.

"Guess what!" they chorused. " 'I slice 'im in two!' "

It was as though they had poured a bucket of ice water over Stanley Dinkle. He went white. He shivered.

"You knew," he said thickly. "I told the Lancers. They told you."

The effect they had achieved was more shocking than

anticipated. Wide grins faded from their faces, and merriment from their eyes. They sat down again as the officer stood up, tipping over his chair. He had sobered in an instant, but in order to support himself, as though he were ill, he crooked an arm around the center pole.

"Ha-ha," he said. "How funny. Invite me here for this. What a good joke. Ha-ha."

By contrast with the pole he seemed shorter and stubbier than usual, amost dwarfed.

"Only wanted tell you about war," he said. "The truth. Nobody tells. What it's like. Never the same again. You'll see."

He tried to look at them but blinked. He shook his head from side to side.

"Thank you for the food and drink. Gentlemen. For everything. If this is what gentlemen do, don't want to be one. Rather be me. A soldier."

He let go of the center pole and lunged for the door of the tent.

"G'night," he said. "Stan' guard."

Up the slope he trudged to his house. He was grievously hurt. He'd never been wounded, but this was what it must be like, a bullet passing through. In darkness he undressed and sat on his cot in BVD's. The night was noisy with insects more concerned about provender than pity. He put elbows on knees and face in hands. Stanley Dinkle was about as miserable as he cared to be.

He had pegged the Philadelphia Light Horse from the day they flivvered into his life and responsibility. They were spoiled rotten. And they were snobs. To demean him, to rub his simple nose in their sophistication, they'd built an elaborate trap into which he'd walked tail wagging to sit up and lie down and roll over and speak for his supper and get, finally, a smart-aleck boot in the butt. On the other hand, Biddle had sized him up exactly. Congress might ordain him a gentleman, but the Light Horse were the real McCoy. The situation was bass-ackwards. They were officer material, he was an enlisted man to the core. They had every social grace, he was a square peg in a world of round holes. They were Good-time Charlies, he was a stick-in-the-mud. They could charm a lady out of her corset, he was a born wallflower. They pranced. He pulled a plow. And to make the cheese more binding, he knew these things in his very guts. He envied Pugh his blue blood, Thayer his tenor voice, Den Uyl his wealth, Darlington his convivialty, Phipps his self-confidence, Biddle his looks. By comparison with the Philadelphians he was a hick, a boob more at home at a brawl than a ball, a gent by fluke and an officer by statute. He groaned. Because if he'd pegged the Light Horse, and Biddle had sized him up, Flossie Grebs had also hit the nail on the head.

I really am a lorn man, thought Stanley Dinkle.

I have been called everything in the book: Stub, Carrots, a tarantula, Stanley Steamer, a banty rooster, etc. Sticks and stones have broke my bones, names have broke my heart, but there's a broken heart for every light on Broadway.

He jumped up, fighting tears, and with a fist punched a gaping hole in the screen.

My real name is Stanley H. Dinkle. I have a passable horse. And a Postal Savings account. And some very good qualities. I write home every month. I ain't mean. I keep my nose clean. If I think about sex too much, why, that is natural. I know my business, which is soldiering. I try to be fair and do unto others. So to hell with those jitney jockeys. If they are the high and mighty of the earth, I am the salt. I may have to mingle with them in a military way, but from this night on I wash my hands of 'em as human beings.

Also I am a brave man.

9

"Hello, Central, Give Me Heaven"

Texas seemed to have a penchant for honoring its early settlers by lending both their Christian and surnames to its small towns. Edhogg had borrowed its multiple cognomen from those of the first mercury miner in the area. One would have been enough for Edhogg, however, since it boasted only one structure, a general store which served as supply center for miners, now few in number, as a saloon for ranch hands between there and Marathon, as post office, and as a communications center. It had a telephone.

In the morning after the Light Horse soiree, the CO of Patrol Post #2 drilled his troopers until he had sweat the last drops of champagne and arrogance and the last laugh out of them. That afternoon he saddled up and rode into the metropolis. This he did once a week, to see the sights, check his mail, and report by telephone to Fort Bliss, HQ of the Department of the Southwest, at El Paso. The store was a squat adobe building with a wooden ramada out front and several indigent dogs taking a siesta in its shade. Looping reins over the rail, the officer entered the establishment and was greeted with cordial disinterest by Mr. and Mrs. Harley Offus, a lank, malarial couple who shared living quarters in the storeroom with bins of staples, cases of canned goods, and a colony of termites. Treating himself to a bottle of grape soda and counter-shopping a box of shiny new Ingersoll watches, he passed the time of day with the proprietors. It passed slowly. They had no news. Neither did he. Harley Offus took that back —one of the dogs had produced a litter. In his own person, Harley Offus was the principal drawing card in

Edhogg. To get him to gab was worth the price of a pop, for he had a remarkable Adam's apple. When he spoke, one was reminded of the movement of a pump handle on a hot day. Dinkle handed over a letter home, which reminded the postmaster. There was a letter for the lieutenant.

It was the officer's monthly pay voucher, in the amount of $166.80, which worked out to $5.56 daily for a second lieutenant with eight years' service. Out of this bonanza he must put uniforms on his back, food on his table, and a roof over his head.

Dinkle pocketed the voucher, polished off the grape soda, went to the wall telephone, pulled down the mouthpiece, and putting receiver to ear, twirled the crank. After several energetic spins he got Central in Marathon, identified himself and the call as Army, and asked to be put through to Captain Claude Mapes, Adjutant 8th Cavalry, at Bliss. It took some doing, even though the fort was less than a hundred miles away by wire, but after cacophony and a cutoff and negotiations with the El Paso operator, Dinkle had his party.

"Captain? This is Dinkle, down at Number Two."

"Oh, yes. Hullo, Dinkle. Coma esta?"

"Fine, thank you."

"Seen anything of Villa?"

"No, sir."

"Neither has Pershing, if that's any consolation. All quiet on your front?"

"Yes, sir."

"How you getting along with the Philadelphia Light Horse?"

"Well." Dinkle frowned. He'd met Mapes only once, passing hastily through Bliss on his way here, and you had to watch your p's and q's with superiors. Besides, if walls had ears, so did telephone operators. "About as well as you'd expect, I guess."

Mapes's chuckle came through clearly. "Wowsers, are they?"

Dinkle was reassured. "They drove down here in Model T's."

"You don't say."

"And we stand Retreat to a Victrola."

"I'll be damned."

"I thought the Keystone Lancers were the limit, Captain, but I tell you, this bunch takes the cake."

"So I've heard."

The line squawked.

"Dinkle, how long have you been stuck down there?"

"Six weeks. Starting seven."

"Going a bit bug, I'll wager."

"Well."

"Tell you what. You've earned a break. Why don't you come on in here and have some fun? Take seventy-two hours, relax."

Dinkle was rendered speechless.

"Dinkle? Are you there?"

"Captain, would you please repeat?"

"I said, pack up your troubles in your old kit bag and come on in to El Paso. How does that sound?"

"Music to my ears, sir!"

"Fine. Come on tomorrow, then. I'll have orders cut—you won't need 'em—but you can stop by here and pick 'em up on your way back. To make it legal."

"Sir, I can't tell you! Thanks a million!"

"Poor nada, my boy. Just be good and stay out of Juárez, and if you can't be good, be careful. Heh-heh. I'll see you out here when you've sobered up. So long, Dinkle."

"Good-by, Captain. I really appreciate!"

A click at the other end. Stanley Dinkle turned, tipsy with joy. Payday, leave, a bed, a bath, wine, women, song—his cup ranneth over. Receiver still in his hand, he weaved toward the door until the line went taut, turning him again. When he realized why, and realized the proprietors were staring at him, he grinned and tossed the receiver onto its hook.

"Going to El Paso," he said.

"Don't take no wooden nickels," warned Harley Offus.

"C'mon, Baby. Here's Your Rattle!" grinned Stanley Dinkle.

" 'Make not provision for the flesh,' " said Mrs. Offus, " 'to fulfill the lusts thereof.' "

But the officer was already out the door, where he stopped on a dime. To his consternation, Flossie Grebs was hitching her mule at the far end of the ramada. He shrank into the shade, but in so doing, trod inadvertently upon the tail of a sleeping canine, which emitted a dolorous yip. The miner's daughter squinted. He was caught.

Expecting an assault, he put his back to the store wall. Instead, she came to him almost diffidently, hands in pockets and scuffing boots.

"I'm 'shamed 'bout the other day," she said.

"Going to El Paso," he said.

"Get any buckshot in yoor ass?"

"On leave."

"I jus' wanted you t'love me a little," she said. "Then Pa spoilt it, goddam him."

"Got to go," said Stanley Dinkle. "Got to pack up my troubles in my old kit bag."

She took his hand and led him to the hitch rail. "No, set with me a spell, please."

"Miss Grebs," he protested.

"Oh hush. I won't hurt you."

Reluctantly he sat beside her.

"El Paso," she said. "Is it big?"

"Not very. Not compared to San Francisco or Seattle."

"You been t'those?"

"Several times."

"Do they have trolleys? In El Paso?"

"Yes."

"I never seen one. How do they work?"

"By electricity. They run on rails, like trains."

"Be they dangerous?"

"No."

"Do they have stores just for ladies?"

"I suppose."

She was silent. He continued to be surprised by the difference in her today. Her questions were those of a child, while her demeanor, loud and crude in her natural habitat, a cave or a sty, was in this civilized setting almost feminine. She even heaved a sigh.

In the shade, dogs drowsed. Down the rail the mule had gone to sleep, ears forward. Nearer his master, Hassan whickered. Flies and fools and gunfire did not concern him, but he wished to express an innate perturbation about mules.

Then, as though Edhogg had a main street thronged with curious passers-by, Flossie Grebs glanced up and down. Furtively she thrust into a pants pocket and pressed something into the officer's hand. "Here. Here's ten dollars. I come in t'buy vittles with it. What I want you t'do is, in El Paso, take it into one of them ladies' stores an' buy me the best dress they got an' bring it back. Then I'll wear it for you an' maybe you'll change yoor mind an' britches."

"Miss Grebs, I couldn't do that." He tried to return the bill.

"Why not?"

"Because I simply. I've never."

"Stanley Dinkle, look at me."

He would not.

With firm but gentle thumb and forefinger she took him by the ear and compelled his face to hers. "You look," she said.

Her eyes were green.

"What d'you see?"

"A shotgun."

"Look again, you ninny."

He looked.

"Underneath," she said. "Somethin' live."

Under the green were glints of gold, swimming. He recalled the green water of a pond in springtime, and a boy bent over it, bewitched by tadpoles.

"Oh," he said.

"There's a woman in there sure as hell," she said. "It's me. Can't you take no pity on 'er?"

"Miss Grebs," he said.

"Stanley, d'you know I'm thirty-one years old an' never had a store-bought dress?"

His face was on fire.

"We got t'see me in a dress!" she whispered.

His earlobe cried out.

"Stanley, what if I'm beautiful an' we don't even know it!"

Her eyes rounded with wonder at the possibility. In one appeared an anticipatory tear. And as within the oyster, a grain of irritant sand may make a pearl, deep within the soul of Stanley Dinkle was born a tender, irritant doubt.

"I'll buy the dress," he groaned.

"Goddam," she breathed.

She kissed him.

Stanley Dinkle went off the rail like a rocket and around it to his horse. Flossie Grebs rushed in sweet flustration into the store. The officer spurred, to no avail, for in his haste he had neglected to unhitch. With an oath he stood on his head, unlooped the reins, and red face hidden beneath his hat brim, kicked the willing Hassan into a trot.

It was some time before either regained his composure. The man was as glad to be rid of the woman as the horse of the mule. With his necktie he rubbed her kiss from his lips, and in the process discovered a ten-dollar bill in his hand.

It will be a cold day in hell, swore Stanley Dinkle, when I buy glad rags for a dame. I will leave the money for her in Edhogg on my way tomorrow.

Tomorrow! He would sail into El Paso the way Dewey sailed into Manila Bay. You may fire when ready, Dinkle!

But the bill was like a grain of sand in his oyster. A pitiful crumple of paper, grimy with ore dust, he could picture how much backbreak and loneliness had been required to wrest it from the Dryass Mine. He wondered what Champion Grebs would do to his darling when she returned without "vittles" and how they would subsist for the next month. He wondered what on earth had come over him when he looked into her eyes. He wondered. From long experience with horses, he doubted you could take a defective mare and turn her, presto, into a serviceable mount. You could have a mole removed, you could scrub her down and curry her up, you could tie a ribbon round her tail. But you might more sensibly sell her for glue and buy a sound animal in the first place. On the other hand, the green of Flossie Grebs's eyes did hide something vital and alive, just as her dirty shirt veiled those phenomenal Hanging Gardens of Babylon. And she had certainly been a horse of a different color and temperament today. A man could almost talk to her. And it would be nice to have somebody to talk to besides Hassan, even if she were homelier than a hedge fence. Stanley Dinkle had difficulty carrying a tune, hence never essayed one in public. But now, reining his steed to a walk, he raised his voice in pensive song:

Hello, Central, give me heaven,
For my Mamma's there,
You can find her with the angels,
On the golden stair.
She'll be glad it's me who's speaking,
Call her, won't you please,
For I want to surely tell her,
We're so lonely here.

10

When the Cat's Away, the Mice Will Play Polo

Although they had executed it perfectly, the Philadelphia Light Horse were of several minds about the prank played on their commander. Phipps said it was a gem, but ever conscientious, added that he wasn't sure it was sporting of them to kick a man in his dignity. Den Uyl snorted. Dinkle's dignity be damned—if they had let some steam out of Stanley's boiler, he richly deserved it. Darlington's admission, that the Battle of Mount Bagsak had been a rather rousing yarn, Pugh countered with the statement that he hadn't swallowed a word of it, particularly the part about slicing a goo-goo in two. Thayer's reaction was mixed. He disliked Dinkle as much as any of them, but practical jokes frequently backfired, and the CO might be even more the martinet now. He asked what Biddle thought and Biddle said he didn't, he had more momentous things to ponder than shit shavetails. On second thought, Dinkle was less than that, for shits often had style, and could therefore be tolerated. Dinkle was only a turd. On one point, however, the six were unanimous: for worse or worser, in cussedness and health, the little lieutenant was theirs to endure for two more interminable weeks.

Which was why, when they presented themselves on the parade ground at seven the next morning, mounted and prepared to drill or be sent on patrol, they nearly keeled from the saddle. For he awaited them in his best bib and tucker, boots shining like a nigger's heel. At his side was a cardboard suitcase.

"Ahem," he said. "It may come as hard news to you, but I am going to El Paso on leave. For seventy-two hours, counting travel time. This is Tuesday. That means you'll be on your own hook till Friday afternoon."

It took a superhuman effort to restrain themselves from whooping, drawing pistols, firing, and galloping deliriously off in all directions.

"Corporal Phipps," the CO went on, "I leave you in charge of Fort Dinkle—I mean, of Patrol Post Number Two. You will carry on exactly as I have. Patrol, drill, inspect, post guard—and if you don't get the discipline and obedience to orders you should, I'll have your stripes. Is that clear?"

"Yes, sir."

Darlington poked Pugh in the ribs while Lieutenant Dinkle paused to rub his chin. "Before I go, I want to tell you another story. You seem to enjoy stories," he commented. "But this one has a moral. The Thirteenth Cavalry was stationed at Columbus a long time. It got fat, and careless, and lazy as a pet coon. Then one night—well, you know what happened. By morning seven soldiers were dead and five wounded. Eight civilians were dead, men and women. The town was up in smoke. And this happened at Columbus, New Mexico, a place nobody ever heard of, a place too unimportant to get hurt."

He looked about him, at his purple house, at the Sibley tent, at his pink pagoda in its arbor of cane, at the Rio Grande lustrous in early light. It was as though he were leaving them for months rather than days. In the interval, Thayer yawned for Biddle's benefit and Den Uyl put a boot in Phipps's ankle.

"So do your duty," he said solemnly. "Keep your eyes peeled and remember my order—don't cross that river. And remember something else. An old man and a woman and a mule made complete jackasses of us the other night—let's have no more Keystone Kops affairs like that. I remind you. You're doing more than guard this post, or Edhogg, or even the state of Texas. You're here to defend the United States of America. Very well, defend it."

It occurred to him that a simple announcement of departure had become a patriotic exhortation. Self-consciously he checked the crease in his sleeve. "Are there any questions?"

Den Uyl could not resist. "Sir, I assume you're riding up to Marathon to catch the train. That's a long ride. Would you rather drive? We'd be glad to lend you a Lizzie."

"Of course not," said the officer.

"By the way, sir," said Biddle, "do you know how to drive?"

"Of course I do," snapped the officer. "Dis-missed," he snapped, and picking up his suitcase, marched toward the grove.

The Light Horse took every precaution. Phipps assumed command and pretended to put them through the Manual of the Pistol, Revised, Mounted, while they gave the CO ample time to saddle up. When he emerged from the trees they seemed busily engaged. When he was around the grove and apparently on his way, they gave him a full five minutes to be safely gone, for it would be typical of the tarantula to double back and sink his nippers into them. Then the Philadelphians could wait no more.

"Hoooooray!"

The cheer burst from their throats, and bumping stirrups they sent the Morgans into a gallop, wheeling in wide and rapturous circles about the parade ground. Dinkle had decamped! For three splendiferous days they were free as the breeze!

Like schoolboys at recess they raced and waved hats and made the welkin ring with glee and then, on simultaneous inspiration, gigged the animals into line and charged the pecan grove. Peeling from saddles they ran to "Henrietta" and "Olivia." Down came canvas tops and side curtains. Behind each wheel a trooper took his place and set the hand brake firmly and pulled the carburetor choke and set the spark and throttle levers, while before each radiator yet another trooper bent and braced himself.

They cranked and cranked. They cursed. They spat into palms and took turns.

They cranked and cranked. They cursed. They rolled

up sleeves. But the Model T's had been too long stored to be this easily reanimated.

Out of toolboxes came the jacks, and one rear wheel of each auto was raised, thus bypassing the transmission and allowing the rear wheel to act as a flywheel connected directly to the engine, a stratagem frequently resorted to by desperate jitney owners and one which rarely failed.

They cranked and cranked. They cursed.

There was one last hope. Out of the toolboxes came a bottle, and with a medicine dropper a hypodermic shot of ether was administered to each intake manifold. They said a silent prayer.

They cranked and cranked. Two cylinders caught, then three. Like sleeping beauties wakening from a witch's spell, the flivvers shimmied with enthusiasm. And then—Eureka! The grove was rent with euphony, the earth itself was shaken by forty combustive horses!

11

"He Saith Among the Trumpets, Ha, Ha"

To a soldier and a horse accustomed to little more exertion than hops, skips, and jumps up and down a parade ground, it was indeed a long, dry ride to Marathon. To while away the miles and hours they amused themselves with divers recreations. They counted pebbles in the road. They snorted at the gall of an offer of a flivver for the journey. They tried to list the capitals of the forty-eight states. They berated themselves for having forgotten to leave Flossie Grebs's grocery money with Harley Offus. They fought for the Union at Yellow Tavern, and with distinction. They dozed. They lost themselves in reveries of Zamboanga, in the Philippines, laved by warm winds and waters of the Sulu Sea, and of its sandy streets and scarlet hibiscus and fragrant ylang-ylang trees. The houses, set on stilts, were roofed with galvanized iron, and now and then, in the night, a cocoanut would fall on an iron roof with a fearful bang.

Arriving in Marathon, which bustled by comparison with Edhogg, the officer stabled an exhausted Hassan and ordered him fed oats. Declining to enter The Pray-For-Us, the saloon, he went directly to the depot, purchased his ticket and an El Paso paper, sat on a bench, opened his suitcase, and economized by supping upon what he had brought with him: hardtack and a can of tomatoes. According to the paper, the German artillery assault upon Verdun continued, resulting in an awful carnage among the Frogs, while Pershing had split his indefatigable forces in Chihuahua in order to effect the capture of Villa, which was imminent.

At 6:14 the bell and wail of the 6:02 sent a shiver up

his spine. He climbed aboard and ensconced himself for the hour's ride at a coach window next to a patent medicine salesman whose biggest item was "Lobelia" and across from a grass widow whose biggest items caused him to loosen tie and collar. It was still daylight when the train entered the outskirts of El Paso. These were tent cities housing the thousands of National Guardsmen called up for the duration of the border emergency, and there were three—Camps Cotton, Pershing and Stewart, the latter the abode of the Keystone Lancers and their successors, the Philadelphia Light Horse. Closer in, Lieutenant Dinkle's attention was caught by a wide expanse of desert void of human and habitation and cleared of much of its flora. Two men in knickers, however, were flailing industriously away at a greasewood bush with clubs.

"What the heck they doing?" he asked the salesman. "Killing a snake?"

"Shucks, no," was the answer. "Playing golf."

Leaving the station, the officer was accosted by three panhandlers within two blocks and heard an appeal new to him. Their brethren elsewhere claimed to need only ten cents for carfare to leave the city, but since El Paso's altitude and dry climate attracted consumptives, these unfortunates wheezed that they were "lungers," unable to work.

Seeking accommodations, he first tried the Paso del Norte, the town's largest and finest, only to learn that the daily rate for a single with bath was an exorbitant $2.50. Spurning this, he located the more modest New York Hotel and moved into a Spartan single at $1.50, bath down the hall. Quickly he unpacked his suitcase, quickly headed for the bath, and after waiting until a female with henna hair and challenging eye had performed her ablutions, unlocked the door, and emerged, he took possession of the facility. Drawing a hot, deep, almost a lascivious tub, he entered it and disposed his limbs.

"Aaaaaaah!"

With this sigh, this baptism of bliss, courtesy of Captain Mapes and Pancho Villa and Newton D. Baker, Stanley Dinkle began his leave.

Later, after his first real bath in six weeks, he slipped into a real bed between real sheets and lay for a time in a state adjacent to Nirvana. For some olfactory reason he was reminded of his boyhood bed under the eaves of the farmhouse near Horeb, Wisconsin, which was not far from Madison, which was not far from Milwaukee. Besides lye soap, those sheets had smelled of butter—a logical association since the family enterprise was a dairy farm. The elder of two brothers, from puberty he milked twenty cows before breakfast and twenty before supper, and after high school graduated to thirty. As his comprehension of cows increased, so did his apprehension of the future. This, he perceived, was how he might expect to spend the remainder of his life: in a barn, on a stool, relieving a herd of Holsteins of their bovine burden. On the night before his twenty-first birthday, therefore, he collected his belongings in a feed sack and lowered himself out the window of the room under the eaves.

He couldn't sleep. Being in El Paso excited him. He lay rigid, and on an imaginery Bible swore three solemn oaths: not to go to Juárez, not to let the Light Horse cross his mind during leave, and not to think about sex until the morrow, when broad daylight would have a salutary, saltpeter effect.

I muffed it, thought Stanley Dinkle. That grass widow on the train and the hooker coming out of her hot bath. Ready, willing, and able.

There is no joy in Mudville, as the poet says, mighty Stanley has struck out twice.

He decided to read himself into the arms of Morpheus. Taking up the *Cavalry Journal* he'd brought along, he began an article laudatory of the horse as a historical vehicle and scornful of the automobile as a potential substitute. Would fabled Troy, demanded the author, have fallen to the device of a wooden Peerless? Could one visualize Jerusalem redeemed from the infidel by Crusaders riding Pope-Tribunes? Stanley Dinkle nodded vehemently. Sentiments such as these were right up his alley, and he still smoldered at Den Uyl's snide invitation to substitute one of their Model T's for the proud Hassan. He wondered what the Light Horse were up to at this moment. Up to no good, probably, but they'd damned well better be soldiering. He returned to the article. When a sorely afflicted Job asked God to prove His infinite power and wisdom, of all His creations, which had the Almighty chosen as example? "Hast thou given the horse strength?" spake the Lord from a whirlwind. "Hast thou clothed his neck with thunder? He mocketh at fear, and is not affrighted; neither turneth he back from the sword. He saith among the trumpets, Ha, ha."

Stanley Dinkle drifted off, the good book in his hand, a righteous smile upon his face. He dreamed a recurring dream. Dancing barefoot o'er a field of udders, he bounded high in lacteal delight. But the field on which he tripped tonight was miraculously altered. Vanished were the udders, and in their stead were breasts, enormous and pneumatic. The teats had been replaced by rosy nipples. "Aaaaaah!" he sighed, and swooning, sank supine amongst the glorious boobs of Flossie Grebs.

12

Tragedy at Fort Dinkle

Rifle across his knees, a dissipated smile upon his face, Pvt. William A. "Phew" Pugh drifted off. It was two o'clock in the morning and his turn to stand guard, to keep vigil over Texas and defend the United States, but it had been a day to fatigue even the most patriotic trooper, and so, seated near the Rio Grande, his back to a small cottonwood, he snoozed.

It had also been their best day since the Philadelphia Light Horse had arrived at Fort Dinkle. With their black beauties, "Henrietta" and "Olivia," finally started and hitting sweetly again on all four cylinders, they scrambled aboard and roared up and down the parade ground in a series of Mounted Model T Pistol Attacks, shouting war cries, sighting .45's over the Motometers, and emptying magazine after magazine into the targets. Tiring of that sport, they drove down the sand road into Edhogg and toasted each other in sarsaparilla. After a leisurely lunch, they enjoyed a long siesta. Arising refreshed and eager for athletic endeavor, on Biddle's suggestion they unlimbered mallets and balls, saddled the Morgans, divided into teams, and whiled the afternoon away with several warmly contested chukkers of polo. That evening they quaffed from the flowing bowl, banqueted, quaffed again, and indulged in revelry of various sorts. Pugh's recollection was hazy, although it seemed to him the six of them found themselves at a late hour in the middle of the river, naked as jaybirds, divinely drunk, saluting the stars with a song dear to the hearts of National Guardsmen and popular, in fact, the length and breadth of the land:

I didn't raise my boy to be a soldier,
I brought him up to be my pride and joy.
Who dares to place a musket on his shoulder,
To shoot some other mother's darling boy?
Let nations arbitrate their future troubles,
It's time to lay the sword and gun away,
There'd be no war today,
If mothers all would say,
"I didn't raise my boy to be a soldier!"

Since they had neither drilled nor patroled nor cleaned equipment, since the entire day had been devoted to celebrating their manumission from bondage, it seemed inconsistent to post guard that night. But Phipps, left in charge and sometimes a stickler for the proprieties, insisted. Pugh couldn't recall, either, how he had been drafted to pull the first trick, but somehow, sans shoes, he was expelled from his bed and pushed into the lonely night in his BVD's, where he promptly found a comfortable tree and fell into a deep, inebriate sleep.

What he dreamed of, he would not himself know in the morning. "Phew" Pugh III was the most abstracted of the Philadelphians. He woolgathered. He dwelt in marble halls. His wits were thumbs, which he twiddled perpetually. Asked what career he would like to pursue, he had responded variously that of a cigar roller, a missionary, a troubadour, and the captain of a clipper ship. A Chi Phi in his junior year at Franklin & Marshall, he still hadn't the foggiest notion what he would prefer to be, if anything. Secretly he was glad to have been called from college to active duty, since this deferred his eventual graduation a semester, perhaps a full year, which would in turn defer the necessity of making any decision whatever about his future. "Phew" was also careless, clumsy, and uncoordinated when not installed in a saddle. A gun or saber in his hands imperiled everyone in the vicinity. He never knew what hour of day it was, or what day of the week. When a formation or a drill or a carouse went awry, he was invariably to blame. In the ointment of military life, he was unfailingly the fly. Yet for several reasons his chums tolerated these shortcomings. If he mooned, he did not annoy. If his laugh was a whinny, it made others laugh. If he were gangling and horse-faced, at twenty he was the retarded infant of the Light Horse, so must be spoiled, and the least affluent, so must be pitied. The iron foundry which had supported his family for five prosperous generations had finally puddled out, and after his elder sisters had contrived to marry money, "Phew" was left to fend for himself in the cruel world with little more to his name than a trust fund—and his name. Fortunately for him, this was a not inconsiderable resource. In the Commonwealth of Pennsylvania, no bloodline ran more blue than that of Pugh.

Unfortunately for him, however, the influence of his name and lineage did not extend to the state of Coahuila on this night in May 1916, or the bandidos would never have the temerity to disturb his slumber. Without warning, in the darkness before dawn—no one had troubled to relieve the sleeping sentry, of course—they poured across the Rio Grande, discharging weapons and shouting "Viva Villa!" and "Arriba! Arriba!"

Private Pugh struggled out of dreams and assumed a posture of challenge.

"Halt!" he mumbled. "Who goes there?"

A rifle butt to the side of the head rendered him hors de combat.

A lamp was lit in the Sibley tent.

It was immediately shot out.

Horsemen were everywhere. They seemed to know precisely where to go and what to do.

Shouting and shooting, riding in circles about the tent, gigging their animals into the ropes, they pulled the pegs, and with a sigh the Sibley collapsed about the center pole, which toppled.

Cries and oaths were muffled by canvas. Under it, the five Light Horse were prevented from taking effective retaliatory action by the profusion of personal effects with which they had furnished their pavilion.

"Freddy" Den Uyl was partially suffocated by the poster of Mary Pickford.

"Lex" Phipps could not untangle himself from his mosquito netting.

"Stew" Darlington's cot had overturned. Crawling from beneath it, his way was barred by two chairs, the table, and a half case of whiskey.

Taking command, in a hoarse voice "Bid" Biddle ordered everyone to get his rifle and fire at will.

"Luce" Thayer, nearest the rack, seized a Springfield, put one round through the walnut washstand and another through the horn of the Victrola.

One by one, on hands and knees, breathless but profane, frightened but resolute, the young troopers wrestled their way out of the farrago of netting and furniture and tenting into the night, each soldier fully expecting to be brought down by a fusillade of lead as soon as he emerged. Determined to fight to the last man, nevertheless, they commenced firing as soon as they could work bolts, sending volleys at the CO's house, into the grove, over the Rio Grande into Mexico, and riddling the officers' latrine. Nor did they cease until, during a lull to reload, it struck them that their fire drew no response.

The bandidos were gone.

They heard a groan near the river. Rushing toward the sound, they discovered the injured Pugh, his arms enfolding a small cottonwood, who apprised them of the fact that Fort Dinkle had been attacked.

In the silence which followed this communique, they then heard rifle fire in the direction of Edhogg.

Phipps cried boots and saddles.

In a body they stampeded into the pecan grove to saddle up and ride to the rescue, only to find that the picket line had been cut.

Their horses were gone.

13

Taking in the Sights of El Paso

Lieutenant Dinkle slept late, shaved, dressed, went directly to the nearest bank, cashed his pay voucher, went directly to the post office, presented his account card, answered queries about his mother's maiden name and his father's birthplace to identify himself, and deposited $86.80. The remaining eighty dollars he pocketed, confident it would cover nicely the cost of a three-day spree and his next month's living as well.

He was immensely gratified by the new total on his deposit slip. Almost nine hundred dollars now, it represented eight years of savings as an officer at various posts. Stanley Dinkle did not believe in banks. Postal Savings was as solid as the government he served, and paid in addition a solid 1.5 per cent interest. Only after his finances were in order did he permit himself to breakfast in a Chinese restaurant and to take in the sights.

There was much to see. The town had modernized itself. Most buildings were now brick-fronted, with fancy tin cornices painted to imitate marble, and the principal thoroughfares, El Paso and Stanton and Santa Fe and San Antonio, were paved with bitulithic asphalt. They were also thronged with National Guardsmen in on pass from the several camps to rubberneck and cram the ice cream parlors and saloons and be painlessly separated from their pay, a process handily accomplished by the swarms of Barnums, fakirs, and lingo artists which, like locusts, had descended on the harvest. Warlike boys from Michigan won Kewpie dolls in shooting galleries and at the same time perfected their marksmanship. Acquisitive boys from Rhode Island bought puppies for company mascots, sets of longhorns as souvenirs of the Wild West, and boxes of Mexican fleas for later release in each other's beds. Shrewd boys from Nebraska picked up bargains in diamond rings sold at a sacrifice by "ranchers" pressed for funds. Sophisticated boys from Connecticut wandered about with armloads of genuine Indian blankets and trinkets manufactured in Chicago. Most of the Guardsmen also invested heavily in picture postcards of the bodies of Villa victims, bullet-riddled by firing squads. Upon receipt of these, worried families in the East would be assured of the safety of their sons and the tranquillity of the border.

El Paso was full as a tick with history. Here was the "News Tree" to which pioneers nailed man-wanted and pig-for-sale signs. There was the "Heroes Marker," erected to honor seven citizens who perished in a rough-and-tumble with Apaches. Here, in this rooming house, the celebrated gunfighter John Wesley Hardin practiced the fast draw from dawn to dusk. There, in the Acme Saloon, he was shot after dark by law officer John Selman. Here a conference between President Taft and President Díaz of Mexico had been held. There, from the roofs of buildings near the Rio Grande, El Pasoans had observed the forces of Madero seize Juárez from those of Díaz, and those of Villa seize it from those of Madero.

Satiated with history, our hero seated himself on a bench under the pepper trees in San Jacinto Plaza to watch the trolley cars go by and to wait, as all soldiers immemorially do, for something wonderful to happen.

I'll be a suck-egg mule, thought Stanley Dinkle. I am just as lorn in El Paso as I was in Edhogg.

He was as solitary at thirty-two as he had been at twenty-one, the night he lowered himself out the window of the room under the eaves and bid adieu to farm and family. Following the seasons and the end of his nose and Horace Greeley's injunction, he went West, threshing wheat in the Dakotas and digging potatoes in Idaho and picking apples in Washington. A yen to see the deep blue sea took him then to Seattle, where he stopped before a recruiting poster which urged young men to join the Army and serve in the exotic Philippines. Enlisting forthwith, he was shipped to the 14th Cavalry at exotic Fort Kearney, Wyoming, where he learned to drill and shoot and equitate rather than harness a horse, if not to make many friends. A year later, however, in 1907, the regiment embarked upon the briny deep, bound for Zamboanga and the ylang-ylang trees.

I would certainly like to get my ashes hauled, thought Stanley Dinkle, but I am not going you-know-where to do it.

Juárez was off limits to enlisted men. Officers were requested not to go there, but most did, and brought back tales of debauchery which curled the hair, not to mention a miscellany of loathsome diseases beyond classification or treatment by medical science.

To get his mind above the belt he checked his exchequer, and there, in his wallet, besides his own money, was the grimy ten-dollar bill Flossie Grebs had forced upon him and he had forgotten to leave with Harley Offus. Snapping the wallet shut, he stuffed it into a breeches pocket, irked that he should feel responsible for it or her.

I need a whore with a heart of gold, thought Stanley Dinkle, and a rump of purest rubber.

Rising from his bench, he strolled across the street to stand idly before an emporium with "The Bon Ton" in gilt letters on the window and a potpourri of female frippery behind them. Glancing circumspectly up and down, he sidled into the store and pretended to be interested in the mesh baskets gliding back and forth on a system of wires and carrying sales slips and change between the counters and a cashier's cage suspended from the ceiling. Presently he was assailed by a gushy matron with a gold tooth.

"Good morning, Lieutenant, may I help you?"

"Ahem," he said. "I want to buy a dress. For a lady."

"Of course, of course!" she trilled. "Right this way. Did you have a particular fabric in mind, or color?"

"No, ma'am. Just a dress."

"On what occasions will the dress be worn?"

"Darned if I know."

"Really? Well, can you give me her size?"

"Size?"

She was horrified. "Lieutenant, Lieutenant," she clucked. "Well, can you describe the young lady? What are her proportions?"

Stanley Dinkle removed his hat and with a sleeve swabbed his brow. "How do they get into that cage?" he asked.

"Cage? Oh, up there. Why, there's a door in back, a dear little door."

"Oh," he said. "Well, she's taller than I am and about as hefty."

"Really?" She surveyed him from carrot hair to brown boots. "Well, perhaps a fourteen, then. Yes, I think a fourteen. Now, let me see." Opening a door into a kind of cupboard, she brought forth on a hanger a dress which she draped against the background of her own ample proportions. It was ankle-length and pink velvet with mut-tonchop sleeves and a "Bertha," or lace collar, attached. "There! Isn't it lovely?"

The officer stared at it. "Ma'am, were you here when John Wesley Hardin was shot?"

"Who?"

"I'll take it," he said.

"Splendid!" she gushed. "Now then, does the lucky girl have a hat to match?"

"I don't think so. But she can read and write."

"Really? Well, come right along." Ushering him into another area, she removed a chapeau from a hat block and perched it on her head. It was a black velvet fedora with a pink ostrich plume. "Isn't it adorable, Lieutenant? And it's a Gage, too, the very best."

It occurred to Stanley Dinkle that he might as well be slaughtered for a sheep as a goat. "I guess she'll need a hat," he agreed.

"Splendid! Will that be all?"

"Yes, ma'am."

"Oh, wait, we're forgetting!" She gave him the gold tooth set in an intimate smile. "Petticoats! She simply must have petticoats, at least two."

"She must?"

"Of course, of course. Here." And leading him into still another department, she bent under a counter and unsheathed two made of iridescent taffeta. "Aren't these sweet? And how they rustle!"

"She works in a mine," he said. "Crushes ore."

"A mine?"

"Wrap 'em up," he said.

"Splendid!" Taking a pencil from her coiffure, the matron busied herself with a sales slip. "I love to wait on men," she confided. "They know what they want and when they see it, that's that, price is no object. Men are so, so masculine, don't you think? That will be seventy-five thirty-five."

"Seventy-five thirty-five," he said, reaching for his hip.

"Seventy-five thirty-five," she repeated.

"Seventy-five thirty-five!" he said.

"Seventy-five dollars and thirty-five cents," she repeated.

"Seventy-five thirty-five?" he said.

"Seventy-five thirty-five," she repeated, showing him the sales slip. "The dress is forty-nine fifty, the hat seventeen ninety-five, and the petticoats are three ninety-five each."

Stanley Dinkle opened his wallet and gave her his eighty dollars and, while she dispatched the slip and currency up the wire to the cage, leaned on the counter for lack of a place to sit down.

"I do hope she has shoes to match, your young lady," said the matron, tissueing dress and petticoats into a carton and the fedora into a hatbox. "It would be a pity to spoil such a stunning ensemble with the wrong shoes."

The basket descended with his change. Since he seemed incapable of handling it, she placed it in his shirt pocket.

"It's been a pleasure to wait on you," she said. "Do stop in again."

Stanley Dinkle did not hear her. Laden with hatbox and carton, his face ashen, he stepped through the door into a world he never made.

14

The Tin Lizzie Troop Is Formed

"They ran off our horses!" brayed Corporal Phipps.

"They stole 'em, you ass," snapped Biddle.

In bare feet and BVD's the six young soldiers stood in the grove, their faces as gray as the gray of dawn which filtered through the pecans. They had actually been attacked by an armed foe. One of their number was a casualty. Pugh examined his skull. Darlington bit his lips. Thayer quivered. All of them were excited and frightened and in shock. Shame would come later.

"We've got to get to Edhogg!" lisped "Freddy" Den Uyl.

"I know!" exclaimed "Lex" Phipps. "We'll go in the cars! It'll beat walking—and maybe we'll get there in time!"

They flapped about like chickens with their heads cut off. Biddle and Den Uyl dashed to the collapsed tent to fetch everyone's shoes and weapons. Thayer and Darlington cranked furiously. But the Fords were balky. Yesterday they had purred, but now, in a crisis, like fractious mares they put their backs up and resisted. Returning laden with leather and armament, Biddle and Den Uyl bent to the cranks, and eventually the jitneys snorted and started, everyone donned shoes and belted a .45 about his middle and piled on, and brandishing rifles, armed to the teeth, the Philadelphia Light Horse roared out of the grove. Not until they were speeding down the sand road did it occur to them that the pistols held only a single magazine and that they had forgotten to reload the Springfields.

They were too late.

The bandidos had done their deadly work and vamoosed. The general store, Edhogg's single edifice, was a smoking hulk of blackened walls pitted by bullets.

"Oh, by jingo," mumbled "Stew" Darlington.

"Oh, my head," groaned "Phew" Pugh.

Then, out of a thicket of cactus and greasewood behind the store, two scarecrow creatures tottered. Only when they neared the autos were they recognizable as the owners and proprietors, Harley and Mrs. Offus, the former supporting his spouse. At the somewhat belated appearance of the garrison of Patrol Post #2, Mrs. Offus ran toward it, waving her arms and shrieking.

"Where was you? Where was the Army when we needed you?"

The soldiers were silent, for one reason because she seemed bereft of her senses, for another because she was bereft of so much as a stitch of clothing.

Corporal Phipps felt it incumbent upon him to say something. "What happened here?"

"What's it look like?" demanded Harley Offus, attempting to control his wife and his Adam's apple. "They come along shootin' an' me an' the missus clumb through the back windy an' hid out. They cleaned out the store, then set 'er afire."

Mrs. Offus broke free of him and ran around the Fords. "Everything we got in the world gone up in smoke and where was the U. S. Army? Drinking sody pop, that's where! Off to El Paso on leave!"

"We'd better phone Fort Bliss right away," suggested Den Uyl.

"Help yourself," said Harley Offus, indicating either his wife or the ruins of his establishment.

" 'Vengeance is mine, saith the Lord!' " continued Mrs. Offus. "Well, it better be His'n—the Army won't lift a finger!"

"Maybelle, you'll have a heart attack," reproved her husband, reaching over a fender for her nude waist.

The distraught female eluded him and leveled an accusing arm. "Taxpayers near murdered in their beds and what do the soldiers do?" she shrieked. "They sets in their undywear in their fancy autos and gawps at naked wimmen, that's what!" With each adverb she pounded on a hood. "Why? Why? Why?"

The gentlemen had no answer. But they did avert their eyes.

"Listen, you better git on down to the Dryass," advised Harley Offus. "After them bandidos done for us, they went thataway."

At the helm of the lead car Phipps nodded, pushed a pedal, and away they chugged down the sand road into the fire of the rising sun. No word was spoken in either Ford. They entered the region of black ash and ocher streaks and abandoned shafts. The hopelessness of the earth here seemed an omen. They came to Old Man Grebs's hand-lettered signs, which were not amusing now, but in their crudity and defiance pathetic. Phipps turned into the tracks made by the miner's mules and wagons, and almost at once, with the sun out of their eyes, they saw the smoke. Phipps speeded up. The vehicles plowed a field of ash into clouds. At the edge of the depression the corporal stopped, cut his engine, leaped out, and began to walk down into it. The others followed. When they caught up with him, on perverse impulse all six broke into a senseless, pell-mell run. They were too late again, they knew it but could not help themselves. In excess of life, they raced death.

They ran into heat as into a wall and were thrown back, faces burning. What had been a shack constructed of railroad ties and ice molds was a glowing, heaving mass of coals and shapeless iron.

They turned from it, and drawing together instinctively, moved past the cannon-barrel smelter and the retort table where the crushed ore was worked with lime.

The dead mules lay side by side. Too decrepit to be worth stealing, they had been used for target rpactice.

Champion T. Grebs was sprawled upon his back, a double-barreled shotgun under him. He had not been shot down, but in some way subdued physically. The bandidos had then lifted his beard and slit his throat to such depth that the head was almost severed from the trunk. Blood had gushed from the old miner's body in quantity sufficient to make it appear that he was covered by a crimson blanket.

The Light Horse looked upon him. His head was twisted to one side. His toothless mouth was wide open, as though even in death he indicted them with a yell.

Stricken, they turned away.

There was no trace of Flossie Grebs.

They stood aimlessly for a moment. Then Darlington did a strange thing. Unsnapping his holster, he slid out his .45, raised it high and south, and fired seven times, emptying the magazine into the morning air over Mexico.

After that, in single file, the young soldiers scuffed across the depression to their automobiles.

The mile to Fort Dinkle might have been ten. Phipps drove as though leading a funeral procession. They were still in a state of shock, too dazed and horrified by what had happened and what they had seen to comprehend even vaguely its meaning. When the touring cars reached the pecan grove, they got out and leaned on fenders or sat down on running boards. It was some time before anyone had anything to say.

Thayer opened the chamber of his Springfield, then clicked it shut. "They took her with them."

Biddle flicked ash from his BVD's. "Old Man Grebs," he muttered.

With his fingers, Pugh measured the lump on his head. "Nothing left of Edhogg."

Darlington toyed with the rubber bulb of a horn. "Six good horses. Morgans."

It was an inventory of disaster.

"I need a drink," Den Uyl said. "I'll unlimber a bottle."

He left them, and in a moment shouted. They whipped pistols out and sprang to the edge of the grove, but it was all right. Den Uyl was burrowing from under the canvas, dragging one of their muchachos after him. While they watched, he seated himself on a table, draped the struggling culprit over his knees, and proceeded to spank him. The boy bawled bloody murder. Den Uyl attended to his behind with relish, spacing his blows to allow time between them to ask something in execrable Spanish. Satisfied, he yanked the muchacho upright and sent him across the river with a climactic swat, then walked to the grove to rejoin the others.

"Looter," he explained. "Dinkle was right—we shouldn't have hired the little blighters. Spies and thieves —they probably tipped off the bandidos when to hit us, and how. Anyway, I pounded a name out of him. Encarnacion Contreras. Not that it does us any good."

It did not. They leaned on fenders again, and sat down again on running boards, and for a time were mute and motionless. They might have been small boys in hiding, afraid to leave the refuge of the trees and the companionship of their cars.

It was Phipps, finally, who cut the picket line of their pride—Phipps who uttered it for them all. "Oh, God," he said suddenly, "what we've done!"

And with his words, pegs of recognition were pulled in them at last. A tent of shame collapsed over the Philadelphia Light Horse. Under it they groveled in guilt, bumping youthful egos into the unyielding furniture of fact. A nobody named Contreras had come out of Mexico in the night and played ring-around-the-rosy with a detachment of the U. S. Army. He had overrun a patrol post, robbed and burned and killed, made captive and carried off a woman for purposes indubitably foul. The tragedy at Fort Dinkle was more total than that at Columbus. There, though taken by surprise, the 13th Cavalry had fought with tooth and nail, driving the raiders back across the border, even pursuing them to exact a fine revenge. Here, caught napping, cavalrymen had been made complete chumps of. Had they given even a feeble account of themselves against the bandidos, a town might not have been wiped from the map, an old man might not lie dead, his daughter might not have met a fate worse than death. But they had not, and the implications of such failure were profound.

The United States could be invaded with impunity—provided the Philadelphia Light Horse defended it. For six of its members had blotted the scutcheon of America's most illustrious military unit. They had watered down their own pure blood. They had sold their birthright for a mess of polo.

Apprised of this fiasco, their fathers would put firearms to their foreheads.

Their grandfathers would groan in their graves.

General Washington would tear his wig.

"Hell's bells, Pugh!" Thayer burst out. "Why weren't you on your toes?"

"Me? Don't you blame me!" Pugh turned on Phipps. "You were in charge! Why wasn't I relieved?"

Phipps excused himself. "I tried to wake somebody! They were all drunk!"

"Blast it, you were just as soused as the rest!" Den Uyl accused.

Darlington dared to attack Biddle. "You and your polo!"

"If you can't hold your liquor," Biddle glowered, "hold your tongue."

"Dinkle warned us!" Thayer reminded. "He stood right over there on that parade ground and told us about Columbus!"

"Oh, dry up about Dinkle!" sniffed Den Uyl.

"Oh, my head!" lamented Pugh.

"If you'd been on your toes!" Thayer charged, completing the circle of recrimination.

They were on their feet, fists raised, glaring at one another.

"There's no point trying to pin the tail on the donkey," said Phipps. "We're all to blame. What we have to decide now is what next. The only thing I can think of is get dressed, crank up, and drive to Marathon and phone Bliss. Tell 'em what's happened and ask what we should do."

"We can't," Thayer objected. "They'll have our heads on a platter."

"They will anyway," said Darlington gloomily. "We're in for a court-martial, I know it."

"Then we're in the papers," added Den Uyl. "The front page. Pictures of us in dress uniform before a firing squad. We'll look simply smashing."

"The *Bulletin* and *Enquirer* both," seconded Pugh. "Our names'll be mud."

"Disgraced," Darlington moped.

"Disowned," worried Thayer.

"Mud?" Biddle said. "Dirt."

"We can't help it, we have to let the Army know," Phipps argued. "It's our duty."

Den Uyl made the name an oath. "Contreras. How I'd like to lay hands on that greaser."

They tugged mustaches. They kicked tree trunks. They tossed pebbles.

"Why not?" Biddle asked himself out loud.

"Why not what?" someone inquired.

He was thinking hard. "Why not lay hands on Contreras?" He strode up and down, his black brows knit. "I tell you frankly, this makes me mad as hell. I don't cotton to being caught with our BVD's down. It's not our style." He seated himself on a bumper. "I propose we do something about it—something a damnsight more manly than boohooing to the Army."

His magnetism drew them near.

"I propose we snatch victory from the jaws of defeat."

"Hear, hear," said Den Uyl.

"Lend him an ear," encouraged Thayer.

"Talk's cheap, deeds are dear," Phipps grumbled. "How?"

"How?" H. Horace Biddle was around the auto and onto a running board before they could blink. Pausing for oratorical effect, he shot each man a look which slapped like a glove. "I propose we take these cars and go after the bastards! I propose we bring 'em back dead or alive!"

The hush of history fell over the grove. They could have heard a pecan drop. On a similar occasion, millennia ago, someone had posited the utility of fire, and later, someone else had conceived the wheel.

"Take the cars?" they gasped.

"Which is faster?" Biddle countered. "A horse or a flivver? Contreras can make ten miles an hour mounted. We can do thirty. If we ride out now, we'll have him in the bag and back here before night."

Phipps was aghast. "You mean cross the river? Dinkle ordered us absolutely not to!"

Biddle reddened. "Dinkle me no more Dinkles. I don't know where he came from, but I'll wager a barnyard. He's certainly no gentleman and I told him so. Furthermore, I'll whip the man who mentions his name again. And further than that, it's Stanley Steamer who's always prating about cavalry dash and initiative—well, let's show him some. What can he say if we pull it off? What can the Army do to us if we bring home the bacon?"

Below him, several of them seemed to rise on tiptoe. The line between inspiration and insanity was a narrow one to walk. Pugh teetered. "We don't even know how many! I didn't see 'em—what if it's six of us against twenty Mexicans?"

Biddle turned up his nose. "For the Light Horse, those are excellent odds."

"Maybe we could get that Grebs woman back," mused the gallant Thayer. "I hate to think what they're doing to her."

"That great bitch?" Biddle scoffed. "I'm more interested in our animals. And our reputation." Slamming a hand upon the plunger, he forced from the Klaxon horn a loud and martial moo. "What say, lads? Let's bring the Army up to date! Let's make Dinkle eat his words! Let's give it a go!"

It was an idea whose time had come. It was a chance at which they must jump. In one stroke they might redeem themselves, hoist themselves by their own unprecedented petard. And it was also a shenanigan so bold and so rambunctious that no young man worth his youth dared resist. They could sink no lower in self-esteem. The only way to go was up, and one of their own hotspur number had shown the route.

"C'mon, fellows!" cried Den Uyl, who invariably played the moth to Biddle's flame. "Remember—Fords rush in where angels fear to tread!"

"Count me in!" whooped Thayer.

"Me, too!" decided Darlington.

"I'll go along for the ride," Pugh consented.

Phipps alone was dubious. "We've already disobeyed every order in the book. Now we're getting ourselves in deeper and deeper."

They called him a spoilsport, a non-commissioned pain in the pratt, but he was adamant.

"Then you stay, dammit, you hold the fort—what's left of it," Biddle told him contemptuously. "But with you or without, we're hitting the saddle."

Phipps threw up his hands. "Oh, very well. You're all wet but I'll go. There's nothing to lose—it's already lost."

At that they cheered and clapped each other on the back and would have cranked up then and there, but Phipps refused to go off half-cocked. If they were setting out on their own punitive expedition, he argued, they should be as well prepared as Pershing was for his. They might brag about being back by nightfall, but in case they weren't, he wanted them ready for any contingency. They beefed as usual, but granting his logic, set to work like whirling dervishes.

They hauled the Sibley to one side.

They attired themselves in gleaming leather puttees and their newest tailor-made uniforms.

Dashing back and forth between belongings and the autos, they threw into the tonneaus armloads of blankets, boxes of ammunition, razors, rifles, ukulele, and whatever rations were handy.

Into the luggage carriers went ten-gallon milk cans of spare gasoline, one of water, and a five-gallon can of crankcase oil.

Den Uyl thought of it at the last minute. Digging out two polo mallets and the two pairs of bloomers they had originally flown on the way down from El Paso, he lashed the mallets to windsheld uprights and presently each Model T was equipped with a guidon.

It was half past nine o'clock in the morning of a fine, hot, propitious day. They cranked up. Eager for the fray, the flivvers responded joyously.

Corporal Phipps took "Henrietta's" wheel, Thayer that of "Olivia," and two men sprang into each tonneau. Turning out of the grove, they ground along in low gear to the brink of the river, where Phipps halted. Only now did the watery obstacle, a mere ninety feet wide and no more than two feet deep at any point, daunt them. Thayer was consulted. Since his father had purchased one of the first Fords on the Main Line, he was the nearest thing they had to a mechanic, and his advice was to back off and take advantage of a flying start. This they did, but when they were in position, Thayer held them up again.

"Hey, just had an idea'!' he called ahead. "We better pep these babies up a little. Open the gas tanks!"

While the others removed front seat cushions to expose the tanks underneath, he rummaged in a toolbox. When the caps were off, he dropped into each tank a dosage of one, two, three mothballs.

"It's the camphor," Thayer explained professionally. "My father let me in on the secret. You mix mothballs and gas and hot-ziggety! A Ford thinks it's a Cadillac! We'll make it now, you bet!"

Caps were replaced, and cushions. Every man hunched down and held on.

Phipps gave the hand signal—Forward! Opening spark and throttle levers wide, he slammed the low-speed pedal to the floor.

Engines roared. Transmissions screamed. Bloomers whipped.

Hell-bent for election, into the Rio Grande and a veritable hallelujah of spray and foam charged the Tin Lizzie Troop.

It foundered halfway across. Carburetors flooded, axles buried in gravel, running boards awash, the flivvers rested on their laurels, "Henrietta" in Mexico, "Olivia" in the United States.

15

Get Thee Behind Me, Satan

That night Lieutenant Dinkle went out on the town, an undertaking not inconsiderably hampered by the lightness of his purse and the darkness of his mood.

After wandering the streets for a desultory hour and indulging in a chocolate sundae, he took in a movie in one of the several tent theaters set up for the recreation of the military. For ten cents he was admitted to a double feature: on the one hand a silent epic starring Bobby Vernon, Gloria Swanson, and Teddy, the Sennett dog, and on the other, continuous sound effects provided by the National Guard audience—boos for the hero, cheers for the villain, catcalls for the dog, and a deafening osculatory chorus during the love scenes.

Later, after a caramel sundae topped with peanuts, whipped cream, and a cherry, he happened by the Hotel Paso del Norte. The ground floor windows were open, and through them the strains of violin and cornet wafted. On tiptoe, he had a peek inside, and another, and another. An officers' ball was in progress. Under festoons of ribbons, the brass from some eastern regiment in its swankiest uniforms waltzed the flower of El Paso pulchritude about the floor in graceful, gay terpsichore. Lieutenant Dinkle tried to picture himself in attendance, and could not. He had never learned to dance passably, to hold a punch cup properly, to bow and scrape and whisper sweet nothings into delicate ears—la-de-da deficits to which his lack of promotion might be in part attributable. It was too late now. You couldn't teach an old Sennett dog new tricks.

The billowing skirt of a ball gown brushed his face. The gown was pink. And that was too much. Angrily he dropped to his heels. $75.35 for a dress and a hat and a couple of damned doo-hickeys—almost half a month's pay flung to the four winds because he didn't know how much women's duds cost and when he did find out was too proud to admit he couldn't afford them. Angrily he stalked to the New York Hotel and up three flights of stairs and into his room and switching on the light, confronted carton and hatbox on the bed. He'd return them first thing in the morning, that's what he'd do. He'd sashay in and inform Gushy that he knew overpriced merchandise when he saw it and she had two options: his money back or a squawk to the El Paso Chamber of Commerce to the effect that the Bon Ton was robbing the sons of Uncle Samuel.

The idea relieved him, and thinking he might as well have a last look-see at the goods, he untied the strings. He looked, and experienced a sinking sensation. The dress and hat were actually crackerjacks, no doubt about it, fit for the Queen of Sheba, but far too highfaluting for a Flossie Grebs. To imagine her in them was as daffy as to imagine himself at a fancy dress ball. You simply couldn't make a velvet purse out of a sow's ear. He touched, and experienced a sexual sensation. He hadn't dreamed material could be that soft, or an ostrich feather that fragile, or petticoats that rustly. Live and learn. So the rig probably wasn't overpriced after all, and he'd never get away with claiming it was.

Packing them up again, he had a better idea. What he'd do first crack in the morning was, he'd put on a sorrowful phiz and say the young lady he'd bought them for was his sweetheart, and he'd just learned she'd been run over by a train, or died of the grippe, or been taken by force across the border to be a white slave, and that under these tragic circumstances he hoped the Bon Ton would accept them for refund.

Leaning out the window of his room he was able, from that height, to discern a few feeble lights on the International Bridge connecting El Paso with Juárez. They seemed to beckon.

A little poontang now and then, thought Stanley Dinkle,

is cherished by the wisest men. But an officer is supposed to set a good example for his men, and how can I cross the river when I ordered mine not to? Besides, I'm not a wise man, I am wishy-washy. I said I wasn't going to think about the Philadelphia Light Horse but I do. I swore on a stack of Bibles I would get my mind off sex but I can't. And I am over a barrel. If I keep those clothes I am a total fool, but at least I won't have enough dough to go to Juárez, which is good. But if I'm sensible and return 'em, I'll have plenty, which is bad, because I'll probably succumb and go and come back with a platoon of crotch crickets.

I may be a rolling stone, thought Stanley Dinkle, but I sure am gathering moss. Two days of my leave are up and I've had two ice cream sundaes and seen one movie and tomorrow is all she'll write.

He undressed and got into bed, and taking up the copy of the *Cavalry Journal* sought solace in the article extolling the horse and ridiculing the auto as a replacement. "The great body of men who are the bone and sinew of a mighty nation," declared the author, "who are upright, God-loving men, who love their neighbor, peace, and justice, see, when they look at a horse, something to be cared for and cherished as a choice possession, a being that is next to man in the scale of life." Could one conceive of Paul Revere giving "the alarm through every Middlesex village and farm" mounted on a Locomobile? Would the Bard have been Immortal had he chosen to have his Richard III utter this desperate appeal? "A Stutz! A Stutz! My kingdom for a Stutz!"

16

A Cold Patch in Time Saves Nine

"By George if I'll be the only patcher in the crowd!" declared "Luce" Thayer.

It was early the following morning, and less than ten minutes south of the Rio Grande, and "Henrietta" had just had her first flat tire. Thayer got out the jack and kit. They'd have more flats, warned their mechanic, and told them to observe him while he demonstrated the fine art of cold patching.

Jacking up the Ford's front end, he unclinched the 30 x 3-inch tire, pulled the tube, removed a large nail, applied rubber cement to the area of the puncture, blew it almost dry, slapped the patch on with a flourish, replaced tube and tire, then suggested the others take turns pumping her up to sixty pounds pressure.

"By George if I'll be the only pumper in the crowd, either!"

Over the handle they huffed and puffed—Phipps, Darlington, Biddle, Den Uyl, even poor Pugh, whose head still bore a painful memento of the raid upon Fort Dinkle. They were already in bad humor. How, they grumbled to themselves, could one possibly pick up a nail in a wilderness? Why hadn't the state of Coahuila, like the state of Texas, begun to build a highway system? Finally, what in Hades were they doing here, a mere two miles south of the border, almost twenty-four hours after setting out when according to schedule they should by now have captured Contreras, retrieved their horses, rescued the woman, and be back in the U.S. telephoning their triumph to Fort Bliss?

To this last, they gave a bitter answer. After bogging

down yesterday in the Rio Grande, they had been unable to restart the Fords. In water up to their knees they pushed. Neither car would budge. Unloading the autos, splashing everything to the Mexican shore, they pushed again until exhausted. They then spent the remainder of the day scouring the vicinity for help, but located neither houses nor people—a fine how-d'you-do. Where had their muchachos come from? Where were their fathers and brothers? As a last resort, where was the girl who had one evening entranced them by her beauty? That was one of the many mysteries of Mexico, they decided: when you wanted Mexicans, you couldn't find them, and when you didn't, they were in your hair. Just at dusk, however, a peon appeared, then another, then three, out of nowhere, and after an extortionate demand for ten dollars had been met, five *pacíficos* and six soldiers together shoved the vehicles onto dry land.

There, thirty yards into Mexico from its starting point, the Tin Lizzie Troop camped for the night, and there had its first difference of opinion. Den Uyl wanted to cross the river for a bottle of whiskey. Corporal Phipps would not allow drinking in the field. Darlington wanted to fetch his cot. It was stupid, he said, to sleep on the ground when comfort was only ninety feet away. Phipps refused. It was time, he decreed, that they begin accustoming themselves to hardship, an excuse Biddle considered idiotic. Thayer and Pugh sided with Phipps, whose stripes won, and so the six rolled up in blankets and hard feelings on the riverbank.

The night passed uneventfully. But in the dawning, to their chagrin both bloomer guidons were gone, and one of "Henrietta's" spare tires, and "Olivia's" toolbox. They cursed Phipps for failing to post guard. They cursed a nation in which public morality had sunk so low that innocent motorists could not park for the night without having their transport stripped. And they loaded up, still cursing, and proceeded southward for ten minutes without mishap along what passed for a road in these parts—two ruts worn into sand and alkali soil by generations of carts with wooden wheels. Then came the telltale pop and hiss of air under "Henrietta."

They finished pumping.

"We've lost a whole day already," fretted "Lex" Phipps. "We've got to step on the gas."

"How can you on a road like this?" "Phew" Pugh wanted to know. "You'll tear these buggies apart."

"The dirty greasers could be in Mexico City by now," said "Freddy" Den Uyl.

"Bid" Biddle took charge. "Let's use our heads. Contreras won't go far—why should he? He's got our animals, he knows we can't pursue. My guess is he'll hole up in the nearest town, divide the loot, and go on a toot."

"And pass that poor Grebs woman around," reminded "Luce" Thayer.

"There must be a town," insisted "Stew" Darlington. "This confounded road has to go somewhere."

A grim Phipps climbed into "Henrietta." "We're wasting time. Everybody look sharp for some sign of 'em—hoofprints, fresh manure, anything. Let's go!"

Away they went, but Pugh had been right: the condition of the road made it impossible to shift into high. And after several miles of creeping along the ruts in low gear, both drivers, Phipps and Thayer, noted with alarm the red line in the Boyce Motometers rising from "High Efficiency" to "Danger-Steaming!" In another half mile, both radiators boiled over.

"Turn 'em off!" Thayer shouted.

Phipps obeyed. "What's the matter? We're barely moving!"

Wrapping his hand in a handkerchief, Thayer unscrewed the Motometers until the radiators wailed geysers of steam. "That's the trouble—drive too long in low and Fords overheat. You just have to wait till they cool off, then fill 'em up again."

They waited impatiently.

"I'm thirstier than they are," said Pugh.

"The cavalryman takes care of his mount first," recited Thayer.

"You and your silly mothballs," jeered Den Uyl.

When the engines were cool and the radiators filled, they cranked up and moved on through terrain as monotonous as it was inhospitable. At "Olivia's" wheel, Pvt. Lucien T. D. Thayer was preoccupied by three of his organs. To the sound of the engine he gave his ears, listening to the regular 1-2-4-3 firing order of the cylinders. To the necessity of watching over his brother-in-law-to-be, "Stew" Darlington, he gave his conscience. To memories of "Livvy," his betrothed, the dear girl after whom he had insisted a Model T be named, he gave his melancholy heart. A stag at her debut at the Philadelphia Assembly, the glittering ball at which each year the flower of the city's girlhood was presented to society, he had fallen head over heels with Olivia Darlington at first fluttery sight, and told her so during their first dance. He was engaged to her within two weeks, was to be wed in June, next month —until the notice from the War Department that the Light Horse was called up for active duty on the border. Torn from his intended, his marriage bed short-sheeted, "Luce" had languished. Love by interminable letters had not sufficed him, nor strumming a doleful ukulele, nor lifting his fine tenor voice in song. The overflow of his affections he had therefore lavished upon her younger brother, "Stew," tying his shoes and wiping his nose and driving that individual to distraction.

"Luce" Thayer relished the role of lovelorn soldier. He pined well. Tall and handsome, wearing a mustache as lustrous as a raven's wing, he considered himself a romantic, and temperamentally unsuited for anything as mundane as the law. Twenty-three, a Deke, a graduate of Lafayette, and a second-year law student at Penn, he would nevertheless join Thayer & Thayer, founded by his great-grandfather and the oldest firm of attorneys practicing in the city, and knew he would. For he was as enamored of tradition as he was of "Livvy." Join the firm he must, and ride the Paoli Local, and waltz in white tie and tails at the Ritz or Bellevue, and one day deliver his own daughter into the arms of a romantic youth who had a taste for torts and played a mean ukulele.

"Look out!" cried Pugh, beside him.

Thayer jerked the emergency brake almost out of the floor. He had nearly smashed into "Henrietta's" rear end. Phipps had stopped at a fork in the ruts, one set leading southeasterly, the other southwest.

An argument ensued. Some were of the opinion Contreras had headed left, some right. There was no one to ask—they hadn't seen hide nor hair of a human being since leaving the river.

"I say east," said Phipps.

"I say west," said Biddle.

Den Uyl interceded. "Pshaw, flip a coin."

They flipped, Phipps won, but within a mile wished he had not. This route led them into a garden of rocks and boulders through which the going was so rough that the flivvers dissented vociferously in every member. Just when it seemed bodies must part forever from chassis, Thayer shouted ahead to Phipps:

"Mine's missing! Is yours?"

"Missing what?"

"Mis-firing!"

"Oh? So?"

"We'll eat up too much gas! We could burn out a bearing! Fiddle with your coils!"

"Coils?"

"In the box on the firewall in front of you! Take off the cover and tickle 'em a little!"

They came to another fork and halted. This time the debate was savage and prolonged. Now Phipps wanted to go west, declaring Contreras would certainly avoid this rock pit, but Biddle and the others argued that the western ruts would take them back where they had come from, which was where Contreras obviously wasn't. Den Uyl suggested they flip another coin, and when Phipps assented, Biddle blew up, saying that conducting a punitive expedition by coin toss was not only unmilitary but moronic.

"I'd better check our oil," said Thayer, getting down on his knees before "Henrietta."

"If there were just someone to ask," said Darlington.

Den Uyl took out a gold watch. "I thought so—it's almost noon."

With a pair of pliers, Thayer opened the top petcock in the flywheel housing. No oil ran out, which meant the supply was low.

"This is ridiculous," remarked Biddle. "Chasing our tails in the middle of nowhere."

"But there isn't anyone to ask," said Darlington. "No one lives here."

Thayer opened the lower petcock, with the same result, then went to "Olivia" and knelt.

"I'm famished," pouted Den Uyl. "Can't we have some lunch?"

"I think Contreras went to St. Louis," said Darlington. "If he came down here, he'd die of loneliness."

"I thought so," said Thayer. "Out of oil—or too close for comfort. They're eating it like pigs. I'll get the can—you chaps fill up the gas tanks."

"Can't you get these machines in running order?" Biddle demanded. "How can we pursue if you can't get us into high gear?"

"That damned Dinkle," said Pugh, "having a ritzy time in El Paso while we suffer in the field."

"Shut up!" everyone yelled, releasing tensions in a rare unanimity. "Shut up about Dinkle!"

Phipps had been cogitating. He resented any criticism of his tactics, and threats to his authority only made him more obdurate. "I've made up my mind," he announced. "I'm in charge and we're going west."

His choice turned out to be the more desirable in one respect. They left the rocks and boulders and made better speed, covering several miles in high gear until they tried to ascend a gentle grade. Both drivers shifted into low, but the Fords shuddered and were clearly incapable.

"What's wrong now?" Phipps yelled.

"Losing power!" Thayer responded. "Shut 'em off!"

Phipps came back to "Olivia."

"They're hitting on about two cylinders," Thayer explained. "Must be the ignition."

"Well? What do we do?"

"Clean the timers. And maybe the spark plugs."

"How?"

"I don't know."

"You don't know!" yelped the Light Horse. "You're the mechanic!"

Thayer slumped. "I'd better tell you. I never worked on our flivver at home. Albert did all that."

"Albert?"

"Our old coachman. When my father bought a Ford, we made Albert chauffeur. But he hated cars—called 'em horseless carriages. He didn't care to learn."

They glared at him. "Well, you'd better care," warned Phipps. "And start learning right now. That's an order."

"Luce" Thayer swallowed, got out, opened "Henrietta's" toolbox, spread an assortment of wrenches, screwdrivers, and pliers on "Olivia's" fender, took off his hat, rolled up his sleeves, raised one side of the hood and propped it, spit on his palms, and ducked his head into the engine compartment.

Phipps joined Biddle and Den Uyl in "Henrietta."

Pugh and Darlington remained in "Olivia."

For five minutes they sat in the vasty desert, under an implacable sky, then ten. They hadn't put up the touring tops in case they should encounter the bandidos unexpectedly and need a full field of fire for the rifles, and now the sun was high. Shirts darkened with sweat, and hatbands. For a moment, Thayer ceased to work. The sounds of his tools were stilled. A silence closed in upon the Tin Lizzie Troop, a silence more absolute than they had ever known. They heard an ant laugh, and a stone sigh. They heard the beat of wings. Black butterflies attended them. They did not move, could not speak. They sat in miscreations of steel and brass, alien and terribly alone. And suddenly they were afraid. Fear melted them from men into boys.

This is the most awful place I've ever been, thought "Stew" Darlington. If God is all-good, why would He make a place as awful as this?

A sticky wicket, thought "Bid" Biddle. I'll be badly

sunburnt. We're out on the end of a damned thin limb, and I talked them into it. But I can't say so, I can't.

I have to fix this ignition system, thought "Luce" Thayer, I simply have to. Henry Ford, you fiend. Albert, you old geezer. Everything depends on me. It's either plugs or timers. If I can't find out which, I don't know what'll become of us.

Well, we're really in the vichyssoise now, thought "Freddy" Den Uyl. Bid's to blame, too—this was his brilliant idea. But if I tell him so, he'll cut me cold. I'll lose a true friend.

Dinkle was dead right, thought "Phew" Pugh, and nobody dares to say it. And if we should run into Contreras we'd pee in our pants. And nobody dares to admit that, either.

Lord, Lord, what are we going to do, thought "Lex' Phipps. A whole day wasted and we haven't come more than fifteen miles. And I'm in charge, I'm responsible. That damned snob Biddle and his damned oratory. If we botch this, on top of what we've already botched, none of us can ever show his face in Philadelphia again. We can't even go back to the U.S.A. We'll have to hide out in Mexico the rest of our lives. We'll be men without a country.

17

Over the River, Perfumed and Passionate

Today's the day, thought Stanley Dinkle, bounding late from his bed in the New York Hotel. Today's the day something wonderful happens to me, and if it don't, I'll make it! So hold your hats, folks!

To ready his corpuscles he did a few calisthenics, then shaved, dressed, left the hotel, and ankled to the Chinese restaurant, where he breakfasted.

To ready his mind he bought an El Paso *Morning Times,* seated himself on a bench under a pepper tree in San Jacinto Plaza, and perused it diligently. The German Zeppelin L-7 had been downed in the North Sea, the Prince of Wales was visiting the Italian war zone as the guest of King Victor Emmanuel, and the Levy Grocery Company was running a special on canned pie peaches, two gallons for 55¢.

"Stanley," she had said, "d'you know I'm thirty-one years old an' never had a store-bought dress?"

Putting down the paper he went to the post office, to the same clerk, presented his account card, answered the same questions relative to his mother's maiden name and his father's birthplace, and announced his intention to withdraw twenty dollars.

The clerk glanced at the card. "Say, you was in here yesterday—deposited eighty-six eighty. Back an' forth costs the gover'ment money," he grouched.

"I pay my taxes," said the officer briskly.

To the Bon Ton he next betook himself, and was presently face to face with Gushy and her gold tooth. "Lieutenant, how nice to see you again!"

"Likewise, I'm sure, ma'am. I believe you said something yesterday about matching shoes?"

"Of course, of course! Right this way."

In two shakes of a lamb's tail he had obtained for $16.95 a pair of Selby highlaces of black kid with pointed toes and Cuban heels.

"Thank you, Lieutenant!" warbled the matron. "Are you sure the young lady has a proper corset?"

"Special on pie peaches at Levy's," responded the officer. "Two gallons for fifty-five cents."

After storing the shoebox in his room at the New York Hotel he strolled the clamorous streets to the YMCA Center, one of many established along the border for the convenience of servicemen far from home. Entering, he took a chair at one of the long tables where, at any hour of the day, National Guardsmen were supplied free of charge with the materials by means of which they might correspond with families and best beloveds. But not until he had pen and paper in hand did it strike him that he had no epistolary purpose. He had absolutely no one to write to. Every month for eleven years Stanley Dinkle had mailed his parents and brother a long letter recounting his adventures and begging forgiveness for his boyish dereliction of duty. On both sheets and envelopes he had printed a return address, but never, in those eleven years, to those more than one hundred entreaties, had he had a reply. Since the letters had not been returned, they had certainly been delivered, but whether read or not, saved or burned, he could not know. It was as though his father and mother and brother and the dairy herd and Horeb, Wisconsin, did not exist. He had been cut off at the roots. Given the least encouragement he would have gone home on leave, but he was vouchsafed none whatever, and the reproach of silence was sometimes almost more than he could bear. He turned inward. In the Philippines, at Fort Kearney, Huachuca, Sam Houston, and Riley, the Army became his home, a horse and saber his brother and sister.

Pen in hand, paper before him, young men everywhere about him blotting and squirming in the throes of composition, Stanley Dinkle sat not writing. He stuck out like a sore thumb. Down the table a sergeant stared. To keep up appearances, the officer dashed off three notes in rapid succession:

Dear Miss Grebs,
I love you. I have bought you an ensembel that will knock your eyes out. Will you marry me?
Sincerely,
Stanley

Dear Phipps, Biddle, Pugh, Darlington, Den Uyl, and Thayer,
I am having a hot time in old El Paso. If I have been too hard on you I am sorry And I hope you are sorry about the other night because six against one is unfair. Let us bury the hatchet and start over and serve our country to the best of our ability and also be friends because everybody needs friends, me especially.
Sincerely,
Lt. S. Dinkle, A.U.S.

Dear Pa, Ma, and Brother Tipton,
Go to hell.
Sincerely,
S. Dinkle

Folding the three sheets, and prudently taking a stock of stationery for the future, he left the table, dropped the three sheets into a wastebasket, and departed the YMCA.

On a street corner he paid a quarter for a family of four Mexican fleas, thinking he might find them a new home in the beds of the Philadelphia Light Horse on his return. "Las Pulgas, The Fleas," read the inscription on the tiny boxtop, "Papacito & Mamacita & kids Willie & Ethel," but when he started to open the box the peddler warned him to desist, saying that afforded the slightest opportunity the occupants would flee, and guaranteeing that a family of four, parents and two offspring, boy and girl, were indeed resident therein.

Seated once more in the plaza under a pepper tree, and noting that his boots were dusty, he engaged a ragamuffin to shine them, after which he paid the nickel asked and tipped another.

"Stanley," she had whispered, her eyes round and a trifle teary, "what if I'm beautiful an' we don't even know it!"

Rising, he went to the post office, where the Grouch awaited him with a belligerent air. "You back again?"

"I want to withdraw five dollars," said the officer, presenting his account card.

"Why don'tcha make it ten and save shoeleather?"

Dinkle was not in the least discountenanced. "I see by the papers," he said, "that they shot down a Zeppelin."

He was beginning to feel very much at ease in the Bon Ton, and the little change cars gliding to and fro on wires between the counters and the cashier's cage continued to fascinate him. Gushy sold him one of her best-brand corsets, a "Tendertruss," for $4.95, but he balked at forking over $1.95 for a silk vest and settled instead for a cotton at 69¢. On the way out she was tactless enough to inquire, in a shrill voice and to the delectation of the other shoppers, "Does your sweetie have bloomers?"

Dinkle blushed red as a beet. "Ma'am," he said, drawing himself up to his full five feet eight, "I have never been in a position to know."

He took the vest and corset to the New York Hotel, went out again to lunch on a milkshake and a tortilla, returned to the hotel for a siesta, and by three o'clock in the afternoon found himself on a bench under a pepper tree in San Jacinto Plaza.

For a time he studied the life-size replica of the immortal Mandy the Mule and the car she drew along El Paso's streets until 1902, when mule cars were replaced by electric. After that he counted trolleys clanging and grinding round the plaza till several seemed so familiar that he realized he was counting the same ones twice.

I am going bug, thought Stanley Dinkle.

I remember what my grandfather used to say. "If I had

some ham," he'd say, "I'd have some ham and eggs if I had some eggs."

I have come to a pretty pass. Today is my last day and today was supposed to be the day something wonderful happened and if it didn't I'd make it. Well, nothing has and I ain't. But it's not too late to stir my stumps. "I am the master of my fate," as the poet says, "I am the second looey of my soul." So pardon my dust, El Paso!

He departed the plaza, walked a block or three, turned in under a sign "FORD LIVERY," and telling the manager, a small, oily individual named Tucker, that he wanted to learn to drive a Model T, was advised that the cost of basic instruction and an hour's rental would be two dollars, which he promptly paid. A late-model roadster with top down was then pushed out of the garage and the officer's education commenced.

He was first acquainted with the emergency handbrake set at the driver's left, and the position and function of the three floor pedals—clutch to the left, reverse in the center, and brake on the right. It was a lie and a calumny, Tucker declared, that one needed three legs to operate a T. Once you got the hang of it, two were aplenty in practically every situation. Putting the officer behind the wheel, he demonstrated. A Ford had two speeds forward, low and high, and halfway down on the clutch pedal was neutral. To start off, you pushed the clutch full down, engaging the low gears, and away you went. When you gained speed enough, you let the pedal full up and away you went. To back up, you depressed the left pedal with your left foot and depressed the center with your right. To brake, you stomped on the right pedal with whatever foot was available at the moment. It was as simple as falling off a log.

The next lesson was in the use of the two levers set on the notched quadrant on the steering post directly beneath the wheel—spark to the left, throttle to the right. There were nine different position patterns: starting, idling, low; ten, twenty, thirty mph, and full speed; hill climbing in low, hill climbing in high. Again Tucker demonstrated, and his pupil seemed to comprehend as though to driving born, positioning the levers easily and nodding vigorously at each explanation. Once you got the hang of it, he was assured, you could set 'em in your sleep.

Tucker stepped from the auto, motioned the officer out, and put a confidential hand on his shoulder.

To start a Ford, he said, was the ticklish part. It was more than a knack, it was an art. One would assume that such machines, turned out by the thousands daily and painted an identical black, would be as similar as sardines out of a single can, but that was the everlasting riddle of the T: each one was unique, each one had its own personality and temperament. Tucker dropped his tone to one of saloon intimacy.

"Gonna let you in on the secret, Lootenant," he said. "And here she be—Love Yer Lizzie."

"Oh-oh," said Dinkle doubtfully. "I don't know about that. I'm a cavalryman."

"Love Yer Lizzie," Tucker repeated. "Don't go by guess and by gosh, get to know 'er inside out, her ups and downs, her good days and bad. Fight 'er and she'll fight back. Coddle 'er and she'll snuggle up to you come the hottest day or the coldest night. Now, take this roadster here, Floss I call 'er."

"Floss!" cried Stanley Dinkle.

"Fer short," said the manager. "Had me a gal once name of Flossie."

"Why, I know a girl named Flossie!"

"Small world, huh? Rhoda and Emily, they're back there." He pointed into the garage. "Anyways, like I say, Floss here's a dear. Easygoing, a hard worker, and the disposition of a dove. Treat 'er right and she'll start before you can say Jack Robinson. Let's try 'er. First off, you pull the hand brake all the way back, then set the spark and throttle."

Dinkle hauled on the brake, retarded the spark fully, and opened the gas four notches.

"Now come round here in front."

Dinkle opeyed.

"This here's the crank. Here's where you take hold of 'er so she knows you mean business." He winked. "You know how it is with a gal. Don't come at 'er like a bull out behind the barn, breathin' hard and pawin'. Just talk to 'er gentle and keep yer pants buttoned and pretty soon she'll close 'er eyes and spread 'er legs and howdy, partner, there you be."

Tucker drew a deep breath. "There's one catch. After she starts hittin', you gotta get back around and re-set them levers before she dies on you. Step lively and move the spark ahead three notches and the gas back two—that's for idle. And you better be spry. Ready?"

"Ready," said Dinkle.

"O.K. Now get right down there and take a good holt of the crank. Hey, unwrap yer thumb, I seen many a sprained thumb."

Dinkle unwrapped.

"O.K. Now crank to the right, and, Lootenant, don't never push down, always pull up. A Ford'll kick like a mule, and you push down she'll snap yer wrist like a match. O.K. now, to the right and pull don't push—O.K., pullaway!"

Dinkle put his back into it and cranked, and within three revolutions the engine sputtered into a roar.

"Back, back! Re-set!" Tucker hollered.

Dinkle raced to the wheel, advanced the spark, retarded the throttle, and the engine slowed to a contented chatter. The manager opened the door, bowed, and the officer took his seat behind the wheel, hands gripping it with such resolution that the knuckles whitened.

Tucker slammed the door, backed off, and waved an arm. "Let 'er rip!"

Dinkle pushed the clutch pedal into neutral, opened both spark and throttle five notches, pushed the clutch to the floor and into low gear and instantly, with such ginger that it took his breath away, he was off and into the street as slick as a whistle.

Keeping the auto in low gear, sitting bolt upright and concentrating on his task with every fiber of his being, Stanley Dinkle covered several blocks without mishap. Then a concatenation of near misses almost nipped his novitiate in the bud. An imperious Pierce Arrow hogged several feet of his half of the street, and steering to avoid a sideswipe and the amputation of a fender he swung too far to the right, coming so close to collision with a horse-drawn bakery wagon that the animal reared and the driver leaped from the seat, shaking a fist at the officer, who, taking his eyes from his course to extend an apology, was galvanized by the alarum of the bell of the streetcar which bore down upon him at an intersection and which he would strike broadside unless he got busy as a one-armed paperhanger and stopped in a fraction of a second, a feat of chauffeuring he essayed by shouting "Whoa!" and stomping with both boots everything that would stomp and yanking with both hands everything that would yank, thereby producing a volley of backfires, an objection of brakes, an agony of gears, a precipitate halt, and a stalled engine. These brushes with disaster, heaped one upon the other, rendered him limp as a dishrag. The trolley passed, its passengers berating him from the windows, but he had reposed his forehead on the steering wheel, and might there and then have given up the automotive ghost had his pride not been pricked by the horselaughter of loafers on the corner. Pale, trembling, with what little aplomb he could muster, he re-set the spark and gas levers to starting positions, got out of the vehicle, genuflected to the crank, and whispered ardently, "Floss, girl, start. Please start, Floss, and I will take back every nasty thing I ever said about flivvers." He spun the crank, the engine came to immediate life, he sprang to re-set the levers, and was once more under way.

Within half a mile, however, and thanks to a change of course, he began to enjoy himself. To the north of the city Mount Franklin towered, and on the principle that it must represent the wide open spaces, he headed for it and soon dusted out of traffic and onto a smooth gravel road, enabling him to pedal the Ford into high gear and reposition spark and throttle for ten, twenty, then thirty miles per hour. Equitating an automobubble, he found, wasn't half bad, provided you had as many appendages as a centipede. The razor of wind upon his cheeks, the babble of pebbles under his running boards, the incredible combustion beneath his feet—these exhilarated him. He gained confidence, he developed daring. Opening spark and gas all the way, he let the jitney run flat out, reaching a penultimate speed of forty, even fifty death-defying mph. He became the sprout he had once been in Wisconsin, whizzing down a wintry hill on a Flexible Flyer. He squeezed the bulb and bawled the horn. He shouted, "Whoeeeeeee!"

At the foot of Mount Franklin the good road gave way to a sandy trail which looped the lower slopes. Dinkle throttled down, shifted into low, and chugged another quarter mile, climbing perhaps a thousand feet until the grade increased and the engine coughed and suddenly conked out, he knew not why. The grade was steep, but not too steep for twenty horsepower, and the rear wheels had ample traction. Letting the auto roll backward to a level stretch, he cranked up and the engine responded, but no sooner were they on the grade again when it wheezed its last. Twice more he tried. He addressed the dashboard in endearing terms, he patted the radiator and scorched his fingers, to no avail. He cussed the roadster out as he might have a recruit, with the same incomprehensible result. Grinding up a hundred yards or so, to his indignation the flivver failed him. As a hill-climber the Ford was a frost. How it could perform as happily on the level, then fizzle out on a grade, was beyond him.

Love Your Lizzie ha, thought Stanley Dinkle.

If I had a nag here, any old nag, we'd toss our tails and hop this dinky hill like a frog.

He was determined, however, to have a view from Mount Franklin while he was here, and leaving the car he clambered along a spiny ridge and seated himself on a boulder, facing south. From this height he had a splendid prospect of El Paso and the valley of the Rio Grande, and over the river, perfumed and passionate, the sprawl of Mexico. Her breasts were stony hills. Dark ranges in the distance were her thighs. She excited him. The mystery of her, the otherness of her flesh—these caused a subtle agitation in the groin. He leaned forward on the rock.

Toward exotic Mexico he tilted. He was reminded of how, their first night at the post, he'd snubbed the Philadelphians up short when they waded for the forbidden side of the river, and how he'd put them over his knee and applied the hairbrush of his tongue. Perhaps he had indeed been too hard on them, for that tomfoolery and for pulling the Philippine rug out from under him after the feast. Boys took to high jinks like ducks to water, which was truly what they were, boys, saplings yet to be bent by the storms of life. In his mind's eye he watched them now, going about their chores at Fort Dinkle, doing their unheralded duty while he cast dull care away on leave. He leaped to his feet.

Leave! It's my last night on leave! cried Stanley Dinkle to himself.

If I could go down from Mount Bagsak to slay the googoos of Sulu, I can go down from Mount Franklin to bed the bitches of Juárez!

Bismillah!

Descending the ridge, he checked his watch and wallet. If the Ford behaved, there was enough time. But when he cranked up, the roadster crept forward affectionately at the first explosion, so that he was forced to hold it at bay by the headlamps. Evidently the hand brake was not set firmly, and with the engine running, the transmission bands urged the machine on to nuzzle him as Hassan often did when begging a handful of oats. His heart softened. "Whoa, Floss, steady, girl," he coaxed. "I know you're sweet on me, but wait'll I diddle your levers a little." To his surprise, the flivver seemed to understand, easing up while he made a dash for the wheel. He backed down the mountain then, turned around, and together they set out for El Paso. Once they reached the good road, Dinkle drove like Barney Oldfield, throttle open wide, until, at the edge of town, he traversed the last mile in low gear. It was uneventful except for a close shave between a Columbia sedan and a wagonload of baled hay.

"Come back in one piece, huh?" said Tucker at the livery. "You and Floss must of got along jimdandy."

The officer allowed they had, although she'd stubbornly refused to climb Mount Franklin for him.

"Shucks," said Tucker, "should of told you. That's one catch to a T—no gas pump. Tanks under the seat, so all's you got is gravity flow down to yer carb. Get 'er nose up too high and she'll plumb die for a drink. Word to the wise, Lootenant. You see a steep grade ahead, turn around, put 'er in reverse, and she'll climb like a scared cat."

Dinkle thanked him and bade farewell to Floss with a final fondle of the steering wheel and quick-marched past the plaza to the post office, arriving at five minutes to five o'clock, closing time.

"I want to withdraw twenty dollars," he announced.

"Why not take it all, Diamond Jim?" asked the Grouch.

"What kind of car d'you drive?"

"Why, a flivver, what else?"

"So do I," said Dinkle.

In the Bon Ton he was given a choice by Gushy: pongee bloomers at $5.50 or muslin at $1.35. "Let's have the pongee," said Dinkle. He winked. "As the poet says, 'There's nothing known to man that beats, A little pongee 'tween the sheets.' "

18

"I Didn't Raise My Dog to Be a Sausage"

Meanwhile, that afternoon, Thayer having succeeded in reviving the ignition system of both autos, the Tin Lizzie Troop pushed on into Mexico. Their noon meal they ate en route and al fresco, since the ruts here ran through packed sand and they could tear along at twenty miles an hour. They had not as yet seen any sign of the bandidos, but at this rate, both cars agreed, they must soon catch up with mounted men.

Then, roaring out of a dry wash, they spotted beside the ruts their first human being. Taking one terrified look at the mechanical monstrosities bearing down upon him, the pacífico took forthwith to his heels. They braked, leaped, and chased after him, but in seconds the desert had swallowed him up, and they returned to the jitneys wondering if he had been a mirage.

Then "Henrietta" had a flat tire. No sooner was it patched and pumped up when "Olivia," perhaps out of a sisterly empathy, had her own.

Then, when they were rolling again, two pacíficos appeared ahead. These gaped at the Fords but stood their ground as Phipps drew up beside them.

"Buenos días, señores," he greeted them.

"Días," they replied.

"Dondey," he began, *"dondey es los bandidos?"*

"Los bandidos?"

"Si. El bandido Encarnacion Contreras."

"Ah, Contreras!" The peons glanced at each other. Fear and guile narrowed their eyes.

"Dondey?" pressed Phipps.

Each extended an arm. One pointed north, one pointed south.

"Torture 'em," snarled a disgusted Den Uyl. "Take 'em along and make 'em fix flats."

"Tell them this," said Biddle. "Say to them, 'May your mothers become prostitutes and take their remuneration in counterfeit pesos and come down, in addition, with an incurable case of the clap.' "

The peons smiled and nodded.

By late afternoon, the desert sand had changed into dry, powdery soil which exploded under the wheels. Those in the second car were whitened and choked with dust. Darlington, who was asthmatic, began to wheeze, and they halted to move him into the lead car. Despite the use of goggles, so thick was the dust that Thayer was unable to keep proper interval between himself and "Henrietta," with the result that when Phipps stopped again, there was a minor rear-end collision. Thayer went forward.

"Sorry, couldn't see you."

Phipps glared at him. "What the devil's wrong with this junk pile now?"

"You tell me, pal."

"It just went dead on me, for no reason."

Thayer tried the crank, but couldn't turn it. Attempting to raise one side of the hood, he singed his fingers. Making a glove of his handkerchief, he propped up both sides, averting his face from the heat. He shook his head.

"Frozen," he said. "She's frozen cold."

"Frozen!" cried Phipps and Biddle in exasperation. "It's hotter than the hinges of Hell!"

"That's what they call it," explained their mechanic. "Block gets so hot that everything expands. Pistons freeze in the cylinders, you can't even turn the crankshaft. But why did she overheat?"

"You tell us, kiddo."

Masking his face with the handkerchief, Thayer inspected the engine compartment. "Oh-oh. I was afraid of that."

"Afraid of what?"

"We've got a lousy leak in the radiator. Two or three lousy leaks."

"What do we do?"

"Sit. Till she cools off. And while we're sitting, figure out a way to plug the holes."

But they could not sit. Except for Darlington, who was too short of breath to do anything but gasp, they paced hither and yon about the cars, to and fro, back and forth. They were dusty, parched, and cramped from confinement. Inwardly they were as locked, as inoperative as "Henrietta's" twenty paralyzed horse-power. Frustration expanded them. The pistons of their energy and determination were stuck fast. In thirty-six hours they had averaged less than a mile an hour .They hadn't fired a shot. Contreras was turning out to be as elusive as Villa himself. Most aggravating was the proof before them that they had been hoodwinked by Henry Ford.

"If we'd bought Chandlers instead of these struggle buggies," predicted Pugh, "we'd be there and back by now."

"If we'd only brought the Vic," regretted Den Uyl, "we could spin a few records."

"If we had some ham," said Phipps sarcastically, "we could have ham and eggs if we had some eggs."

"Eureka!" Thayer snapped his fingers. "You said it—the rations!"

They thought he'd gone goofy. But bringing the water can and a paper sack, testing to be sure the engine had cooled, he poured into "Henrietta's" radiator half a pound of ground coffee, filled with water, cranked up, and the flivver sprang to life as though fresh off the assembly line in Highland Park, Michigan. Dropping the sides of the hood he checked underneath for leakage, rose, and grinned at them.

"Grounds plug the holes like a charm! Step right up, hot coffee a nickel a cup! Let's go!"

Then, a mile or two down the ruts, they encountered still another human—if that was what he was. This customer stood erect and tall as a telephone pole beside the ruts, unperturbed by the arrival of machines such as he had never imagined. He seemed to be waiting for them, to have a rendezvous with them, like Grim Death. He was a very old, gaunt man. Under his black sombrero they could see only a slice of his face, while the rest of him, from cheekbones to bare, gnarled feet, was shrouded in a black serape. His forehead was lined, his eyebrows were gray. Yet the obsidian eyes which fixed upon them like a pair of pliers were as youthful as their own.

An uncomfortable Phipps inquired as to Contreras's whereabouts, at which the old-young gent beckoned with a skeletal finger. Phipps eased from behind the wheel and followed him to the top of a rise, then double-timed back in high excitement and ordered everyone out, rifles and pistols and no noise, they had the bandido trapped. The others sprang to arms and let Phipps lead them round the rise, where he pointed at a small mud hovel, or jacal, some two hundred yards away in the desert.

"He says Contreras is in there. So, so, so," stammered the corporal, "so we'll surround it and I'll demand he surrender. Don't shoot unless I do. Thayer, you take Biddle and Pugh around to the other side, then we'll close in. All right, men, stay down and ssssssh."

Crouching low, hearts misfiring at the prospect of their first combat, the Tin Lizzie Troop deployed. When it was in place, Phipps shouted:

"Contreras! This is the United States Army! We've got you surrounded! Come out with your hands up!"

Contreras kept mum.

"Come out, Contreras, or we'll come in after you!"

After a pause to let this threat sink in, Phipps waved his forces forward. Springfields leveled, faces pale under their burn, they closed in on the hut. At the final instant, with the traditional selflessness of those whose hard duty it is to lead men into battle, Phipps himself rushed the door and kicked it open.

The jacal was empty.

"Horsefeathers!" roared a mortified Phipps.

Whirling out the door, bumping into them, he made for the autos on the run, the rest at his heels. "I'll shoot that old liar!" he cried. "I'll execute him!"

But the inscrutable ancient had disappeared, as had the Boyce Motometer crowning "Olivia's" radiator.

It was almost the last straw. Silent and sullen, they mounted up again and chugged across a barren expanse which twilight painted purple. They stopped beside a tiny structure of weathered wood. It was a roadside shrine, complete with cans of expired flowers about the base of a table on which stood a statue of the Virgin of Guadalupe and a shiny brass Motometer. They stared at it open-mouthed. Why the old man had stolen the accessory, why he had enshrined it here, how he could have reached this place on foot faster than they had on wheels, there was no point in conjecturing. Mexico was a land located somewhere outside the latitudes of probability. Phipps brought the gadget back to "Olivia," screwed it on, and they proceeded without a word.

Then, five dusty minutes later, they ran head-on into the stone wall of their military situation. Taken by a sudden and severe attack of asthma, "Stew" Darlington slumped over in the tonneau and passed out. They had the cars stopped and "Stew" stretched out on blankets on the ground in jig time, but he was blue in the face. They fanned him with hats, they sponged his face with wet handkerchiefs. Eventually the spasm of his bronchi ended, he breathed again, oxygen was pumped to his brain, and he regained consciousness. He would be in no condition to travel for a while, however, and they used the enforced wait to dine on the last of their beans and hardtack, washing it down with hot coffee drawn from the outlet of "Henrietta's" radiator.

Phipps took Thayer aside. "I want you to do something for me. Tell me how far south of the river we are and if we've got enough gas to get back."

Thayer hefted the milk cans of gasoline in the luggage carriers and checked the gas tanks under the front seats by means of a dipstick, then reported. "I'd guess between twenty and thirty miles. And I'd say we've got just enough juice to get back. But that's a guess, too. It's the oil and water I'm worried about. We're low on both."

"Thanks."

To be by himself, to think through the implications of his predicament, Phipps took a short stroll. It was getting dark. The outlines of the Model T's resembled those of two bony, incongruous cows put out to pasture on sand. Someone had made a fire near them, which was dangerous and which he should order doused immediately. But would he be obeyed? Noncommissioned officers in the Philadelphia Light Horse were elected rather than appointed. Pull rank on your peers once too often and they might dis-elect you. Phipps walked into a greasewood bush. Did Lieutenant Dinkle bear ultimate responsibility for the debacle night before last, and for the conduct of his men later, now, here? Or had he been relieved of that responsibility by delegating it to another in his absence? In short, in the event of legal proceedings, which might spend more of his declining years in Leavenworth—Dinkle or Alexander M. Phipps? The latter stumbled over a cactus. He simply must come to some kind of decision. To be or not to be, that was the question—to be authoritative and let it go on, let it compound its original folly, let it make a jackass of itself as he had of himself this afternoon, assaulting a mud hut and shouting "Horsefeathers!"

Making up his mind should be a mere bagatelle for a "Lex" Phipps, "Lex" Phipps assured himself. He was twenty-four, the eldest. He was a corporal. He was married. He was a businessman. He was the most mature and level-headed of the bunch and looked it. He was stoutish. And he parted his brown hair in the middle. But the difficulty was, "Lex" Phipps had never made an independent decision in his life. He had matriculated at Harvard and cultivated a Boston accent because his father and grandfather had done so. He presided over a desk because his great-grandfather had founded a shipyard. A determined girl from New York counted cadence while she marched him to the altar. His robustness was impending corpulence, his composure a premature middle age, and his sobriety would turn him, in later years, into a crashing bore. His heart might be in the right place, but his head would soon be bald.

He listened. To lift their spirits, Thayer was singing one

of the many parodies of "I Didn't Raise My Boy to Be a Soldier," accompanying himself on his uke:

I'll let you take my dog out for a ramble,
But you be sure and bring him back to me;
Steer clear of Bertha Krupp,
She'll blow the poor pup up,
He likes to chase the chickens when he's free.
Among the fields of clover let him gambol,
Why, you can even trust him on a bridge;
But look out, he is French,
Don't go in a German trench,
I didn't raise my dog to be a sausage.

In the breast of Alexander M. Phipps the song rang a inspirational bell. If someone cared enough about his mutt to save it from the Hun, he cared enough about his men to save them from themselves, no matter what it cost him in rebellion. To be a commander, one must command.

He returned to his troop. "I've made up my mind," he announced, standing authoritatively beside the autos. "We're on a wild-goose chase. I was opposed to it from the start, but I didn't want to be a wet blanket. Anyway, we're going back. Thayer tells me we've got enough gas to make the river—but if we go on, even another mile or two, we won't have. So everyone into the cars."

No one moved. They were weary and chopfallen. It was night now, and the chickens of their recklessness were coming home to roost.

"If I don't have a bath pretty soon," said Den Uyl, "I'll go absolutely nertz."

"Didn't you hear me?" Phipps demanded. "We're also low on water and oil. And d'you know how much food we have left? Two cans of tomatoes!"

"We have to think of Stew, too," reminded Thayer. "His lungs won't take much more dust."

"Bunk." Darlington, his brother-in-law-to-be, sat up angrily. "You look out for yourself, Luce. Leave me alone."

"Bid" Biddle yawned, stretched, and added a twig to the fire. "I'm not in favor," said he.

Phipps couldn't believe his ears. "You're not in favor! Who talked us into this mess in the first place? We'd have Contreras in the bag and back by night—baloney! This is our second night out and we're in Mexico up to our necks and we don't even know where!"

"Good point," Den Uyl derided. "But if we don't know where we are, how can we find our way back? Let's 'fess up—we're little lost lambs, baa-baa-baa."

"Well, we can try!" asserted Phipps. "And furthermore, I won't listen to any more run-around. I'm your corporal and I'm giving an order—everyone into the cars!"

Biddle rose. "Don't be such a stuffed shirt, Phippsy. In case you're curious, we elected you for our convenience, and we can break you back to private whenever you're inconvenient." He leaned against "Henrietta's" fender. "Here's what I am in favor of. Going on. Right now. We have headlights, after all. There must be a town somewhere—these ruts must lead to something. At least we've seen people today, and that shrine. Reach civilization and we can gas up and get some intelligence on Contreras. The case I made day before yesterday is even more valid today. If we had damned little to lose then, we have less now. In fact, to save our skins, we have to go on."

"Biddle, I've swallowed enough of your banana oil." "Phew" Pugh was the last to be heard from. "I don't care if you do whip me. Dinkle was right, but we're too stubborn to admit it. Well, I admit it. We don't know anything about war. He may not be a gent, Bid, but he's a soldier —and you're not and we're not. And I wish like hell he were here—if he were, we wouldn't be."

Biddle appraised him coolly. "I've half a mind to acquaint my right hand with your kisser."

"Touch him," warned the gallant Thayer, "and you'll have me to reckon with." He held his ground and struck a defiant chord on his uke. "I say, go back, while we're still able."

That decided Darlington. "I say, go on."

"I gave an order!" cried Phipps.

"Go jump in the lake," Den Uyl advised him.

"I say, let's be democratic, let's vote," Biddle suggested. "All in favor of going on?"

But they had already chosen up sides, and the result was foregone—Biddle, Den Uyl, and Darlington for the motion, Phipps, Thayer, and Pugh against.

Biddle smoothed a satisfied mustache. "A tie, eh? Corporal, you're fired."

"No I'm not," quoth Phipps, with as much poise as he had ever mustered. "I hereby resign." And reaching, he tore the stripes from his sleeve and dropped them grandly into the fire.

"By George," said Thayer.

They were not a little awed, even embarrassed. Friends in their formative years, social and cultural equals, troopers together in peace and hooch, the self-demotion shocked them, and the threat of fisticuffs. After an uneasy pause, Den Uyl suggested that since they were evenly split, they divvy up the gasoline and go their separate ways in the two cars, one north, one south.

"And what'll you do if you bump into the bandidos?" Phipps inquired. "Three against Lord knows how many. No, we'll tag along in case you do. But I wash my hands of the whole rotten show. From now on, it's Biddle's baby."

A proud Biddle accepted the challenge. " 'Lay on, MacDuff,' " said he with a bow, " 'and damned be he who first cries, Hold, enough!' " Lithely he leaped to a running board. "Very well, gents. Let's toddle down the pike a few miles. Mount up!"

"Henrietta" and "Olivia" sprang to life, the eight-and-a-half-inch electric head lamps, which had replaced acetylene gas on the Model T only the year before, were switched on, and the caravan crawled onward, Biddle driving the lead vehicle. The occupants were soon made aware, however, that the advent of electricity, under these circumstances, was a dubious blessing. The bulbs took their current directly from the flywheel magneto, and since the magneto voltage ranged, according to engine speed, from eight to twenty-eight volts, a fairly high speed was required to keep the voltage up and the lights bright. But in ruts such as these, and on a night as Stygian as this, the flivvers were incapable of more than five miles an hour, the bulbs flickered and faded, and neither driver could see his hand before his face, much less the natural impedimenta of the terrain. Only by stopping and racing the engines were the beams intensified. It was start-dim-stop-bright-damn Detroit-denounce the night. Biddle wandered out of ruts into sand so deep that "Henrietta" had to be pushed. Thayer drove "Olivia" into a staghorn cactus, the spines of which reciprocated by puncturing a tire. Thayer refused to patch. "Henrietta" boiled over. Den Uyl refused to pump. Pugh insisted they could make better time on shanks' mare. Darlington was wheezing again. Finally, after an expectoration of oaths more erudite than they had ever heard, Biddle ordered lamps and engines cut. They would camp here. They would sleep in the cars, and upon their arms. To guarantee that the greasers did not entirely dismantle the autos by morning, he was posting guard, Phipps to stand the first watch. They opened and shared one can of tomatoes. Phipps went his solitary way. With rifles for bedfellows, the others bundled themselves into seats and blankets. What lay in store for them, wondered the Tin Lizzie Troop, in the black, foreboding night?

19

A Goat with a Heart of Gold

What lay in store for him in the dark, illicit night Lt. Stanley Dinkle could not know, but clean-shaven and shirted he set out from the New York Hotel refreshed in body and immaculate in spirit. To resist temptation is human, to give in to it divine.

His intentions were humble. He would be properly disgusted by Juárez. Having wisely secreted the bulk of his funds under his mattress, he would spend wisely as few as possible of the ten dollars in his wallet. Juárez, it was common knowledge, was infested with women of the lowest type, and these he would spurn, paying instead for the favors of someone more toothsome and certainly more sanitary. Above all, he would be a cool customer, remembering his rank, gratifying his glands, and returning to his native land edified and uncorrupted.

After a ten-minute walk down Santa Fe Street he neared the International Bridge, where a six-man guard was posted to prevent enlisted men from slipping into Sodom on the other side and turning into pillars of salt on this. A corporal advanced, but catching sight of the gold bar on Dinkle's collar, let him pass. Halfway over the rickety bridge he looked down from the rail and was surprised that the Rio Grande, a clear swift stream at Fort Dinkle, was here but a muddy trickle. He went on, and reaching the far end of the bridge squared his shoulders, made sure of the wallet on his hip, and entered the cesspool of vice, intrigue, and danger that was Juárez.

He was at once appalled by the ruin five years of revolution had wrought. What had not been put to the torch by Maderistas had been burned by Villistas—the customs house, railroad station, post office, bull ring, even Kettelson & Degetau's wholesale hardware, long a landmark. Blackened walls were pocked with bullet craters where Villa's machine gunners, to save ammunition, had executed prisoners in rows of seven. The dusty street was illuminated only by lamps within the surviving places of business, through the doors of which piles of guns could be seen. Mexicans armed to the teeth stood watch over these arsenals, while Carranzista cavalrymen trotted bony ponies up and down, grimacing ferociously at any gringo incautious enough to have crossed the line.

Dinkle slunk down the street, solicited at every step by small boys crying *"Chicletas! Chicletas!"* He shook his head, deploring the evil that lurketh in the hearts of men. Pushing through swinging doors, he sallied into the Black Cat Bar, a den of iniquity if he had ever seen one. Under guttering candles, and to the strains of a violin and *guitarrón,* several scrofulous couples swayed in what appeared to be a comatose or inebriate condition. Stepping to the bar and ordering a beer, paying for it and counting his change, he had scarcely sampled the brew of Cuauhtemoc when he was greeted by a harem of hideously painted *filles de joie,* who made clear the import of their salutation by thrusting hands under his belt and down the front of his breeches. He was insulted, not to say revolted. Leaving his beer, he moved next door to the Tivoli, only to be victimized in the same foul manner, whereupon he tried the Monte Carlo and the Big Kid. In despair he took to the street again, and walking warily another block, reached the white-walled haven of the Cathedral of Guadalupe, a monument that even blasphemous war had not yet dared profane. Loitering near the steps, he became aware of movement in the shadows, and presently a girl leading a goat came toward him timidly, holding out a tin cup and indicating the goat and murmuring *"Leche fresca, señor? Leche fresca?"*

He stared at her. For all he cared, she might have been peddling fresh milk from a mastodon. She was lovely. The mantilla over her head outlined a cameo face. Her chin was dainty, her lips formed a rosebud, her eyes were large, brown, luminous, and innocent.

"Leche fresca, señor?"

He nodded vigorously.

Falling to one knee the girl milked the animal, an act which, by its poignancy, so personal to him, and by the memories it induced, brought moisture to his eyes even as she induced milk into the cup. She rose, offering the potion to him.

Dinkle drank. It was the vilest stuff he had ever tasted, but with a heroic effort he somehow got it down his gullet and returned the cup.

"Delicioso!" he enthused. *"Cuantos pesos, señorita?"*

"Veinte centavos."

"Twenty cents?" He was into his wallet like a flash, and out with a dollar, which he pressed into her tiny hand.

"No, no, señor!" she demurred.

"Si, si!" he insisted.

"Muchas gracias!" she smiled.

"Beh-heh-heh!" bleated the grateful goat.

Into the lacy top of her blouse the girl tucked the bill, granting the officer, despite the gloom of night, a glimpse of two tender, pristine tacos which made his mouth water.

I've picked a peach, exulted Stanley Dinkle, a pippin, a pearl of great price. But then again, if the cost of the cup was any indication, maybe not.

It is time, Dinkle, he told himself, to take this Lizzie by the levers.

"Como se yama, señorita?" he asked.

"Conchita," said she.

"Conchita," he sighed. *"Tu es mucho hermosa, mucho* beautiful."

"Oh, señor," said she, dimpling.

He hesitated. She could not be more than sixteen. To take carnal advantage of such a child, and one in obviously straitened circumstances, would be heinous. At the same time, faint heart ne'er won fair lady, and it might be that generosity and gilt-edged gringo currency would spare her a far worse fate at cruder hands than his.

"Ahem," he said, coming closer. "Conchita," he murmured, "I'm a lorn man. Also, I am still young, and as a young man I have certain physical, I mean natural, needs, which have long remained unsatisfied." He drew her into a corner near the cathedral doors. His arms encircled her sylphlike waist. "That is to say, Conchita, you're just the sweet patootie I've been looking for, and I'd lay good old Americano dollars on the barrelhead to make love to you."

"Dólares? Americanos?" she whispered, lifting her petal face to his. *"Amor?"*

He seized her with such abandon that the tin cup was crumpled between them. He kissed her. And then, to his consternation, and to his bliss, she pushed her tongue into his mouth practically to his medulla oblongata. A wriggling serpent, it sent a heavenly poison into every vein and fiber of his being.

"Oh, Conchita!" he choked.

"Oh, mi General!" she gasped.

"Beh-heh-heh!" bleated the libidinous goat.

She released herself. *"Vamanos,"* she said, and leading him with one hand and the goat with the other, slipped from the cathedral down the street and into an alley black as the ace of spades. Girl and animal seemed to know the way, but Dinkle stumbled, intoxicated by lust, assailed by conscience, and half-asphyxiated by the stench of the barrios of Juárez. Eventually, however, the trio came to some kind of hovel, and tethering the goat, the girl opened a creaking door and bade the officer follow her. The door seemed to close behind them by itself.

Stanley Dinkle blinked. They were in a gloomy room, and over a bed, on the wall, small religious candles smoking before each, were a lithograph of the Virgin of Guadalupe and a glossy photo of Fatty Arbuckle. Piously he removed his hat. He took Conchita in his arms. " 'There's a Little Bit of Bad in Every Good Little Girl,' " he whispered. And as he urged her pliant form to the keg of his chest and pressed his burning lips to hers, he was transported sensually to distant Zamboanga, wafted away once more upon the perfume of the red hibiscus and the ylang-

ylang trees. To the rustle behind him he was oblivious. And then, as in those tropic nights a cocoanut sometimes descended upon an iron roof with a fearful bang, the blow descended on his head.

20

The End of the Main Line

When, in the virgin light of dawn, the Tin Lizzie Troop awoke and descended from their autos, it was to ascertain that another of "Henrietta's" spare tires and both of "Olivia's" head lamps were missing.

"They're stealing these cars right out from under us!" Biddle exploded. "How in the name of God Almighty can this happen when I post guard?"

"If you recall, that's what I said when Contreras attacked," said Phipps dryly. "If you also recall, that's what Dinkle said the night the Grebs woman came courting him."

"One of you went to sleep at the switch!" Biddle snarled at them. "Which one? Who?"

Phipps managed an alum smile. "Ah, the loneliness of command," he sympathized.

In silence the six breakfasted on the remaining can of tomatoes, the last of their rations. Starvation could not stay them now, nor theft nor respiratory ailment nor mechanical failure. By using precious fuel to try by night another futile mile or two they had passed the point of no return. They were committed. Cranking up, creaking aboard, the Philadelphians once more traversed the wastes of Coahuila. But though the spirit of the flivvers was willing, their flesh was weak.

Run too long in low gear, "Olivia" boiled over.

"Henrietta," too, overheated next, not from low speed but from a cause which took Thayer, their mechanic, an hour to assign and repair. Her oil line was clogged with lint from the transmission bands, in which event one needed only to unscrew four bolts, loosen the bottom hose, remove the radiator, uncover the timing gear, blow out the line with a tire pump, cover the timing gear, reset the radiator, fasten the bottom hose, tighten four bolts, refill the radiator, and discover, to one's dismay, that this lowered the water can to a single, stale gallon.

Darlington was next prostrated by a second attack of asthma. They laid him out in the tonneau of the lead Ford and covered his face with a damp handkerchief.

Next, exhibiting the contrariness of her sex, "Henrietta," whose oil line had just been cleared, signaled Danger-Steaming! on her Motometer again, and for no apparent reason. Not until Thayer had tested everything else did it occur to him to get down on his knees, open her petcocks, and check her oil. She was dry as a bone, but the ground beneath her was black. Something, a boulder perhaps, had punched a hole in her pan. He plugged it with a stick, went for the oil can, uttered a groan, and sank to a running board, head in his hands. The others gathered.

"Luce?"

"Go 'way."

"What's wrong?"

"Lost her oil."

"Well, fill 'er up."

"We're down to one quart."

"Well?"

"She takes four."

"What'll we do?"

"Go 'way."

Seemingly comatose, he sat for several minutes, then shot to his feet. "Excelsior!"

"What?"

"When you mix oil and water, which rises?"

"Oil."

"Right! So all we need is enough on top to keep the flywheel oiled!" His elation vanished. "But we're down to a gallon of water. We have to choose. Walk and drink, or ride and die of thirst. Which'll it be, boys?"

They were cavalrymen. "Ride," they said.

Thayer emptied the water can into the crankcase, emptied the oil can into it, cranked up, and on a lubricative potion of four quarts of water and one of oil, "Henrietta" purred.

But the triumph was short-lived. Within another mile there issued from "Olivia's" hood a tunk-tunk-tunk, a sound as excruciating as that of a female giving difficult, multiple birth. Thayer cut the engine and got out. Pugh and Phipps got out. Biddle and Den Uyl stopped and got out.

"Drat it, what now?" lisped Den Uyl.

"Luce" Thayer removed his hat. His expression was that of a young man at the breaking point. "She's burned out a bearing."

"What's that mean?"

"The end of the line."

"No."

"Yes."

Their mechanic suddenly took hat in hand and with it strode about "Olivia" raining blow after blow upon the perfidious machine.

"Jezebel!" he yelled.

This example set, the rest cut loose with their own hats, flailing at "Olivia" with might and main, taking out on her doors and fenders all the mortification and frustration of two nights and days in Mexico.

"Hussy!" yelled "Freddy" Den Uyl.

"Hooker!" yelled "Bid" Biddle.

"Whore!" yelled "Phew" Pugh.

"Ford!" yelled "Lex" Phipps.

While they vented their spleen and dilapidated their hats, Pvt. Stewart H. Darlington lay on a pile of blankets in "Henrietta's" tonneau, recovering slowly from his seizure and hating his brother-in-law-to-be, "Luce" Thayer. He was twenty, and high-strung, and spoiled, and rich. His family had long been pillars of the Pennsylvania Railroad, his grandfather, in fact, having conceived the idea of a spur line west from Philadelphia along which the affluent might build their mansions, later called the "Main Line." At this moment, "Stew" had just hit upon the cause of his asthma. It was not dust. It was the mere physical presence of "Luce" Thayer. And the realization that, as "Livvy's" brother, he was destined to spend his future, as he had his past, in that same propinquity, brought him to a boil. "Luce" it was who persuaded him to attend Lafayette when he preferred Princeton. "Luce" it was who hot-boxed him into pledging Deke when what he wanted was Phi Psi. "Luce" it has been who, out of lovesickness for "Livvy," has delegated himself to big-brother "Stew's" health and deportment on the border. Lowest blow of all, it was "Luce" who urged him to apply for membership in the Light Horse, and helped him through training, and got him elected. In short, had it not been for that prig, that flat tire, that general human gyp "Luce" Thayer, Stewart H. Darlington would not be in his present pickle.

Someone approached. He sat up and took the damp handkerchief from his face. It was "Luce," laden with a solicitous expression. Darlington saw red. Unsnapping his holster, he drew his .45 automatic and leveled it.

"Another step and I'll kill you!" he shouted.

His brother-in-law-to-be halted. He smiled, but warily, then continued.

"Stew" slipped the safety and fired a round. The bullet ricocheted from the ground, singing, and "Luce" blanched while the others hopped for cover behind "Olivia."

"I told you to stay away, Luce Thayer! Leave me alone!"

Thayer collected himself. "Stew, Stew," he soothed, "you mustn't overexert yourself. You're in a weakened condition, my boy."

"Rapsberries!" howled Darlington, drawing a bead. "One more step and I'll fill you full of lead!"

"What's wrong, Stew?" Thayer implored. "What have I done?"

"What've you done? You got me into this mess, that's what!" Rage and relativity strengthened "Stew's" lungs. "If you hadn't talked me into this outfit I wouldn't be here!" he shouted. "And if I weren't here I wouldn't have asthma! So you're to blame for my asthma!"

Thayer shook his head. "Stew, Stew," he sorrowed. "We mustn't think of ourselves, Stew, we must think of dear Livvy."

"Livvy's a bitch!" her brother bawled. "I know her and you don't, you dumbbell! She'll henpeck you to death and I hope she does! She's a bitch, a bitch, a bitch!"

Shocked, wounded grievously in soul if not in flesh, "Luce" Thayer turned away.

Darlington waved his pistol and fired a final, vocal shot. "Not only that—I hate horses!"

Thayer returned to the others. "He's out of his mind, poor chap. Sunstroke, probably. I'll never, never forgive myself."

It was already past nine o'clock, the day would be another scorcher, and they held a council of war—the question being whether to leave "Olivia" by the wayside or to tow her. Biddle favored abandonment. The gallant Thayer would not hear of it. Already estranged from poor, addled "Stew," he refused to part with any object, however inanimate, named after his beloved "Livvy." Such an act, he said, would desecrate the tenderest emotion of which man is capable. And besides, if spare parts for "Henrietta" were needed in future, "Olivia" could supply them.

This tipped the scales. They backed the lead Ford up, joined the twain with a towrope, and Biddle put "Henrietta" into low gear and to the supreme test. She met it bravely, groaning in every planetary band of her transmission, shuddering from radius rods to side lamps, but managing on level ground an agonizing four mph. For a full mile she struggled, then gave up the combustive ghost. All of them heard her death rattle—that mortal tunk-tunk-tunk which had signified "Olivia's" demise—all heard and knew. "Henrietta," too, had burned out a bearing. Literally and figuratively, the Tin Lizzie Troop had reached the end of its rope.

Under a burning sun, somewhere in the state of Coahuila, "Bid" Biddle, "Freddy" Den Uyl, and "Stew" Darlington sat in one auto, on her door the warning "Danger, 100,000 Jolts!" In the second, emblazoned with the invitation "C'mon, Baby, Here's Your Rattle!," sat "Luce" Thayer, "Lex" Phipps, and "Phew" Pugh. The game was over. Both vehicles were broken down beyond their poor power to repair. Reserves of water, gasoline, oil, and food were exhausted. And they themselves were burnt to a crisp and worn to a frazzle. Their mustaches wilted. They sat in a kind of stupor. It seemed to them they dreamed. Where they were they could not be. What they had done they could not have. They had but to pinch themselves and they would wake within the groves of academe at Lafayette and Princeton, Harvard and Cornell, Franklin & Marshall and Penn. But those were not mirages in their minds—smoke rising from the ruins of Edhogg, and Mrs. Offus naked, the bloody throat and beard of Champion Grebs, his daughter's piteous cries as even now, brute men took their will and fill of her. Those sights and sounds were real. Therefore where they were and what they had done were real. For the first time it occurred to the young Philadelphians that they might die here, six soldiers fallen in a foreign land, sacrificed to the gods of war and progress and entombed forever in coffins of tin. It was just as well. It was preferable, perhaps. Better to have their bones bleach here, 'neath alien skies, sharing a common grave with the chassis of their comrades, than return disgraced to face court-martial music. And so they sat in the last extremity, awaiting the blessing of oblivion.

Resigned to their fate, how long they sat they never knew. What roused them was the happening along of a peon driving two emaciated burros pulling a cart overloaded with wood. Bursting from the touring cars, they greeted him like a long-lost brother, pumping his hand and almost kissing his feet.

"Señor! Señor! Buenos días! Wow, are we glad to see you! *Dondey* in hell *es* a town? *Un ciudad?"*

"Una ciudad?"

"Si, si! Por favor, señor!"

"Derecho, derecho." The pacífico indicated the ruts ahead.

"That means straight on," Phipps translated.

"La ciudad Delicias."

"Delicias?" they whooped. They clapped each other on the back. "Delicias! Delicias or bust!"

Swallowing pride in lieu of water, stooping not to conquer but to survive, they made the man a proposition. But despite their best Spanish and most fluent hand language, they were unable to make him understand what they intended. A twenty-dollar bill, however, seemed to pave the way to comprehension with instant macadam. The burros were unhitched from the cart. The cart was hitched to "Olivia's" rear bumper. The burros were hitched to "Henrietta," who was already hitched to "Oliiva" and the cart. The soldiers remounted their autos. And soon, under the impetus of profanity and abuse, the diminutive beasts provided a motive force by which the caravan—burros before Fords, Fords before cart—proceeded slowly southward.

21

Lieutenant Dinkle Reports to Fort Bliss

When, in the morning, Stanley Dinkle recovered consciousness, he was laid out in an alley as though for burial, hands folded upon his chest, campaign hat over his face. On his head was a knot as big as a hen's egg. His wallet was gone. About his prostrate form were clustered numerous citizens of Juárez, bowing heads and whispering concern until, like Lazarus, he performed the hocus-pocus of ascension.

Somehow he staggered to the International Bridge, maneuvered himself over it by means of the railing, planted boots again on solid American soil, and directed them uptown. The night before was a blur, an improbable juxtaposition of girl, goat, and Fatty Arbuckle, about which the less he recollected the better.

Into the New York Hotel he stumbled, a mechanical man. He washed and shaved, nicking himself only twice. He changed shirts and tied his necktie thrice. He packed his suitcase, adding to razor, dirty laundry, pistol and holster, *Cavalry Journal,* Postal Savings account book, and YMCA stationery a dress, hat, pair of shoes, two petticoats, corset, vest, and a pair of pongee bloomers. Fumbling his last few dollars from under the mattress, he went down to the lobby, paid his bill, left the hotel, ambulated to San Jacinto Plaza, and got aboard a streetcar bound for Fort Bliss.

It was a two-mile ride to the fort, where he was to report and pick up his leave papers prior to returning to El Paso to catch the 2:02 train to Marathon, and his condition, dire to begin with, deteriorated steadily. Each time the bell clanged his head clanged. Each time the wheels rang upon the rails as the car rounded a corner the sound reverberated in his stomach, hollow because the very thought of breakfast had made him ill. There was a bulge in the breast pocket of his shirt. Reaching in, he brought out the tiny box with the inscription "Las Pulgas, The Fleas, Papacito & Mamacita & kids Willie & Ethel." There was nothing whatever in the box, he knew now. Like everything else, it was a fraud and a delusion. And since it was empty, to confirm what needed no confirmation he opened it and peered inside. Perhaps his vision was impaired, too, but for a split second he sensed a scatteration, an infinitesmal fuzz of flight. He squinted, but the box was indeed bare, and tossing it out the window he wished the flea entrepreneur a short life and an unfaithful wife.

Vee get too soon old und too late schmart, philosophized Stanley Dinkle.

I don't know what in Sam Hill is to become of me. I can handle a squad, a platoon, or a troop, but I can't handle Stanley Dinkle for even three days. What I need is to get married and settle down, for as the Good Book says, a man shall cleave unto his wife and she shall darn his socks.

Except for the sentry at the gates, Fort Bliss was strangely deserted. Suitcase in hand, he hiked along the parade ground, extensive enough for a regimental review or four simultaneous polo matches, green in winter but browning now in the May heat. Bliss had once been home base for the legendary 7th Cavalry, wiped out with Custer at the Little Big Horn, and later, yet not so long ago, the old red brick officers' quarters on the west side of the parade ground housed men who fought Apaches. On the east side were two barracks for enlisted men, a mess hall, and his destination, the large building which served as headquarters for both the Department of the Southwest, Major General Frederick Funston commanding, and for the 8th Cavalry, the regiment to which he, Dinkle, had been assigned temporarily then detached temporarily for duty down the Rio Grande. Today, however, Bliss was a ghost post. The 8th Calvary was conspicuous by its absence. Dinkle couldn't conceive where it had gone or why, nor did he give a tinker's damn. He felt lower than a snake's hips. All he wanted was to thank Mapes for his leave— thanks ha—then crawl in a hole and pull the hole in after him.

He entered the 8th regimental HQ on the first floor and identified himself to an enlisted clerk.

"Lieutenant Dinkle?"

"That's right."

"Dinkle!" The clerk tipped over his chair and called to an inner office. "Captain, it's Lieutenant Dinkle!"

The other clerks had risen. Dinkle could not have created more stir had he been Marshal Foch, dropping in from France via balloon.

Mapes rushed out of his office. "Stanley, I persume!"

Dinkle saluted. "Nice to see you, Captain."

"Never mind that rigmarole—Dinkle, where in Hades have you been?"

"Why, on leave."

"But where?" Mapes persisted. "We've looked high and low for you for two days!"

"Well, sir," said Dinkle, lowering his voice, "I was over in Juárez last night."

"Sacre bleu!" The adjutant wrung his hands and cracked his knuckles. "You haven't heard the news?"

"No, sir."

"Haven't you even seen the morning papers?"

"No, sir. What's happened? I noticed when I came in— where's the regiment?"

Claude Mapes put both hands on Dinkle's shoulders and shook his head. "Stanley, amigo, what we don't know doesn't hurt us, and I'm not going to be your Brutus. But I hope to heaven you've had yourself a real spree, because you'll need it. In any case, I have my orders. We've been expecting you. And as soon as you show up, I'm supposed to escort you upstairs to chit-chat with the old man. He'll tell you."

"The old man?"

"Funston."

"Funston?"

"Major General Funston," Mapes corrected. "So come

along, lad, step lively. And for God's sake, not a word about Juárez."

Still shaking his head, the adjutant took Dinkle in tow upstairs to HQ, Department of the Southwest, and introduced him to the commander's aide, a major.

"The lost is found, Major," said Mapes with relief. "I deliver him into your tender mercies."

"And about time," said the aide severely ."I'll show him right in."

"Captain, aren't you going in with me?" Dinkle entreated.

"Not for all the tea in China, my boy," said Claude Mapes grimly. "But good luck. *Via con Dios.*"

Stanley Dinkle had never in his career spoken to or been in the presence of or so much as saluted a two-star general. Now, before he could say good-by to Mapes, his mentor, the aide was ushering him through a door and he was facing Major General Frederick Funston and attempting at the same time to come to attention and to salute with the right hand which held his cardboard suitcase by the handle. Fortunately the general ignored him and his contortions. He stood with his back to the room, facing a large window which overlooked the parade ground, and appeared to be searching the skies. Not until the aide had closed the door upon them did he turn to acknowledge a visitor.

"Dinkle."

"Yes, sir."

"Lieutenant Stanley H. Dinkle."

"Yes, sir."

"At ease. Where in hell have you been?"

"On leave, sir. In El Paso."

"Juárez more likely. Swilling tequila and getting yourself a stiff dose of disease. So you know nothing about this?"

"No, sir."

Funston strode back and forth behind his desk. He was a small man, an intense man, with salt hair and pepper eyes, and originally a cavalryman. He wore no necktie, but his shirt and breeches were creased to cut and the shine on his boots could not have been removed with a mustard plaster. He picked up a flyswatter and Dinkle flinched. "You're in command of Number Two, south of Marathon."

"Yes, sir."

"Edhogg's near there, whatever Edhogg is. And you have six men down there."

"Yes, sir."

"This is Friday. Tuesday you went on leave."

"Yes, sir."

"Stop saying yessir like a damned parrot. What did you tell 'em when you left?"

If it were possible, Dinkle's condition had worsened. The lump on his head had expanded, causing his campaign hat to hover like a halo, he was sure, several inches above his scalp. And there was something ominous about his interrogation. The general made him think of a firecracker on which the fuse had apparently fizzled, but which, when you took a chance and picked it up, detonated in your face.

"I told them to do their duty and keep their eyes peeled and not to cross the river. Sir."

"Don't move!" Funston hissed, swatter raised, and suddenly gave the corner of his desk a powerful whack. "Got 'im!" he exulted. "Reflexes of a man half my age." He brushed the trophy off the desk. "All right, Dinkle, let's get down to brass tacks. Eighteen patrol posts between here and Brownsville and eighteen shavetails in charge and of course—it happens at the only one where the CO's off to the fleshpots. Dinkle, if I didn't need you I'd hang you to the nearest tree. Somebody named Offus got word to Marathon night before last and the sheriff there phoned us."

It was all clear as mud to Dinkle. "That's Harley Offus, sir, runs the store in Edhogg, has a very unusual Adam's apple."

"Don't interrupt. You left Tuesday, and Tuesday night bandits crossed the river—I don't know who or how many, the border's crawling with 'em, professionals and amateurs. They caught your men with their pants down, evidently, and ran off their horses. They then burned and looted

Edhogg. They then murdered a miner named Grebs and abducted his daughter."

"Oh, no!" groaned Stanley Dinkle. "Sir!"

"Oh, yes!" the general assured him, swatting the desk for emphasis. "She may be dead, she may be alive, but she's better off dead. In any case, that's not the worst. Your six men crossed the river after the bandits and haven't been heard from since."

"Oh, no!" groaned Stanley Dinkle. "Sir!"

"Oh, yes," Funston assured him, swatting the desk for emphasis. "And there's more. They had no horses. Why don't you ask me how they went after the bandits, Dinkle?"

"How, did, they, go, after, the, bandits, sir?"

"In two Ford autos!"

"Oh, no!" groaned Stanley Dinkle. "Sir!"

"Oh, yes!" the general assured him, swatting the desk for emphasis. "And stop contradicting me! Not only have those nincompoops of yours entered the Republic of Mexico without authorization and contrary to orders, they have entered it in automobiles! And now the joker in the deck, Dinkle. You must not read the papers. They are full of it. Edhogg went out on the wire services and every editor in Christendom's frothing at the mouth for action. They don't know about your men or those cars, not yet, thank God, and neither does Washington, thank God, but they do know I have one hundred thousand men guarding this border and this raid coming on top of Columbus is one damned raid too many!" Funston waved a sheaf of papers. "Telegrams! From the Chief of Staff and the Secretary of War and half the United States Congress demanding I do something! Why don't you ask me why I don't, Dinkle?"

"Why, don't, you, do, something, sir?"

"Because I can't! I've had the Eighth Cavalry at Marathon since yesterday—sent 'em down on flatcars—an entire regiment waiting to ride south and cross the river. You know and I know they won't catch anything but colds, but at least it'll look as though the Army's trying and Washington will be satisfied and the public will forget about it.

So I have four hundred men mounted and ready to go and I can't send 'em. Why don't you ask me why?"

"Why, can't, you, sir?"

Major General Funston sat down. "Because there's also a pack of newspapermen at Marathon waiting to freeload along and play war correspondents, that's why." He put his elbows on the desk, he spoke in a pitch almost sepulchral. "Dinkle, do you have any notion what will happen if I send the Eighth across the river and they run into your men? If those reporters find out six cavalrymen are cavorting around Mexico in Model T's? We will be the laughingstock of the country and the century. And what would be even more tragical would be to have them catch the bandits. Do you follow me? I'm a cavalryman myself, or was." His fingers drummed a tattoo on his temples. "Dinkle, let me put it bluntly. John J. Pershing isn't catching Villa with ten thousand men on horses. What do you suppose will happen to the cavalry as a branch of service if six ignoramuses bring home the bacon on wheels?"

"Sir, do you mind if I sit down?" asked Dinkle. "I'm not in very good health."

"Sit, dammit. Neither am I."

The junior officer drew up a chair and applied the seat of his breeches and, to the extent an aching cranium would permit, contemplated both his cardboard suitcase and the calamity which had befallen Champion T. Grebs and his daughter and the U. S. Cavalry. The general was right: she would be better off dead, for in the fell clutches of bandits she would suffer a fate compared to which a life crushing cinnabar ore would be infinitely preferable.

I should have bought the muslin bloomers, thought Stanley Dinkle.

Phipps, Biddle, Pugh, Darlington, Den Uyl, Thayer, "Henrietta," "Olivia"—if I ever lay hands on them again I will tear them limb from limb.

It was a dark and stormy night, when my Nellie went away, and I never will forget it, until my dying day.

Across the desk, Frederick Funston was similarly preoccupied. Now and then, as though to supplicate heaven, he stalked to the window to peer at it.

"What's your first name again, Dinkle?"

"Stanley, sir."

"How long have you been in grade?"

"Eight years, sir."

"I don't wonder. Stanley, where did they get those flivvers?"

"They bought 'em, sir. They're filthy rich. The Philadelphia Light Horse."

"God help us," said the general softly. "I can't even court-martial 'em. Their families have more influence in Washington than I do."

"Boys will be boys, sir."

"And generals will be jackasses."

"Yes, sir. I mean, no, sir."

Frederick Funston sighed lugubriously. "Stanley, what happens to you is incidental, and to me. And to that miner's girl. And to the bandits, for that matter. What's at stake is nothing less than the reputation and future of the most noble arm of American service. The cavalry may be on its last legs already. We're using trucks for supply, Pershing's riding around in a Dodge. You know the saying —what General Sheridan started, General Motors will finish. Well, there may be more truth than poetry in it. And if wind of this lame-brain escapade gets out, we can put the horse, as an instrument of war, out to pasture forever."

"I know, sir," Dinkle agreed. "Myself, I'm cavalry to the core."

Funston sat upright. "Glad to hear you say so. Because you're going to save it."

"Me, sir?"

"You. Lieutenant Stanley H. Dinkle. You have just volunteered. Since you're responsible for your command being off limits in the first place, you're responsible for getting it the hell out of there. I want those young whelps back in Texas within twenty-four hours if not sooner. Come here."

He motioned Dinkle to a large topographical map on a wall. "This is my Department, the border from Yuma to Brownsville. Here's the river. Those red pins are my patrol posts. Here's yours." The general used his fly-swatter as a pointer. "Now, across the river from you is the state of Coahuila, and somewhere in the state of Coahuila are six troopers and two Ford products. What do you see?"

"Mountains, sir. A few towns. Mostly space."

"That's right, mostly blank space. It's never been mapped. No one knows what's down there. Now, if I saddle you up and send you looking for your men, you'll ride in circles till you're as gray as I am. So you're going to display the old cavalry dash and initiative. You're going to fly."

At this very juncture, in a sensitive sector of his physique, Stanley Dinkle incurred what was unmistakably the bite of a flea. It was a strong, judicious bite, the work of an adult male at the height of his sanguinary powers, probably Papacito, the head of the family. The box had not been empty after all.

"To flea, sir?"

"To fly," Funston corrected. "I've sent for an aeroplane. The First Aero Squadron's been based at Columbus for the last month, carrying mail and scouting for the Punitive Expedition. They're lending me a machine—waiting for it now. He'll land here on the parade ground, take off with you, and if all goes well, you'll be below the river south of Edhogg in less than an hour."

"Fly?" asked Stanley Dinkle.

"From the air you can easily spot two autos—they'll be the only ones in Coahuila—they must be stuck in the sand somewhere. You're to land, turn 'em around, get the damned nuts and bolts back across the river before dark, then telephone me and I'll blow the bugle and the Eighth will go into action at the crack of dawn tomorrow. And, Dinkle, I swear to you on my stars, if you aren't out of Mexico within twenty-four hours you'll go to your grave a second lieutenant."

"Fly?" bleated Stanley Dinkle.

"Curtiss JN-3's. 'Jennies,' I think that's what they're called. Ninety-horsepower engines—when they run. First Aero Squadron started out with eight machines a month ago and now they're down to one—think of it, seven crashes the first month. I wouldn't go up in one for love nor money, but as I said, Dinkle, what happens to you is incidental. So they have one aircraft they can still get off the ground, and it should have been here—wait a minute, what's that?"

A drone in the distance was audible. Major General Funston hopped to the window. "Here it comes! Remember, Dinkle, you won't be alone—Harry Lee and Jeb Stuart and George Armstrong Custer will be up there with you!"

The droning became a violent racket, and what sounded like a Tin Lizzie roared over the roof of HQ, Department of the Southwest.

"Off you go, Dinkle!" cried Funston. "Good luck and happy landings!"

Stanley Dinkle put one hand to his echoing skull and with the other frantically scratched his crotch.

"Fly?"

22

The Tin Lizzie Troop Receives the Key to Delicias

"Walk?"

They were convinced that Biddle, like poor Darlington, had gone goofy.

"Walk," he repeated. "Those burros can't possibly haul us and the cars both. So, off your duffs." He nodded to the pacífico, who was secreting the twenty dollars about his person. "At your pleasure, señor."

Across the deserts of Coahuila the unique procession plodded southward. Under the lash of their master, two dessicated burros pulled a Model T Ford attached to another Model T Ford attached to a cart of firewood. Both autos were clearly casualties of the road, cranks swinging uselessly below the radiators, several head lamps and spare tires missing. Beside them staggered six soldiers in a condition as deplorable as that of their vehicles. Thirsty, shabby, hungry, dusty, weary, dizzy, guilty, they lifted sunken eyes to the consolation of the mountains.

Presently, after a trek of a mile or two, they passed a stubbled cornfield. Unexpectedly, the ruts became a road, and the road a street, and the street the principal thoroughfare of a village of such charm and sanctuary that the soldiers, had they been able, might have thrown themselves upon their knees and thanked the Supreme Episcopal Commander for having brought them out of the wilderness to it. Delicias was aptly named. Tucked away into a mountain fold, it seemed indifferent to time, irrelevant to revolution. There were green trees and whitewashed walls and a running stream. On most days, one knew, it would be possessed of an idyllic somnolence, but this morning, the arrival of strangers and even stranger equipages created a tumult. Men, women, and children, and dogs came running. They had heard outlandish tales of conveyances called "automobiles," but had not willingly suspended disbelief until now, until they could verify with their own senses. They touched iron. They blinked at brass. Children swarmed into tonneaus. Dogs lifted hind legs to authenticate the nickel-plated hubcaps. And slowly, amid much pomp and curiosity, the column entered the plaza, the entire village in its train. Here, in the center, was a covered bandstand, and opposite, a cantina. The burros were unhitched, and the cart of firewood, and as the Philadelphians attempted to reach the cantina through the press of citizens, there emerged from it a small, rotund señor whose mustachio surpassed in length and luster any of their own. He faced them with suspicion.

"My name, eet ees Perfecto Lopez. Of this village I am El Mayor. Joo are soldados, no? *Que pasa?* What ees joor beezness?"

Biddle acted as spokesman. "Delighted to make your acquaintance, Mayor. We're down here on a strictly military mission, in pursuit of a bandit named Contreras. Encarnacion Contreras."

At the appellation, the crowd drew breath.

"We've had a little difficulty with our cars. In fact, Mayor, we've had difficulty in all respects," Biddle admitted. "To be candid, we're desperate. We need food, and something to drink."

At the mention of comestibles, the crowd shrank from the Americans.

Lopez raised his hands, his expression a mingling of pain and pity. "Ah. But thees ees a poor place, señor. We don' have too many turistas. We don' have no food. Five years now we are rob' by Rurales, Federales, Villistas, Maderistas, Obregonistas, Carranzistas, an' other bastardistas. They take what they wan', they don' pay. Our souls only they leave us, señor, but even the soul, eet ees said, has a belly."

This recital was more than "Freddy" Den Uyl could

bear. To reach oasis, and then to have his appetites unappeased, was to look for the last tomato in the can and find it gone.

"But we'll pay, Mayor!" he cried, opening his wallet and flourishing a wad of currency. Stepping forward, he thrust it upon Lopez. "We come from Philadelphia and we've scads of money—real moeny—E Pluribus Unum —dollars!"

A public examination took place at once. About the mayor the crowd surged, gazing upon the greenbacks, as much the wonder of the world's finance as the Model T Ford was of its transportation. The worthy alcalde thumbed the bills, held them to the sunlight, counted them with infinite patience. Then, satisfied, a tear sparkling on his cheek, he raised the blessing in the bowl of his hands. It was as though, by this simple gesture, he wished to say that it was they, his people, who had been saved by the grace of the Americans, not the reverse, and to give thanks to the fickle fingers of war, which had finally let fall a few loaves and fishes upon his village.

"My frans," said Perfecto Lopez emotionally, addressing the entire plaza and speaking largely in English for the benefit of the visitors, "joo don' never see these before. But I have work een Feenix, Ahrizona, peeking froots, an' I know them." His voice quavered with homage. "My frans, thees are the real dinero—gringo dólares. Eet ees honor to welcome such moneys to Delicias—joo have more, señores?" he asked the other soldiers, who nodded. "Much more?" Again they signified, and Lopez spread his mustachio in a broad, benevolent smile and suddenly shouted, *"Vivan los soldados Americanos!"*

"Vivan los dólares gringos!" roared the crowd, carried away by its good fortune. Men tossed sombreros in the air. Women wept. Dogs barked. The Tin Lizzie Troopers grinned their heartfelt appreciation.

"Bring tortillas!" commanded the mayor. "Bring tequila! Bring señoritas! *Viva la Revolucion!"*

23

If God Had Intended Man to Fly

"Lieutenant Edgar N. Carberry," the pilot greeted Dinkle, "just call me Ace." He was equipped with very long arms and legs and in the process of separating himself from the cockpit and uniting himself with the parade ground somewhat resembled an extension ladder. Around his skinny middle was strapped a Colt six-shooter and the ends of his breeches were stuck into high-heeled cowboy boots. "You my passenger?"

"I, am, your, passenger," Dinkle managed to say. "Lieutenant, Stanley, Dinkle."

"Dinkle? Hiya, Dink, put 'er there," grinned the pilot, pushing up his goggles. "Say, you get acquainted with Jenny while I give old Funston some papers. We go on a mission these days, somebody's gotta have papers in case. Next of kin, last rites, so on and so forth—just a joke, Dink. Be right with ya." And he headed for the HQ, taking four feet in each stride, a plume of orange silk streaming from his leather helmet.

Suitcase in hand, Stanley Dinkle stood like a befuddled child. He had never before seen an aeroplane on the hoof, as it were, and the existence of this one he simply disbelieved. The young officer who, but an hour earlier, had been a mechanical man going through the motions of washing and shaving, was now a man imprisioned in a dream. Fact had forsaken him, reality had kissed him bye-bye. Since the cocoanut had fallen on the iron roof of his head in Juárez he had never fully recovered his faculties. It could not be true that Edhogg had been raided, Flossie Grebs abducted, her father murdered, and that the Philadelphia Light Horse were gallivanting about Mexico mounted upon Model T's in pursuit of the raiders. It was a lie of life that he himself was about to be made a human sacrifice to the madness of a departmental commander and the eccentricity of an aviator. And the proof of the whole figmental pudding was that the longer he stared, the more convinced he was that this was not an aeroplane at all, but a *deus ex machina* let down from the skies by gibbering gods—and completely incapable of flight.

The Curtiss JN-3 was a biplane with a wooden, brass-tipped propeller, a snub nose, bicycle-type wheels, coffin-shaped fuselage, and a tail with a red star painted on the fin. On its side was the large number "43." Its wings seemed to be attached to the fuselage, and to each other, by a haphazard tangle of struts and piano wires.

He crept up on the thing. Struts and undercarriage were made of spruce, longerons, rudder post, and tail skid of ash, and the whole skeleton was enclosed in a taut, gossamer skin of Irish linen doped with nitrate. Wood, wire, and cloth, then, were the principal components of the aircraft, in addition to faith, hope, and the charity of Divine Providence.

He peered into the observer's cockpit, unfurnished except for a seat and protected from the heat of the OX5 in-line, single-ignition engine by a fire wall, then into the rear. Three instruments were fastened to the panel—an altimeter, an oil pressure gauge, and a compass, while a hand throttle was clamped to the left side of the pit. It was absurd to think that anyone of Carberry's elongation could cram himself into a cubbyhole so small and so stuffed with controls—and controls, furthermore, so intricate that they required as many arms and legs as a flivver's. A heavy yoke ran from side to side across the driver's lap, with a wheel in the center which operated the ailerons in the wings. Moving the yoke backward and forward actuated the tail elevators, while bulky foot pedals on a crossbar turned the rudder.

A gaggle of curious HQ personnel in his wake, none of whom had ever set eyes on an aeroplane in the flesh, Lt. Edgar Just-Call-Me-Ace Carberry returned. He didn't walk, he perambulated. He didn't talk, he chattered. "Back like a bad penny, Dink! How'dya get along with 'er?"

"Number Forty-Three, I see," observed Dinkle.

"That's just her fuselage. She's got Thirty-Eight's tail assembly, one wing from Seventy-Two, one from Fifty-Six, and her engine's out of poor old Ninety-Four. Put 'em all together they spell Jenny," Carberry sang, striking an operatic pose, "the crate that means the world to me!"

"Seven crashes?" Dinkle asked. "In one month?"

"One month less three days. This is what's left of First Aero Squadron—we lose her and that's all she wrote." With only ninety horses, he said, the Jennies were badly underpowered for flying conditions in the Southwest. There were whirlwinds which spun you like a top and frequently blew the engine cowlings off and wrecked your stabilizer. There were terrific vertical air currents which slammed you down and hung you in the trees like an apple. Any mountain higher than five thousand feet you hadn't enough sap to fly over, so you had to sneak between them through the canyons, many of which turned out, too late, to be box canyons. Sand played hob with the engines, while the dry climate warped hell out of the Paragon props. To top it off, most of the Berling magnetos were defective, as were the Zenith and Schebler carburetors, and the manifolds were forever condensing moisture, which dripped into the carburetor and stopped you cold just when you believed you were really percolating. "But the pesky thing about this baby," he said, "she's out of true."

"Out of true?" gulped Dinkle.

"Yup. Glued together out of so many bits and pieces we can't get her in true. Here, take a look from here." He led Dinkle around to the prop and had him squint down the fuselage to the tail. "See how she's out of kilter? Wings, too. We've used plumb lines and trammeled the wires till we're blue in the face and be damned if we can get her in line. So she's a thrill a minute when you're aloft. I tell you, Dink, nobody knows when she'll fall apart, including me. So I hate to waste her looking for a couple of gasoline buggies in Mexico—like finding a virgin in Juárez." He grinned and snapped his fingers. "But I'll tell you another.

If anybody can get us there and back it's Ace Carberry, because he's got the secret."

"Secret?"

Carberry leaned over him like a lamppost. "Love Your Jenny," he disclosed.

Dinkle made a strange face. "Oh, no," he said.

"That's right, Love Your Jenny," insisted the pilot. "You're a cavalryman, you know how it goes with a filly. Slip her the sweet talk and she'll be sweet to you—that's what they tell me. Now, I pretend like I adore this old whore. I tell her she's young and beautiful and spry as a spring chicken and can take me anywhere if she puts her heart and ass into it. And when she hears that, blimey if she don't turn young and beautiful and blimey if she don't take me!" He winked. "But you don't need advice, you lady-killer. Well, ready to leave terra firma?"

"No," said Stanley Dinkle.

"Whatsa matter, you nervous?"

"I am."

"Who says I'm not?" Carberry demanded. "If I'm not, how come I've lost half my hair in the last month and I'm only twenty-nine years old? Every man to his own poison, Dink. Believe you me, I'd rather go up in one of these flying hearses any day than fork up on a horse!"

"Well," said Dinkle, "I don't remember ever not wanting to do anything as much as I don't want to do this. And I'm not feeling very well today. But I'm whipsawed. I've got to get my men back. I've got to do what I can for that girl, I mean that woman. Not to mention General Funston. So I guess I have to go."

"Attaboy!" enthused the pilot.

Dinkle inflated an obdurate chest. "There's one thing I won't do, though. Yesterday a man told me to love his Lizzie and I wouldn't. Now you tell me to love your Jenny. But I have a good horse, Hassan, so I'll be damned if I will."

"Fair enough," said Carberry.

"Oh, and I have to take this suitcase."

"O.K. You can stow it in your lap. But first we'll use it for a chock." And relieving his passenger of the case he wedged it against a wheel, then ducked out from under the wing, drew the six-shooter at his hip, and gave the cylinder a practiced twirl. "Loaded and ready for bear," he declared, holstering the weapon. "And you'd better be when you put down in Ol' May-hee-co. Now, what we'll do, we'll fly by the seat of our pants and follow the river east. When you spot your post, where they started from, you point and I'll ease off south and you watch for tire tracks and spare parts. We ought to cut some kind of a trail in no time. We'll cruise around fifteen hundred rpm, around ninety per. So let's go, pal. I forgot to tell you, you'll have to crank her up."

"Did you say ninety miles an hour?" asked Dinkle.

"Here's what we do." Carberry rapid-fired a series of instructions, none of which his assistant understood, then called to the clerks mustered about the aircraft. "Give us a hand, buckos. Two of you grab that wing tip and two on the other. When we're rolling, run along with us and hold on till we get up ground speed, then let go and thanks a lot."

He turned to Dinkle. "You go on up front and get set. As soon as she's hitting on a couple, you unchock the wheel and bring your case and hop in. All right, up there and position the prop."

Carberry reached the rear cockpit in two strides, clambered in, and like a contortionist arranged himself. Then, snapping his helmet flaps under his chin and pulling down his goggles, he turned on the gas, made certain the ignition switch was "Off," and shouted "Clear!"

Up front, his mechanic stood like a wooden Indian.

"Clear," said Dinkle faintly.

"Now say, 'Switch Off!' "

"Switch Off."

"Louder!" cried Carberry in exasperation. "Now turn the prop through till you hear her suck gas!"

Dinkle took hold of the great propeller, which, since it was balanced, turned with surprising ease. After two turns the engine gave a gasp of misgiving.

"Ready!" shouted Carberry. "Ready, you guys?" he appealed to the two soldiers at each wing tip. "All right,

Dink, set her for a good downswing and holler 'Contact!' "

Stanley Dinkle bowed his head over the propeller. "Oh, Lord," he prayed, "wherever I'm going, let me get there. Because I'm going up in this monstrosity to do Your work on earth. That is, if I ever get down on it O.K. If I don't, please comfort my father and mother and brother Tipton."

"What in holy hell you doing?" cried the pilot.

Dinkle hurried it up. "Let me locate my boys alive and well, Lord, and bring them back to their own country. Let me find Flossie Grebs in sound condition, too. She has had a hard life and don't deserve to be murdered or raped. And above all, please let me save the U. S. Cavalry from the Ford. Thanks very much, Sir, and amen."

"Goddammit, Dinkle, let's hear it!" shouted Carberry.

"Contact!" yelped his mechanic.

Carberry switched on the ignition, cracked the throttle slightly, and in a tone stentorian enough to topple walls trumpeted, "Contact!"

Dinkle swung the prop.

Internal combustion occurred. The propeller flapped. And then the OX5 erupted in a bombilation of sound and blue smoke. The entire aircraft was taken with the shakes. Jumping out of harm's way, Dinkle crawled under a wing, retrieved his suitcase, crawled out, and promptly had his campaign hat blown from his head. Swaying like a reed in the prop wash, he clung to a strut until a soldier brought the hat, then was backed by the gale to the forward cockpit, dumped hat and suitcase in, and fell in after them. Before he could say Jack Robinson the biplane was moving and enlisted men were running at its wing tips. He was deafened. His hat was mashed beneath his boots. He sank below the cowling. He flung his arms about the suitcase in a last embrace. And as Stanley Dinkle commended his soul to heaven, the JN-3, with its living freight of two men and four fleas, gained speed over the parade ground, outsped its wingholders, and in total defiance of natural law detached itself from the earth and took flight, going to glory be.

I am f-l-y-i-n-g, thought Stanley Dinkle. I am up in an aeroplane looking for motorcars.

I forgot to buy her some stockings.

For some minutes he remained head down, clutching the cardboard suitcase. He was nauseated. The memory of the goat's milk soured in his mouth. He was baked. Even through the fire wall, the heat of the engine turned the cockpit into an oven. His cranium ached, his body boggled. The aircraft vibrated, oscillated, and palpitated. He expected it to disintegrate at any instant like the poet's one-hoss shay. And he was terrified. Over the wail of wind through struts and bracing wires he seemed to hear both harps and a celestial chorus.

Eventually a tapping on his shoulder forced him to raise his head and look behind. Carberry gesticulated over the side of the fuselage, reminding him of his observer's duties. Only then did the cavalryman look down. The Jenny cruised at an altitude of perhaps a thousand feet, and under her the Rio Grande was a rivulet of mercury, glittering in sunlight. Leaning forward, he shielded his eyes from the airstream behind the cowling, and within minutes was able, to his amazement, to make out the salient features of Patrol Post #2 swimming below—parade ground, purple house, even the pink speck of his bladder bungalow. He indicated them to the pilot, who immediately sent #43 into a bank so steep that Dinkle's stomach executed an Immelmann turn.

Southward the two officers soared upon their rattletrap Pegasus, until Dinkle became aware first of lines in the desert which appeared to be tire tracks, and then of what seemed to be, if not a road, ruts worn into sand and rock by generations of wagon wheels, and into which the tire tracks merged. Carberry followed them until, simultaneously, pilot and observer spotted three mounted men, a welcome sight in this wilderness. But when the aviator let down to a sociable three hundred feet and waggled his wings in greeting, too late it was seen that the riders wore big sombreros, that their shoulders were crisscrossed with bandoliers, and that they drew rifles, aimed, and fired at the Jenny! Lashing his ninety horses, Carberry climbed, banked at such a perilous angle that the wing shuddered, drew his Colt, brandished it, and dived upon the dastards! Dinkle hugged the suitcase in horror as the aeroplane plunged to within a hundred feet of its prey—as the daredevil Carberry leaned from his cockpit and emptied the six-shooter—as they zoomed upward out of the strafing run and the bandidos bolted!

After some moments occupied in renovating his nervous system, Dinkle observed that the Jenny was once again on course above the road, if such it could be called, and that it led out of the deserts into a garden of green hidden within the skirts, as it were, of a small mountain range. A closer inspection revealed the existence of a village among the trees, undiscernible except from the air, and in the center of the village, a plaza, and as Carberry buzzed it, parked in the plaza the black, grotesque hulks of two Tin Lizzies. He made frantic hand signals. Carberry nodded, circled the village for a landing site, settled upon a cornfield in which the stalks had been cut close to the ground, throttled back to forty mph, landing speed for the JN-3, and brought them down to bump and bounce through the stubble to a stop. He was out of his cockpit almost before he had cut the engine, reloading his six-shooter.

"Here we are, Dink! First Aero Squadron always gets its Fords! So you go your way, I'll go mine—right back where I came from. Dink?"

Stanley Dinkle's head was bowed again, his eyes were closed. "Thank you, Lord," he prayed, "for getting me here in one piece. Now, if you'll just let me hoe the rest of the row, I'll get my mind out of the gutter and never think about sex again, I mean it. Amen."

He climbed slowly out of the aeroplane. Taking an unsteady step, he stooped low and kissed the earth. Ignoring the aviator, he removed his suitcase from the cockpit, and next his battered hat. Opening the case, he donned his belt and pistol. With due deliberation he then put the hat on his head, trimmed it, tore it off, and slammed it to the ground.

"Damn the twentieth century!" he exploded. "Yesterday I drove an automobile, today I flew in an aeroplane—I've had a crawful of rudders and levers and pedals and dinguses of every damned kind! If I'm behind the times, there's where I'll make my stand! So damn the twentieth century to hell, because that's where it's going!"

Carberry grinned. "That's the old spunk. You find yourself a horse and hang on, Dink. Meantime, let's crank up and I'll get this buggy off the ground again."

"You will not!" barked Dinkle.

The pilot pushed up his goggles. "Did I hear you right, pal?"

"You did. There's more at stake here than you realize, Carberry. I may want to send a message back to Bliss, and I'm keeping you in case I do."

"In case? My orders from Funston were to—"

"Funston's in El Paso," Dinkle interjected. "And my horse is in Marathon. But I'm here."

Carberry extended his ladder. "Now, just a darn minute, Dinkle. I operate this aircraft and I—"

But Stanley Dinkle had replaced his hat and rigged his necktie up like a noose. "Lieutenant Carberry, how long have you been in grade?"

"Three years. What's that got to do with the price of eggs?"

"Aha," said Dinkle. "I've been a second lieutenant for eight. Therefore I outrank you by five years. Therefore you'll take orders from me now and I'll take the responsibility later. Is that clear?"

Edgar Carberry backed off, one hand hovering at his revolver as though in readiness for a showdown. He squinted. Dinkle was as out of true as #43. A knock-knees had become a brass hat, a blithering idiot who could scarcely spin a prop had transformed himself, merely by planting his bowlegs upon the planet once more, into a senior and commanding officer. Suddenly the pilot crouched and whipped out his pistol. "Watch it, Dink," he muttered. "We got company."

Dinkle whirled. Fifty yards from them, above a wall of piled stone at the edge of the cornfield, heads had popped up, a hundred heads, two hundred, men, women, and children—excepting infants, dogs, and certain other individuals later to be specified, the entire population of the village. In each head two round brown eyes were fixed upon the JN-3 in awe. On each face, young and old, were those expressions of revelation with which both saints and simple folk, throughout religious history, have accepted the appearance of a vision or the performance of a miracle.

"It's all right," said Dinkle with relief. "They've never seen an aeroplane."

He walked around a wing tip and spoke to the multitude of heads and eyes. *"Buenos días,"* he smiled. "We are friends, *amigos*. Come on closer if you want to." He invited them with a hand. "Come on, *venga."*

And they came. One by one, then in groups, the people of the village left the protection of the wall to form a reverent circle about the apparition of wood and wire and cloth. It was true: they had never before seen a machine which flew, quite probably had never heard or dreamed of one. They knelt in silence. They crossed themselves.

Dinkle was embarrassed. "Does anyone here speak English?"

"Sí, señor." A small, roly-poly gent rose from the throng with difficulty, due less to the encumbrance of his belly than to the heft and length of his mustachio. "I speek Eengles. I have work' in Feenix, Ahrizona, peekeeng froots. My name, eet ees Perfecto Lopez. Here I am El Mayor."

Carberry joined the conversation. "Mighty pleased to meetcha, Perfect. What's the name of this burg?"

"Thees ees Delicias, señor."

"Delicious? Ain't that a corker!"

"Digamé, tell me, El Mayor," asked Dinkle. "We saw two autos parked in your plaza. How about soldiers, Americano soldiers? Got any of those?"

Lopez smiled benignly. *"Sí, mi Coronel.* We have seex."

"Six? Whew, thank God," breathed Dinkle. "Healthy, are they?"

The alcalde pulled a long face. "Ah, no. They have suffered *mucho*. But they are reech."

"Reech? Oh, rich. Well, I want to get my hands on 'em—I mean, I want to see 'em pronto." He headed for his suitcase. "Let's go, Carberry."

"O.K., but give me a minute. You guys look after your crowbaits, I take care of Jenny first."

From his cockpit the pilot brought a short iron bar, tapered to a thin edge at one end like a crowbar, and strode to the nose of the aircraft. There, under the fascinated gaze of the populace, he removed the safety wire, inserted the bar into the lock ring of the propeller, loosened it, used the narrow end of the bar to unscrew two studs in the hub ring itself, dropped the bar, spread his long arms, took the blades in his hands, uttered what might have been an incantation and, with one abracadabra tug, pulled the prop free of the crankshaft and slung it blithely onto his shoulder.

"Where I go, this goes," he told his sawed-off but senior officer. "I'll explain later. At your service, mi Coronel."

Perfecto Lopez led the procession. And as the citizens of Delicias tagged after them at a venerative interval, Lieutenants Dinkle and Carberry, suitcase in hand and propeller over shoulder, marched toward the village like a mythological Mutt and Jeff.

24

Lt. Dinkle and the Philadelphia Light Horse Are Reunited

El Mayor, Lieutenants Dinkle and Carberry, the suitcase, the propeller, and the inhabitants of Delicias reached the plaza. There they halted.

Opposite a cantina called Mi Corazón Contento, or "My Contented Heart," in a condition hideously indicative of the horrors through which they had passed, were parked two Model T touring cars.

In the bandstand was the remainder of the population of the village. Shaded by the tin roof, six hammocks were strung. In them, shoes and puttees off, and unarmed, reclined Pvts. "Lex" Phipps, "Bid" Biddle, "Freddy" Den Uyl, "Luce" Thayer, "Phew" Pugh, and "Stew" Darlington. Beauteous señoritas attended them, tousling their hair and feeding them enchiladas from dainty fingertips and lifting bottles of tequila to their rapacious lips.

"Ace" Carberry leaned in glee upon his propeller. "Mon Dieu!" he chortled. "If this is the U. S. Cavalry, I'm joining up!"

Stanley Dinkle disregarded the gibe. Slowly he let his suitcase down.

I will not bust a gusset, he thought. A good officer never loses control.

He strolled to a position near the bandstand. "Ahem," he said. "Good afternoon, gentlemen."

He spoke calmly, but at the sound of his voice, as though at a blast of Gabriel's horn, the Philadelphia Light Horse fell out of their hammocks. Choking on enchiladas and spilling tequila and tumbling señoritas, they stumbled from the bandstand. They were not yet drunk, but at the sight of such a ghost their eyes glazed.

"Good afternoon," he said again, playing Stanley to their Dr. Livingstones. "Enjoying yourselves?"

"Oh, Lieutenant!" blubbered Phipps. "We've been through absolute hell!"

"Obviously."

"Are we ever glad to see you!" Pugh enthused.

"I'm sure."

"How'd you get here?" demanded Biddle.

"Sir."

"Sir."

"I flew down. General Funston has put an aeroplane and a pilot at my disposal." He indicated Carberry, who was as diverted by the reunion as were the villagers.

"Did you have a good time in El Paso, sir?" lisped Den Uyl.

"Hotsy-totsy."

"Sir, they overwhelmed us at Fort Dinkle," asserted Thayer. "We fought like the old Harry, but there must have been a hundred of 'em! Pugh was hit on the head."

The knot under Stanley Dinkle's peaked hat commenced to twinge again.

"And they ran off our horses and burned Edhogg and murdered the old miner and took away his daughter!" Darlington added. "Sir, it was really frightful!"

"Is that a fact?" said Dinkle. "Any word on Miss Grebs?"

"No, sir."

I am keeping a tight rein, thought Stanley Dinkle. I am keeping cool as lemonade made in the shade.

"And so you hopped into your runabouts and crossed the river looking for a fight," he said almost affably. "Now, let me see. This is Friday afternoon. I said a fond farewell to you Tuesday morning. You've had three busy days. What would you say you've accomplished?"

"Well, sir, we found out the head bandido's name is Contreras," reported Phipps. "Encarnacion Contreras."

"Contreras." The officer rubbed his chin. "Heard of him, Mayor?"

"Sí, mi Coronel," said Lopez. "Thees one ees very bad hombre. *Muy malo.*"

"Any idea where he might hide out?"

"No, mi Coronel. We don' wan' know."

Dinkle nodded.

"Good work anyway," he commended his troopers. "Always nice to know the enemy's name, I always say. By the way, Phipps, where's your stripes?"

"Oh, we had a slight difference of opinion about tactics, sir, so I resigned."

"Resigned?" The CO smiled. "Sorry, Corporal, we can't do that on active duty, can we? Better get yourself a needle and thread."

"Yes, sir."

With my sunny disposition and self-control, thought Stanley Dinkle, it is a seventeen-jewel, eighteen-carat wonder I ain't a general by now.

"Well, well," he said paternally. "We meet again. In romantic Mexico. Unfortunately, we must leave romantic Mexico. And part with our excess baggage. Henrietta and Olivia, I believe you call them." He turned to the alcalde. "Mayor, we'll need seven horses. I'll sign a receipt. Seven good ones, now, no nags."

Lopez raised his hands, his expression a mingling of pain and pity. "I am sorry, mi Coronel, but we don' got no horses. For five years now our *caballos* ees rob' by Rurales, Federales, Villistas, Maderistas, Obregonistas, Carranzistas, an' other bastardistas."

Lieutenant Dinkle flinched. It was as though he were in an arena, and to weaken him, a banderilla, a dart with a small streamer, had just been expertly sunk into his shoulders. "You have, no, horses?"

"We got burros," the mayor suggested hopefully. "Joo wan' burros?"

"Burros," said the officer. "Ha-ha." He spoke to his forces. "Very well, good soldiers make do with what they have. So load up your autos. I have orders from the

Commanding General, Department of the Southwest, to be back across the Rio Grande by tomorrow morning, and I will be. Gentlemen, start your engines."

The Philadelphians looked at each other.

"Surely you heard me," chided the CO gently. "I said, load up and crank up."

"Sir," said Phipps.

"Corporal?"

"Sir, they won't run. I regret to inform you, but we've burned out a bearing. Or something."

Lieutenant Dinkle flinched again as a second cruel shaft was driven into his flesh, further sapping his aplomb and authority.

"We've, burned, out, a, bearing? Or, something?"

"Yes, sir."

"Ha-ha," said the officer. He began to back off, to retreat toward the wall of the cantina. "Then we'll hike. How far to the border, Carberry?"

The pilot shook his orange plume. "Forty, fifty miles. As the Jenny flies. On foot, I'd say two days minimum, the shape they're in."

"Fifty, miles?"

Stanley Dinkle put his hindquarters to the wall. He seemed to paw the ground.

"Two, days?"

The situation made no military sense whatever. A mere fifty miles from his base, he might as well have been a thousand. And he was immobilized—the one dilemma of which a cavalryman, dedicated to dash and initiative, could not conceive. There was no way on God's green earth, animal, vegetable, or mineral, to carry out his order, to spare his branch of service and his government and his beloved country a monumental and historic contretemps. It was the moment of untruth. A man at bay, Stanley Dinkle faced that clumsiest of all matadors, that rustiest of all swords—cruel, cruel circumstance.

He swiveled his head. He stared at the bobtail bunch of boys in partial uniform before him. He stared at the bell tower of the small church at one end of the plaza, and at the population of Delicias, which was consumed by a morbid and commercial curiosity.

It was at this instant, perhaps out of thankfulness that she had survived the first flight by a flea in a heavier-than-air craft, that Mamacita bit Stanley Dinkle gratefully but inopportunely in the groin. To be stung by men and machines was one thing, to be pricked by a flea another. Bloodied beyond endurance, he came off the wall horns leveled, bellowing.

"Hell? You've been through hell? You'll think it's heaven before I'm through with you and Funston's through with you and the War Department's through with you!" His fury backed them toward the bandstand. "You know what you've done! You've made colossal, cat's-ass fools of yourselves and me and the cavalry! You've disgraced the United States of America! And you're not men enough or soldiers enough to admit it! I'd line you up and shoot you myself but I'd rather let the Army have the pleasure and I'll watch! All right, ten-shun!"

They snapped to, swaying.

"Phipps, get 'em dressed! Pistols on and rifles out! Close-order drill till they drop or I figure a way to get us out of here—take charge!"

"Yes, sir!"

Stanley Dinkle waited while the Philadelphians put on shoes and puttees and pistol belts and formed by two's, Springfields on shoulders, for close-order foot drill—to cavalrymen, the ultimate indignity. Only then, when Phipps started them, did the officer sag. A hand was on his shoulder. It was Carberry's.

"C'mon, Dink, we haven't had a feed all day. They say the cuisine here's Delicias."

With his assistance, Dinkle, suitcase, and propeller were seated at a table in Mi Corazón Contento, which did not lack for local color if it did for cash customers. As honored patrons, carrying an honored currency, they were waited on by the mayor himself, who by coincidence owned the cantina. Carberry ordered. What had been good enough for enlisted men, he declared democratically, was good enough for officers, plus a bottle of the best red-eye, plus a wet rag.

Campaign hat off, his superior had slumped. "No booze," he said hollowly. "No drinking on duty."

The pilot grimaced. "Grounding me again, huh? Well, for your information, I couldn't fly now anyhoo—too late in the day. We may be eagles, but come dark we roost." He placed his helmet and goggles grandly on the table. "Now I'm grounded, though, I like the looks of this no-horse town. I don't even mind lingering a little."

"Why can't you fix those Fords?" Dinkle mumbled. "You can take off a propeller."

"That's the extent, mi Coronel. Oh, and this." Lopez had by now supplied a wet rag. "You think you got problems." Carberry leaned the propeller against the bar and began to damp it down, caressing its curves and laminations with tender strokes. This dry atmosphere played hob with wooden props, he explained. The glue cracked and the layers came apart and the wood warped, so that it had become second nature for 1st Aero Squadron pilots to remove their Paragons and keep them moist, particularly if they cared to be birds again. "That's our motto—keep your powder dry, your prop wet, and Love Your Jenny."

Lopez brought food in large quantities and of such incendiary seasoning that it cracked the teeth and warped the tongue. Carberry tied in with gusto, remarking between tortillas that he had started out in the Army as a Lieutenant of Engineers at Fort Belvoir, Virginia, a perfect whiz at bridges and minefields and barbed wire.

Round and round the plaza marched the Philadelphia Light Horse, with Phipps counting cadence: "One! Two! Three! Four! By the left flank—march!"

Stanley Dinkle toyed with his refried beans. Since he had taken it upon himself to ground the JN-3, and its crew, the least he could do was to offer justification. He therefore passed on to his companion General Funston's account of the raid upon Patrol Post #2, the destruction of Edhogg, the murder of Champion Grebs, and the carrying-off of his daughter by Contreras.

Having volunteered to transfer to the Signal Corps and

submit himself to flight training, first at the Curtiss factory and later at Mineola, Long Island, and having won his wings, Edgar Carberry had come West with 1st Aero to support the Pershing Expedition.

Round and round the plaza marched the Philadelphia Light Horse. Children paraded with them, and dogs, and beauteous señoritas, extending whatever aid and comfort was possible.

Renewed by nourishment, Dinkle deemed it advisable to sketch the dimensions of his tragedy. The raid upon his post, he said, following upon the Columbus fracas, had been the straw which broke the back of American patience. The newspapers were in full hue and cry, Congress demanded prompt punitive action of the Army, and the finger of the War Department pointed directly at Frederick Funston, who even now had the 8th Cavalry at Marathon, prepared to send it charging into Coahuila as soon as he, Stanley Dinkle, got his six stage-door Johnnies and their jalopies the hell out, which he'd been ordered to do by tomorrow morning. At stake were the reputation of the Army and the future of the cavalry itself, not to mention his own career, which was certainly in jeopardy if not defunct.

"Believe you me, chum," responded Carberry, "toting mail and ferrying nuts like you around Mexico takes its toll of a guy. Now, where I'd rather be is over the Big Water—La Belle Fransay! Now, there's a real war for you!"

"Lieutenant, you're not hearing me!" Dinkle snarled. "The Eighth Cavalry's waiting and the papers are waiting and Washington's waiting! The whole world's waiting on me! If I don't have this outfit over the Rio Grande by morning I'll be a private again or behind bars or worse!"

"Strap me into a Spad or a Camel!" cried the aviator. "Gimme twin Lewis guns synchronized to spit through my prop!" He snatched up two enchiladas and aimed them across the table. "Ah-ah-ah-ah-ah!" he stuttered. "Got a Fokker! Down he goes, poor devil! Horrible sight! *C'est la gare!*"

"Thunder and damnation!" Dinkle roared.

"I'd be a legend in a month!" warbled the pilot. "Ace Carberry—Scourge of the Skies!"

"One! Two! Three! Four!" Corporal Phipps's voice was gravelly. His count was almost inaudible now, and his cadence lagged until the detachment marched like men in slow motion.

Stanley Dinkle buried his face in his hands. This is what I have come to, he thought. I am stuck in Mexico with two Tin Lizzies, a Jenny, a pilot who is crazier than a bed-bug, six playboys, and four fleas. I can sink no lower in this life.

Carberry pushed away his plate and emitted an amiable belch. "Tell you what, mon ami. First thing in the morning I'll hop up to Columbus and bring you back a mechanic. He'll have new bearings in those babies in a couple hours, and you'll be off in a cloud of dust. O.K.?"

Stanley Dinkle uncovered his face. The mayor of Delicias had come to clear the table, bringing with him a woman in her late thirties, a señora dark of eye, sensuous of mouth, and abundant of hip.

"Thees ees my sister, Señora Olvera," said Perfecto Lopez. "She work for me een here. She don' know eef she ees marry or a weedow. Her husban', he gone away weeth Rurales, Federales, Villistas, Maderistas, Obregonistas, Carranzistas, an' other bastardistas."

"Pleased to meetcha," grinned Carberry.

The woman flashed an inter-American smile. "I been een Estados Unidos," said she. "Joo call me Conchita."

"Conchita!" said Dinkle sharply.

Round and round the plaza reeled the Philadelphia Light Horse.

Señora Olvera bent over the table. She wore a white, diaphanous blouse. Extending a dimpled arm for his plate, beneath the blouse she aimed at him two Lewis guns of such luscious and lethal caliber that he was simultaneously delighted by his libido and anguished by the memory of Flossy Grebs.

Conchita hesitated. He salivated. It was lust at first sight.

She looked at his hair. " 'Allo, Rojo," she murmured. " 'Allo, Red."

Oh my God, not again, thought Stanley Dinkle. Deliver us from evil. Hold that tiger.

25

"Oh, the Monkeys Have No Tails in Zamboanga"

Lieutenants Dinkle and Carberry shared a room over the cantina which was made available, for a modest rental, by the mayor. In the morning, accompanied by that worthy and the propeller, they crossed the plaza, passing the impotent Fords and the Philadelphia Light Horse. Exhausted by miles of close-order drill, the latter snored in their hammocks on the bandstand. The CO let them sleep. They'd have a long, hard ramble in their runabouts, he said, before this day was done.

On the walk out of Delicias he double-checked arrangements with the pilot. Carberry estimated he'd land at Columbus in an hour. First Aero Squadron boasted mechanics as handy with Lizzies as they were with Jennies. If the wind was right, he'd be back with a grease monkey in another hour, and it would take no more than a third hour to replace the burned-out bearings. By noon the Fords should be off and running, and to be certain they continued to run, the mechanic would accompany them to the border. By late afternoon, then, Dinkle should be in Edhogg, where, provided the telephone line to Marathon was by now operative, he could call Fort Bliss and say the coast was clear, all fools and flivvers were out of sight—at which news Frederick Funston could in turn give Marathon a ring and unleash the 8th Cavalry upon Contreras, thereby satisfying Washington and the press and an apoplectic nation.

They reached the cornfield.

They stopped in their tracks.

What they saw surpassed the power of speech.

The JN-3 was parked precisely where it had been left the day before. But it was no longer a mechanism capable of flight.

#43 was a skeleton. It had been plucked as clean as a chicken. Wings, fuselage, tail—every section, every shred and every thread of its linen fabric was gone.

Aviator and cavalryman moved toward it like men grown old before their time.

"What?" they said. "What?"

They ran their hands along the ribs of spruce. They touched the rudder spine of ash. They looked long at each other.

"Moths," whispered the cavalryman.

"Vultures," whispered the aviator.

"No, señores," said Perfecto Lopez. "Eet was the *gente,* the people."

"The people?"

"Sí. I din' know they would do thees. But I have hear them speakin', las' night. They are seemple people. They don' know 'bout thees aeroplano, what eet ees. They call eet 'Horse of God.' "

"Horse of God!"

The alcalde folded pious hands upon his belly. *"Sí, mi Coronels.* To them, eet ees *sacrosanto.* So they take the skeen of the aeroplano to their homes, to keep. As one keeps beets of the Cross, or the bones of a saint. How joo say, releecs?"

"But they can't!" cried Dinkle.

"Sí, señor."

"But it won't fly!" shouted Carberry.

"No, señor."

Lopez closed his eyes in sympathy and sorrow, then opened them. He smiled. He gave his mustachio a mercantile tweak. "Now joo can stay weeth us in Delicias, no? We don' have too many turistas."

A zephyr blessed the bare bones of the JN-3. The wires keened.

Stanley Dinkle turned in the direction of El Paso and

raised his eyes to the morning sky. "I'm sorry, General," he said. "I did my damndest."

Edgar Carberry took off his helmet and bowed his head. "Jenny, old girl, I'm sorry," he mumbled, close to tears. "Forgive me, cheri."

They turned away. They walked back into town as mourners disperse from a wake. Lopez carried the propeller. Through the plaza they shuffled. The Light Horse were still asleep on the bandstand. They entered Mi Corazón Contento and slouched at a table for a time. It was the aviator who broke the silence.

"Horse of God," he said. "Ha-ha."

"I've written to my folks back in Wisconsin every month for eleven years," said the cavalryman. "They've never answered."

"Bones of a saint. Ha-ha."

"All I've got in the world is eight hundred dollars in Postal Savings."

"I apologize, Wilbur. You, too, Orville."

"I'm not a lady-killer. I've never had a real sweet patootie."

Señora Conchita Olvera undulated to the table. " 'Allo, Red," said she to Dinkle, flashing a compensatory smile.

"Bottle of tequila, per favor," said Carberry.

She brought it, and two glasses, a saltcellar, and the halves of a lemon.

"What are you going to do?" Dinkle inquired.

"I am going to get intoxicated," replied the pilot. "Roofed, lathed, and plastered. Pull rank and order me not to and I will anyway. Who grounded me in this dump in the first place?"

"This is not the time to get drunk."

"This is the perfect time."

"Can't that crate be repaired?"

"Sure, if I ever get back to the U.S. of A. Send down a truckload of mechanics—they'll put on a new skin, the old bitch'll fly again. That's if I ever get back to the U.S. of A."

Edgar Carberry poured from the bottle. On the back of his left hand he made a paste of salt and lemon juice, into which he dipped the tip of his tongue. He gritted his teeth and raised his glass.

"I order you not to," said Dinkle forlornly.

"Remember the *Maine,*" said the pilot, then tossed off the tequila, swallowed, pulled the lobes of his ears, blinked watery eyes, and extended his stilt legs under the table. "Drink, Dink?"

"No."

"When you're being raped, Confucius say, lie still and enjoy it."

"I've heard about tequila."

"Besides, look at it this way. You're doing as well as Pershing. He's stuck in Chihuahua not catching Villa and you're stuck in Coahuila not catching Contreras."

"Right now I'm supposed to be crossing the Rio Grande and getting word to Funston. He put his trust in me. He called me 'Stanley.' He also said if I wasn't out of Mexico in twenty-four hours I'd go to my grave a second lieutenant."

"So have a drink."

"No. You're setting a bad example for my men."

"Not as bad as yours. Being a bit of a horse's ass, I'd say."

"I resent that, Carberry."

"Resent and be damned. You've got no animals, your cars are out of commission, it's too far to hike, and I can't fly. Anyhoo, your men aren't men, they're kids, tired kids, scared kids, and ashamed of themselves. What they need is some rest and some fun and so do I and so do you. When we've had it, we can figure a way out of this jam. But not now, Dink. Now's the time to have a drink. Here, stick out your hand."

His superior said a curious thing. "I don't have any friends, either."

"Hand," said Carberry gently. "Left hand."

In response, Stanley Dinkle's left hand jerked as though by reflex. But the right hand seemed to know what the left was doing. It clamped upon the left at the wrist. But the left continued to rise above the table toward the tempter. There took place under the aviator's gaze a struggle even more curious than the confession. One hand wrestled with the other, one self with the other, dash warred with discipline, will with longing, until it seemed the cavalry man must tear himself in twain. Carberry did not await the outcome. With almost satanic haste he squeezed lemon and shook salt and poured from the bottle and assisted the left hand to the victim's mouth and raised the glass to his lips.

Forgive me, Flossie, thought Stanley Dinkle. "He May Be Old, But He's Got Young Ideas."

He drank.

Into his empty stomach as into the dark of night the tequila crept, then reached with reverent, robber fingers into his heart. In seconds every shred of frustration, every thread of inhibition, was gone. He was relieved of the monotony of Patrol Post #2, of heckling and humiliation by his men, of the girl and her goat and his cocoanut coronation. In seconds he was stripped of the fabric of solitude and a second lieutenancy. In seconds the drab trappings of the soldier were stolen by the claws of the cactus liquor, and the good, honest, human bones of Stanley Dinkle were exposed.

"If I do say so," he admitted, "that stuff's all right. Let's have another."

They had another.

"Say, that's the cat's meow!" he grinned. "Say, let's do it again, Ace!"

They did it again.

Heads appeared in the doorway of My Contented Heart, and young, incredulous faces. The Philadelphia Light Horse had risen. The officer waved.

"Come on in, boys!" he cried. "Say, Carberry here's taught the old dog a new trick—let's have your left hands!"

They accepted the invitation, they tried the new trick, and with the CO's announcement that the drinks were on him, there began a day and night of revelry such as Delicias had never witnessed. Joy reigned. Tequila flowed like water. What the village lost in tranquillity it gained in legal tender. For the rest of his life, Stanley Dinkle would treasure like relics the bits and pieces of its recollection.

Item. Light of boot, supple of leg, he danced the hat dance with Perfecto Lopez over the blades of a Paragon propeller.

Item. He was with Carberry in the cantina. They had dispensed with the lemon-and-salt folderol and were shooting down the tequila straight.

"Now, I ain't a poetical man, Dink."

"Noor am I, Ace."

"But I wanna tell you. First time I ever soloed—in a Jenny it was, at Mineola—I knew what I was put on God's ol' green apple for. T'fly, that's what for. It was like I died and went t'heaven an' there I was, floatin' 'mongst the clouds an' the angels singing in my soul! Know what I mean?"

"I do, I do. Now, I ain't a poetical man either, Ace."

"Noor am I, Dink."

"But I wanna tell you. I'm a farm boy myself. Dairy place near Horeb, Wisconsin. Rode a plow horse or two. Then I got t'fork up on an Army animal—Fort Phil Kearney, Wyomin', it was—an' pulled that pig-sticker an' heard that bugle blow the charge an' took off down the field. I tell you, Ace, I was ridin' with Stuart an' Sheridan an' I could of jumped a mountain an' massacred Sin and slew Corruption single-handed! Know what I mean?"

"I do, 'deed I do."

Item. The Philadelphia Light Horse managed to scrape up an array of tin pans, after which they staged a Moro attack in the streets, banging the pans like brass gongs and waving broomsticks for barongs and shouting "Bismillah! Bismillah!"

Item. Lieutenants Dinkle and Carberry were enthroned in the front seat of "Henrietta," passing the loving cup back and forth and discussing the enlisted men.

"Oh, they look pretty in the Mounted Pistol Attack, Ace, but they are the dumbest, damndest outfit. Good-time Charlies an' polo players. An' how they are fire-eaters—can't wait t'hit the Huns. You think we'll be in that scrap?"

"Darn tootin', Dink. We got to. Show ol' Kaiser Bill what us Yanks are made of."

"Well, if so, they'll get all the raw meat they want soon enough. Some of 'em won't come back."

"I know. We'll go, too, First Aero. Over in a tub, back in a box, some of us. C'est la vee."

Edgar Carberry unholstered his Colt, drew a bead on the bell in the church tower over the windshield, fired six times and missed six times.

"War's hell, Dink," said he.

"You said a mouthful, Ace."

Item. Backed by Thayer's ukulele, the Philadelphia Light Horse presented a concert from the bandstand to a large, enthusiastic audience, vocalizing several dozen verses of the song most dear to the soldiers, sailors, and marines who helped to pacify the Philippines:

Oh, the monkeys have no tails in Zamboanga,
Oh, the monkeys have no tails in Zamboanga,
Oh, the monkeys have no tails,
They were bitten off by whales,
Oh, the monkeys have no tails in Zamboanga.
Oh, we'll all go down to Shanghai in the fall,
Oh, we'll all go down to Shanghai in the fall,
Oh, we'll all go down to Shanghai,
Those champagne corks will hang high,
Oh, we'll all go down to Shanghai in the fall.

Item. Near midnight the CO found himself propped against the bar in Mi Corazón Contento. "Bid" Biddle entered and offered him a cigar, which was accepted, and together, with heroic effort, they performed the feat of striking a match and lighting it.

" 'Quila," said Biddle.

" 'Quila," said the officer.

"Sir, wish t'fess up. My idea t'come down here in cars, catch Contreras. Brillian' idea."

Corporal Phipps lunged through the door, plunged to the far end of the bar, and supporting himself with both hands, edged alongside.

"Lootenan', you were right. We don' know particle, iota, smidgeon 'bout war. All's we know how t'do's make whoopee."

" 'Quila," said the officer.

" 'Quila," said Phipps.

Biddle put his backside to the bar and slid down its front into a sitting position. Dinkle joined him.

"Freddy" Den Uyl came through the door on hands and knees and crawled to Phipps's legs, pulling the latter down beside Biddle and the officer. Four on the floor, they considered the problem of perpendicularity at some length.

"Sir," said Den Uyl, "sorry 'bout your goo-goo story. Rotten show. Good story, ver' sorry."

Dinkle drew on his cigar, which had gone out. " 'Quila," he said.

Den Uyl nodded. " 'Quila."

Stepping smartly in, as though on review, "Phew" Pugh came to attention, saluted, and fell flat on his face. The others sat him up and braced him against a table leg facing the CO.

Dinkle returned the salute. " 'Quila."

"Sir," said Pugh, "said we're glad to see you down here meant what I said really glad knew the nipper'd know what t'do. 'Quila."

Some time later "Luce" Thayer sauntered in, a model of sobriety, and seated himself on a table. "Sir, wish I could fix the cars. Fixed 'em on the road. Fixed flats, timers, radiator leaks, oil lines, holes in the pans, everything but the kitchen sink. But can't fix bearings. Have to have new bearings."

" 'Quila," said Dinkle.

" 'Quila," said Thayer, and toppled forward from the table onto Pugh.

"Stew" Darlington was the last to join the party. He pulled up a chair. "What're we getting down here doing drunk for?"

" 'Quila," said Dinkle.

" 'quila," said Darlington.

For several minutes the officer and six enlisted men sat

or lay or leaned or slumped on the floor or furniture of My Contented Heart in a kind of owlish solemnity, each one contemplating whatever matter, cultural or alcoholic or military or nostalgic, seemed important to him at the moment. Eventually "Lex" Phipps banged a doleful gavel.

"We can' go home," he said. "Court-martial all of us. Ruin our fam'lies. Shame of the Light Horse. Laughin'-stock of the country."

"Noor can I," said Dinkle. "I'm 'sponsible. CO's always 'sponsible. End my career. Man Who Killed the Cavalry."

"No." To a man, the Philadelphians shook their heads. "No. We'll tell 'em, sir. All our fault. You told us not t'cross river. We'll get you off. Yessir."

Their mustaches bristled with sincerity.

"How'll we do that," asked Biddle, "if we never go home?

Their mustaches drooped with doubt.

"Then we'll go," said Phipps.

"Take our med'cine," said Darlington.

"Come what may," said Thayer.

"Amen," said Pugh.

"Hear, hear," said Den Uyl.

Their commander was obviously moved. He sought to fix each man with his baby-blue eyes, now pink and as out of true as a JN-3 which had been too much buffeted by too many storms. " 'Preciate it," he said. "Do my damnest for you, too. Boys be boys. Boy once myself."

"Lootenan'," said Corporal Phipps, "behalf Commonwealth Pennsavanya an' city 'Delphya an' Light Horse, wish t'state you are a good egg."

" 'Preciate it," said Dinkle.

"Sir," said Biddle, to his own surprise as much as theirs, "wish to 'pologize. Insulted you. May be officer but also gent'man. Born gent'man much as we are."

" 'Preciate it," said Dinkle. "Don' forget, unner un'form all soldiers. Same clay."

"Shake my hand, sir?"

"Ever'body shake," said the others.

An attempt was made to stand, to formalize the ceremony, then given up as unnecessary and impossible. Then there was difficulty locating extremities, even distinguishing between left and right, but in time, by a process of elimination, the proper hands of reconciliation and friendship were offered one by one to Stanley Dinkle, and accepted.

"Ahem," he said.

Item. Finally, slowly and laboriously, at some ossified hour between midnight and cockcrow, Stanley Dinkle was ascending the stairs to his room over the cantina when his nose became embedded in a cleft beneath a white blouse. It was the cleft beneath the blouse of Señora Conchita Olvera, who stood, by happenstance, on the step above him.

" 'Allo, Red," said she.

" 'Chita," said he.

He inhaled.

" 'Chita," he sighed, "it has been one helluva long time."

Up the stairs he stumbled her, into his room he bumbled her. Here he deprived her of her clothing, and taxiing her to the bed, chocked her head securely with a pillow. In darkness he stripped to the buff, filled the tank of his chest with oxygen, flexed his biceps and behind, and positioned himself at her engine end.

"Say, 'Clear!' " he ordered potently.

"Clear!" she giggled.

"Say 'Switch Off!' "

"Switch Off!"

Stanley Dinkle gave his Paragon propeller a strong downswing. She laughed. He laughed, and for good measure, gave it another.

"Say 'Contact,' 'Chita!" he cried.

"Contac'!" she cried.

"Contact!" bulged Stanley Dinkle, leaping into the cockpit, opening the throttle wide, getting a masterful grip on the controls. And at his yell, so long stifled, so long thwarted, internal combustion occurred. Dust erupted from the straw tick. The bed, with its freight of man, woman, honor, duty, country, Frederick Funston, the 8th Cavalry, the Congress, and four fleas, bumped and bounced and gained speed and in total defiance of natural law detached itself from the floor and took flight, going to glory be.

26

Enter an Angel of Mercy

Came the dawn. Lieutenant Dinkle sawed wood in his bed, the Philadelphia Light Horse reposed in their hammocks on the bandstand, while Lieutenant Carberry and his propeller lay dead to the world in the tonneau of "Olivia."

At noon there was no change in the situation, nor at two, three, and four o'clock in the afternoon.

Lest it seem incredible to the reader that their slumber should have been so sweet in a setting so urban, it should be recalled that these were soldiers sleeping off a full night and day of debauchery. May it be noted also that Delicias was at great pains to be certain they were not disturbed. This was a logical solicitude. They were the first genuine tourists the village had entertained since the advent of the Revolution, if not in its history. They were Yanquis, moreover—walking, talking gold mines. In two days they had fed a small fortune in gringo dollars into the local economy, and there was more, the residents knew, where that had come from, much more. Were soldiers not, in a sense, officials of their government? They were. Did this not mean an association with Washington? It did. Might this not imply in turn a relationship, even though tenuous, to the U. S. Treasury? It must. The longer they dallied in Delicias, therefore, the better for all materially concerned, and the longer they drowsed this third day, the less likelihood of their decamping till the fourth. And so the serene hours passed, and the townsfolk maintained a conspiracy of silence. Perfecto Lopez posted members of the Chamber of Commerce at each entrance to the plaza with instructions to detour traffic. Guitars were unstrung. The church bell was not rung. Children were hushed, dogs muzzled, birds discouraged. Tortillas were squeezed rather than slapped.

At almost five o'clock a Stanley Dinkle three sheets to the wind stumbled from Mi Corazón Contento, opened his mouth to shout a reveille, closed it, and collapsed on "Henrietta's" running board. Presently his fellow officer awakened and joined him, and they sat together in a fraternity of agony. As though a wand had been waved, burros entered the plaza, the church bell rang, birds sang, dogs barked, and tortillas were subjected to their customary torture. The sudden racket only increased the affliction of the pair. They conferred in grunts, and groans.

Dinkle said there was no use crying over spilt tequila, they had to get out of here.

Carberry agreed.

Dinkle said he was now overdue at the Rio Grande by a day and a half and Funston would have run amuck.

Carberry said as long as #43 sat in a cornfield without skin, the 1st Aero Squadron did not exist.

Dinkle said they had to get out of here.

Carberry agreed.

The reintroduction of noise to the plaza roused the Light Horse. Holding heads in hands, they came to drape themselves over the fenders of "Henrietta."

Carberry said he was convinced the key to the entire problem of transportation was these flivvers. Get them rolling and they could be back in the U. S. of A. in a couple of hours. He asked Thayer if he were sure the bearings were shot.

Thayer couldn't be sure. It sounded like bearings to him. In any event, cause was irrelevant. They were practically out of gas and oil.

Au contrary, said Carberry. They had plenty. He could siphon enough gas and drain enough oil from his Jenny to run 'em to Timbuktu.

A grim and pallid Dinkle jumped to his feet. "All right, we go to work!" he croaked. "Thayer, I want those engines out of these buggies and taken apart nut by bolt till you find out what's wrong! Lieutenant Carberry, you take

Biddle, round up a cart and a burro, load the cans, and drain that aeroplane to the last drop! Everybody move! I want this outfit on the road in two hours!"

It is a tribute to man's indomitable stupidity that he will try, try again when there is no hope whatever of success. Except that its function was vital, the gallant Thayer did not know what a bearing was, or what it did, much less where it might be located. But emptying the toolbox and spreading blankets on the ground for parts and raising the hoods, he stripped to the waist and bent to his task, and hung over, shaking with various miseries, the others rolled up sleeves to assist him. Two hours later, as shades of eve descended, a crowd had gathered upon a scene unprecedented in the plaza of Delicias. Upon the hapless "Henrietta" and "Olivia" major surgery had been performed. Their engines rested upright on blankets amid an et cetera of nuts, bolts, tools, spark plugs, wires, intake pipes, exhaust pipes, commutators, carburetors, cylinder covers, and camshafts. About them stood six soldiers, on their faces expression of infinite futility. Carberry and Biddle had long ago returned with a cartload of milk cans filled with fuel and a reserve of oil filched from the JN-3. Citizens, enlisted men, and aviator stared at the hodge-podge of organs arrayed before them, at the greasy symbols of a new civilization, the Age of the Dingus, the Era of the Whatchamacallit, and their mechanical bubble burst. A good cigar was a smoke, but a flivver without her liver and lights was only a pile of junk.

Lt. Dinkle, on the other hand, knew it all along. His faith in the horse was fortified. His hatred of the dojigger and the thingumabob was rekindled. But it was at this juncture that his elbow was nudged by a small, smooth-shaven Mexican wearing a bow tie, a checkered vest, and a derby hat.

"Joo got trouble, amigo?"

"What's it look like?" rasped the officer. "They say it's bearings, but they don't know. Nobody knows."

"Ah, the beareengs." The diminutive Dapper Dan smiled, offering as though for sale a mouthful of dime store dentures filigreed with gold. "The Ford, she ees like a woman, ver' hard to handle. But there ees a way. Joo mus' Fight Joor Ford."

"Fight Your Ford!"

"Sí, sí. Joo mus' treat her rough an' show her joo are the boss. Then she weel kees joor han'."

The officer was skeptical. "How would you know?"

"I have work' een El Paso, amigo. In the garage. My name ees Angel Salcido. I tell joo, I am one *mecánico terrífico.*"

"Hokum," Dinkle sniffed.

The man bristled. "I weel show joo, hombre." He stepped jauntily to an engine block and with a gesture directed the soldiers to turn it upside down. This done, he selected a wrench, turned three nuts, and tapped off the bottom plate, revealing the crankshaft. Whistling between his teeth, he inserted a crank and turned the shaft to expose the connecting rods and caps, then invited Dinkle and Carberry.

"Joo see? Here ees the bad bearing."

"Well, I'll be," said Carberry. "But it's no help. We're fresh out of bearings."

"Eet ees no trouble, señor." He solicited the crowd. "Weel somebody geev' me a *huarache? Por favor?*"

There was no immediate response. The villagers looked to Perfecto Lopez, but the mayor's mien was negative. To his delaying tactics, the appearance of anyone expert in the maintenance of autos was as dangerous as it was unexpected.

"Somebody geev' me a huarache," bargained Salcido, "an' I will pay heem a gringo dollar."

At the mention of money, real money, the alcalde forgot himself, tore off one of his own sandals, and handed it to the mecánico terrífico, who sliced off the thongs with a long, wicked knife. With another wrench he loosened the nuts of the cap which attached the connecting rod to the crankshaft and picked away the scraps of babbitt with the point of his knife. Then in quick, professional sequence he cut a short strip from the leather sole of the huarache, daubed it with grease, wrapped the strip around the crankshaft, tightened the nuts of the rod cap over it, and wiped disdainful hands on the blanket.

"I'll be a ding-dong daddy," breathed Carberry.

"Una nadita," said Salcido, slipping the knife under his vest. "Eet ees notheeng."

"Will that work?" demanded Dinkle.

"Now she weel take joo to Detroi', hombre."

"Could you fix the other car and put the whole shebang back together?"

The proud Salcido frowned. "I have said eet. I am one wheez-bang."

"How long?"

The Mexican shrugged. "Three, four hour. Weeth the soldados to asseest me."

Dinkle pondered. "Let's see. Out of here by midnight —any luck and we'd hit the river by daylight. All right, Salcido, take my men and go to it."

But the mechanic folded haughty arms. "Joo tell me, hombre? Joo don' ask me?"

Dinkle bit his lip. "Damnation—very well, will you?"

Salcido smiled, but this time his china choppers glistened like the blade of a knife. "I weel do eet for the great Estados Unidos. An' for one hundred dollars."

"A hundred dollars!" cried Dinkle. "That's highway robbery!"

The El Pasoan tipped his derby. "Joo don' pay, hombre, joo stay."

In despair, the CO kicked an engine block. "I don't have it." He turned to Carberry.

"Don't look at me, old chap. I haven't a bean."

In the gathering darkness Dinkle turned next to the Philadelphians, who understood his mute appeal and put heads together, conferring in low tones.

Phipps acted as spokesman. "Lieutenant," he said with ill-concealed emotion, "you may not remember last night but we do. We told you that even if we couldn't afford to go home after the bungle we've made of this, we would anyway, for your sake. We said we'd back you to the hilt and take the blame. Well, sir, we are men of our word. Therefore we'll put up the hundred."

"Thank you," said Stanley Dinkle. "I appreciate it."

A collection was taken up among the Light Horse and the money forthwith paid to Angel Salcido. Dinkle arranged for torches to be brought, so that the mechanic would have sufficient light, and the repair of the Fords was undertaken. Although the CO left Salcido to his own devices, the prospect of pulling out of Delicias by midnight, of actually pointing the flivvers' noses toward the Rio Grande, of finally doing his soldier's duty to flag and country and cavalry, turned him into a whirling administrative dervish.

By nine o'clock he had rotated his men in and out of the cantina and seen to it that they were fed.

By ten o'clock he had superintended the refueling of the Fords and the loading of gear.

By eleven o'clock, cardboard suitcase at his side, he waited with Carberry under the smoking torches in the plaza as Angel Salcido tightened the last nut, reconnected the last wire, and pronounced the vehicles ready to roll.

"Corporal Phipps, crank 'em up!"

"Yes, sir!"

Phipps and Thayer performed the honors. Under the weather for three days, but feminists to their cores of steel, "Henrietta" and "Olivia" shivered and shook and presently took to their new bearings of shoe leather as ducks take to water. "Texas, here we come!" the Philadelphians cheered. *"Olé!"* cheered the scatter of spectators. Dinkle turned to commend Salcido, but the mecánico terrífico had taken his derby hat, his hundred dollars, and his leave.

"Mount up!" whooped Lieutenant Dinkle, heaving his suitcase into a tonneau. "Damn the torpedoes—full speed ahead!"

"Momentito! Momentito!"

Perfecto Lopez came out of his cantina sqeualing like a stuck pig.

"Alto! Stop!" Seizing the impatient Dinkle's arm, the mayor tugged at him. "Come weeth me one *momentito,* plees, mi Coronel! Come eenside!"

"Sorry, Mayor, we're on our way," was the gruff reply. "Thanks for everything and *hasta la vista*."

But the alcalde would not be denied. Hugging the officer to his belly, he put his mustachio to Dinkle's ear. "Contreras!" he hissed. "I have jus' foun' out where he ees! Joo wan' to know? Encarnacion Contreras! Joo wan' heem, joo can have heem!"

27

Love Conquers Lt. Edgar N. Carberry

They were inside My Contented Heart.

"I'll listen, Lopez," said Lt. Dinkel sternly, "but we're pulling out of here now, pronto, comprendey? O.K., where's Contreras?"

The mayor's countenance was caught between greed and guile. "Let us do beezness, mi Coronel. I tell joo where he ees, joo geev' me somethеen'."

"What?"

"Delicias ees a poor place. For five years now we are rob' by Rurales, Federales, Villistas—"

"Cut the comedy," snapped Dinkle. "Speak your piece, now or never."

"Hokay. Joo mus' geev me joor aeroplano."

The officer started for the door and the waiting autos. "So long, Lopez, see you in church."

But the alcalde had a derringer up his cuff. "When joo are gone, mi Coronel, I weel pray for her."

The officer halted. "For who?"

"The gringa señorita. The one Contreras has taken weeth heem from hees raid. But how can joo, a *soldado valiente,* leave her?" the mayor wondered. "Joo know what dose bastardistas do to her."

Stanley Dinkle came to heel. "You saying she's alive?"

Perfecto Lopez nodded gravely. "I have heard eet. Contreras ees hideen' out, ten kilometros from here, an' she ees a prees'ner." He threw up a hand in horror. *"Madre de Dios,* a woman *abandonado!"*

Stanley Dinkle sat down, heavily, in the nearest chair. "Go tell 'em," he said in a voice scarcely audible. "Shut 'em off and come in here."

While the mayor was gone, Stanley Dinkle removed his battered campaign hat and sat like a soldier of stone. He heard the engines stilled. He hadn't let himself believe she could be alive. He closed his eyes and looked into hers. Under the green were glints of gold, swimming. He recalled the green water of a pond in springtime, and a boy bent over it, bewitched by tadpoles. "There's a woman in there sure as hell," she'd whispered under the ramada at Edhogg. "It's me. Can't you take no pity on 'er?" And then, "Stanley, what if I'm beautiful an' we don't even know it!" Her eyes rounded with wonder at the prospect. In one appeared an anticipatory tear. And as within the oyster, a grain of irritant sand may make a pearl, deep within the soul of Stanley Dinkle had been born a tender, irritant doubt. He doubted no longer. His luck had changed at last. He loved. He was loved. Through the deserts of this life she would stride at his side. In sickness she would cool his brow, in health would warm his bed. Her loud voice would be his trumpet, and at its call the walls of his loneliness would tumble. Her homely face would gladden the hearth of his manhood.

Hello, Central, give me Heaven, thought Stanley Dinkle, but I hope it don't answer. I'd rather have my Flossie here.

He opened his eyes. Lopez had led the troopers in, and they stood waiting on him, wondering why, when the throttles were finally open, he should apply the brakes. Propeller over his shoulder, Carberry lounged in a chair.

"The lost is found," the CO told them. "Lopez claims Contreras is hiding out six miles from here."

"Contreras!" Even their mustaches were electrified.

Dinkle frowned at the mayor. "How many in his band?"

"A dozen, mi Coronel, *más o menos.*"

"More or less." Dinkle leaned back. "Well, that's the intelligence. We've got our man if we want him."

"Want 'im!" they whooped. "Let's go, sir!"

"Hold your horses," the CO advised. "Think it over. We wouldn't attack before dawn. That delays getting up to the river God knows how much longer, and we're two days late now. They'll have our hides for that plus everything else." He leveled a finger. "This isn't a polo game we're talking about. This is a real fight, and we're outnumbered, maybe two to one."

"But this is our chance, sir!" cried "Lex" Phipps. "To show some real dash and initiative!"

"Don't you see, Lieutenant?" begged "Luce" Thayer. "We'll make up for everything! Capture the whole bunch, and who'll court-martial us?"

"I'll have my mare back or know the reason why!" threatened "Freddy" Den Uyl. "The greaser cads!"

"Seven Yanks and a dozen Mexicans—very decent odds," judged "Bid" Biddle.

"We'll go home heroes!" rhapsodized "Phew" Pugh. "A parade down Chestnut Street!"

"We'll smite 'em hip and thigh!" shrilled "Stew" Darlington. "Lieutenant, we've simply got to do it!"

When they had run out of babble, the CO spoke again. "There's a catch. We don't know where. Lopez does. In return for the information, he wants a small token of our gratitude."

"What's that, sir?"

"The aeroplane."

"Ha-ha," said Carberry.

"That's what he wants," Dinkle repeated. "And I'm inclined to think he should have it. This is a chance for us to pull out of a manure pile smelling like roses."

So appalled was the pilot that he let his propeller fall with a crash. "Give up Jenny? So you jockeys can play bang-bang with some bean bandidos? Not on your tintype, Dinkle!"

"I mean it, Ace," said his superior. "I could order you to, but I won't. After all, that hedgehopper's no good to anyone now."

"Ace" Carberry slammed the heels of his cowboy boots to the floor. "You're bughouse! I told you—we'll give 'er a new skin! She'll be flying when you're old and gray!"

"All you have to do," Dinkle continued, "is tell 'em you crash-landed. That the thing wasn't worth salvaging. No one'll ever know."

It was as though the intrepid aviator were being asked to betray not only his country but the very principle of flight. And as the CO waited, as the Philadelphia Light Horse looked down their noses at him, his face crimsoned with outrage and injustice. For a minute he went berserk, backing away, upsetting chairs, hand on the butt of his six-shooter. Dinkle might order and be damned, he declared, he'd protect that crate with his life! It was the last operable military aircraft on the American continent—well, almost operable! Give it away and he gave away the entire 1st Aero Squadron! Give it away and the U.S. of A. was the only major power in the world without an air arm! He ripped off his helmet, flung it on the table like a gauntlet, and when the challenge was ignored, flung his arms and legs haphazardly into a chair, and out of breath sat sourly, sucking on a lemon of righteousness.

There was an intermission. The Light Horse stood on one leg, then the other. Stanley Dinkle loosened his necktie and unbuttoned his collar. He twisted in his seat. He heaved a lugubrious sigh.

"Edgar," he began.

"Edgar?" snorted the pilot.

"Edgar, I haven't told you the whole truth. I hate to put things on a personal basis, but I guess I have to. If you won't trade what's left of your aeroplane for the good of the cavalry, will you for me?"

Carberry set his jaw. "Hell, no."

"Then will you for Flossie Grebs?"

"Who?"

"The miner's daughter. You know, the old man Contreras murdered when he raided Edhogg. He ran off with her. I expected she'd be dead by now, and better off dead, but she isn't. Lopez says she's alive. The bandidos have her, just six miles from here. Putting it on a personal basis, Edgar, I'd like to save her," he said simply. "I'd like to very much."

"Personal basis? Applesauce."

Stanley Dinkle got slowly to his feet. "Then I have to show you, Edgar. I'd rather hang my tail on a rusty nail, but I will."

And he left the cantina, to reappear a moment later in the doorway carrying his cardboard suitcase. Into their midst he moved, embarrassed but indomitable. He placed the suitcase on the table. The mayor sidled up to see. The six young soldiers mustered.

"Ahem," he said. "When I went to El Paso, she gave me ten dollars to buy her a dress. It was her grocery money. She's thirty-one years old and never had a store-bought dress. So I bought this." His ham hands unfolded the pink velvet with attached "Bertha." "Then I got in deeper and deeper, the way you did yourself down here with us. You think I don't understand, Edgar, but I do. So I went in over my head and bought her a whole rig." Fumbling, rustling tissue, he spread out on the table the hat and petticoats and shoes and corset and vest and bloomers. He was younger now than they. He was like a boy made under duress to disclose to prying, adult eyes his most intimate treasures—a mash note from a girl, a half-smoked Cubeb, a magic stone guaranteed to eliminate warts, a ring which, when held to the light, revealed a burlesque queen in the buff. "I've got a hundred dollars invested in her," he concluded, "and she's worth every red cent. You may not think she's a female at all, but you can't judge a mount in the show ring. In the field, class tells, and she's a thoroughbred. I forgot stockings, though."

At first sight of the velvet and taffeta and pongee they had been inclined to crude, masculine amusement. But under the influence of fabrics such as these, strong men grow weak, and now the members of his audience were ashamed of themselves. They shuffled shoes and cleared throats and inspected ceiling beams. It is to be doubted there was a dry eye in My Contented Heart.

Carberry dragged himself up, his fingers in contact with the "Tendertruss" corset. "Gee whiz. You saying you love 'er?"

"She's bigger than I am," admitted Stanley Dinkle, "and stronger. And homely as a hedge fence."

"I asked you," demanded the pilot. "Man to man, d'you love 'er?"

"I probably ought not to."

"But do you!" roared Carberry.

The Light Horse held their breath. If cavalryman had asked the penultimate of aviator, one man now asked it of another.

"I damn do," stated Stanley Dinkle.

Edgar Carberry snatched up the orange plume of his helmet and blew a chivalrous nose. "Why didn't you say you're carrying the torch?" he spluttered. "If that ain't the berries—Don Juan Dinkle! Why, I'll swap a Jenny for a Flossie any day! Put 'er there, Dink!"

Ceremoniously the officers shook hands.

"Thank you, Edgar," said Dinkle. "Appreciate it."

"We'll rescue her, Lieutenant!" Corporal Phipps assured him fervently.

"And our horses, too!" added Darlington.

"Ace" Carberry took the Paragon in his arms for the last time. "So long, sweetie," he murmured, and placing hands about its wooden waist, lifted it in presentation to Perfecto Lopez. "O.K. Perfect, Number Forty-Three's all yours. Also the mortal remains of Thirty-Eight, Seventy-Two, Fifty-Six, and Ninety-Four. You take care of Jenny, she'll take care of you."

He turned quickly, truculently, to Dinkle. "Listen, mon ami. I'm doing this foul deed on one condition. I get an invite to the ruckus."

The CO was repacking his suitcase. "What for?"

The daredevil pilot whipped out his revolver and gave it a gunfighter's twirl around his forefinger. "You need beaucoup help, pal," he insisted. "You need a crack shot like me."

Stanley Dinkle shut his suitcase with a click. And with that click he sealed away not only velvet, taffeta, and pongee but his secret self as well, including the personal revelation he had been forced to throw into the bargain. That done, he straightened the gold bar on his collar, stiffened his upper lip, and turned himself once more into the hard-boiled handler of men. "You've got your aeroplane, Lopez," he said with tarantula decisiveness. "Now, where's Contreras?"

The worthy alcalde hugged his acquisition. "He ees at

an *estancia*—how joo say, a ranch, mi Coronel. Eet ees call' El Cuervo."

"El Cuervo?"

"Sí. The Crow. Joo mus' follow the tracks of the *carros,* the carts. To the *este.*"

"All right," said the CO to his troopers with the same sting, "all right, we're going after him." But as he tightened up his pistol belt a notch, they could almost see him trying to suppress excitement. "We'll hit the ranch at dawn, and hard. It's midnight—we ride out at three A.M. Between now and then I want rifles and pistols cleaned. Be sure your ammunition pouches are full. Get what food you need and sleep you can, and no drinking. Phipps, see to it."

"Yes, sir."

"One more thing." The lieutenant's eyes bored into theirs. "I'm cavalry and proud of it. So are you. But we have no animals. Therefore we sink however low we have to. So I want you to swear on your word of honor to keep this under your hats. That the U. S. Cavalry ever went into action on Model T Fords."

28

Confusion at El Cuervo

At precisely 0300 hours on 14 May 1916, a day which was to be momentous in American military history, a day the events of which would effect profound changes in the tools and tactics of warfare, the Tin Lizzie Troop cranked up and chugged out of Delicias.

Lt. Stanley H. Dinkle, commanding, rode in "Henrietta" beside his driver, Corporal Phipps, with Privates Biddle and Den Uyl in the tonneau. "Olivia" was driven by Private Thayer and manned by Lieutenant Carberry and Privates Darlington and Pugh. During their sojourn in Mexico the vehicles had already been relieved of two spare tires, a toolbox, and two head lamps, but now, for purposes of speed and fuel consumption, they were unloaded of all equipment save for weapons and a cardboard suitcase. Despite patched inner tubes, dusty timers, linted oil lines, a pan plugged with wood, weak coffee perking in one radiator, and a bearing of shoe leather in each crankshaft, "Henrietta" and "Olivia" performed admirably. It was more than a mere sense of mission. For on this day they became more than mere horseless carriages. They were the first of their breed to go to war. The average Lizzie was distined for inglorious demise in a junkyard, but these flivvers seemed to shiver with intimations of automotive immortality. They champed at the bit of fame. Their pedals, they believed, might one day feel the heels of kings and presidents. In their brassy breasts they dreamed of permanent pasture in the Smithsonian Institution. Through their carburetors passed an elixir of piss, vinegar, gasoline, and aspiration.

It was a warm and somber night, and black as the ace

of spades. In the west, behind them, too low to provide illumination, half a red moon guttered. They passed the field of stubble in which were parked the struts and tendons of the JN-3, a poor, nude pawn of love, and took to the tracks, or ruts, of cartwheels. According to Lopez, the estancia had long been the last inhabited place east of Delicias, and the expedition would know it had reached its destination once it climbed a ridge and the tracks ended. It was difficult enough to keep to them even now. "Henrietta" had no head lamps, but in any case they would not risk using lights. To one side, then the other they meandered, into cactus and over greasewood, until the CO resorted to the means used by cavalry to follow a trail by night. Dismounting a man at intervals, he had him walk before and scout the way, leading the cars like horses. And so they plodded along, exhausts putt-putting resolutely, and the minutes lagged, and every mile was hardly earned.

They halted only once. "Olivia" boiled over, perhaps with impatience rather than prolonged reliance on low gear, and while they let her ardor cool, Lieutenant Dinkle could not sit still. He prowled about the autos, preoccupied with complex strategical considerations.

Would these four-wheeled velocipedes get them to the ranch by daylight?

If they did, would Encarnacion Contreras in fact be there? It made sense that he might be. After a foray into Texas, why not hotfoot it back to his lair, there to hide from pursuit and enjoy his loot?

How many, más o menos, more or less, men than a dozen did he have?

What was his firepower? Surely more than that represented by a few Springfields and .45 automatics and one hogleg Colt revolver.

Wouldn't his bastardistas be better shots than a collegiate glee club and an aeroplane cowpoke incapable of plinking a church bell once in six tries?

Was he, Dinkle, rattling his ass, and theirs, into a trap?

Only the Good Lord knew the answers, and before a battle He seldom spilled such beans. To the crucial question, however—why a grown man and trained officer had let himself be hurrahed into a stunt as adolescent and dangerous as this one—Stanley Dinkle supplied his own. It seemed to him that until now his life had been a fine kettle of uncaught fish, unmilked udders, unanswered letters, undelivered corsets, unfinished articles, undarned socks, and unpropitiated peckers. And it was possible, just possible, that here, this black and muggy morning, in this outlandish place, he might finally win all the marbles. That if they could pull this off, if they could find the foe and whip him soundly, Stanley Dinkle might amount to something. And if they did, he decided, he would ask her then and there, on the bloody spot, to be his bride.

Hassan, he thought, I wish I was straddling your backbone instead of a gas tank.

I love you, Flossie Grebs.

Transmissions growling martially, forward crawled the Tin Lizzie Troop, into chuckholes and over boulders, into sand and out of gravel. But if the Fords strained at the reins, the enlisted men in them did not. Their mood had changed. It was one thing to get hot and bothered about an idea in a cantina, another to be actually going into battle. Phipps and Thayer could concentrate on steering wheels and spark and throttle levers and the ruts ahead, but Biddle, Den Uyl, Pugh, and Darlington could only bite their lips and grip their rifles. For some reason they were unpleasantly reminded of the night of the raid upon Fort Dinkle, and how they'd hopped about under the canvas like toads and popped away like the Fourth of July and behaved, in general, like blithering idiots. In their minds' eyes they beheld once more the burning ruin of Edhogg, the naked Mrs. Offus, and the corpse of Champion Grebs, upon his chest a bush of beard in crimson bloom. Fire, raving women, and dead men—these were war, about which Lieutenant Dinkle had warned them they knew nothing, and warned them truly. But in an hour or less they'd go to school and learn, and live, they hoped, to take the lesson home. Thinking on these things, the Philadelphians touched wrists, hands, noses, throats. How fond were they of their own hide now, of the fancy envelopes in which they had been dispatched into the world! How precious were they to themselves!

"Henrietta" halted again. The labor of her engine indicated to Lieutenant Dinkle that she was climbing. It might be the ridge. They had ridden almost an hour, ample time to traverse six miles. He reseated Den Uyl and took his place out front to lead and test the incline, the autos panting eagerly at his heels. The slope was gradual, and the ruts worn by wheels gave him a route. Then, unexpectedly, his boots found level ground, and he was back to Phipps and Thayer in a hurry, ordering them to cut engines and set hand brakes, this must be the ridgeline, which would mean the ranch was on the far side, below them—everyone out, no talking, and follow him.

They obeyed, lugging rifles and stringing out in single file until, having taken two steps downward, he backed them up, squatted, and whispered as they hunkered down around him. He'd had enough of this blindman's buff, he said. By his guesstimate they had some twenty minutes before first light, so they'd wait, prone and spread out, and when he could see his hand before his face, he'd give final orders. His plan was to wake Contreras from a sound sleep and serve him bullets for breakfast—so not a cough, not an itch, lie doggo and stay doggo.

He deployed them along the crest, pushing them flat and ten yards apart, Carberry in the center, three on either side of him, and took his own position near the pilot.

They turned with the earth like worms. In the west the moon waned. The stars were pinched out one by one. Now they lay with Mexico at last. But this was not the perfumed and passionate wench across the Rio Grande for whom they had once yearned. The real Mexico, they had found in a few dreadful days, was a hag. Barren mountains were her bones. Fever wasted her, sun had dried her ancient skin. She nourished no existence other than that of ant and lizard, bird and beast of prey. They were young and strong and soldiers, but her darkness stole away their arms, her spaces made them insignificant, and since her withered lips were sealed, she could not tell them what it was they waited for, whether glory or irony or tragedy.

Some were brave before the impending hour, others craven. Some fell in love with life, others introduced themselves to eternity. For twenty minutes they lay with her, this true, this terrible Mexico, and turned with the earth like worms.

From his wallet Thayer took a lock of "Livvy's" hair and tucked it into a pocket near his heart.

Biddle drew deeply on an imaginary cheroot and conceded that the curtain might be rising on his last act.

Pugh embraced his Springfield. He would identify the bandido who had parted his hair with a rifle butt and do a bit of barbering himself.

Carberry counted the rounds in his cartridge belt. There were seven. Seven and six in the revolver made thirteen. Thirteen.

Lieutenant Dinkle kicked himself. He had trained them in the Mounted Pistol Attack. Now he was taking them into their first fight dismounted.

Phipps touched the homemade stripes on his sleeve. He was the only non-com, hence must set an heroic example for the lower ranks.

Ashes to ashes, dust to dust, if the greasers don't get me, the dollies must, versified Den Uyl. He loathed lying about in the dirt.

Darlington listened to his lungs. The exertions of combat might be very bad for asthma.

Then a wind wafted in from the south. Suddenly the night was pierced by a sound so fearful that it erected the hair on their scalps and took the starch totally out of them. It was a long, loud caw, exactly like that of a crow. It was the voice of El Cuervo. From the depths below it called to the soldiers, reminding them of loss and agony, of mold and autumn, of wills and codicils and final testaments. And every horrid monosyllable of the black bird made them writhe and bathed their brows with new and clammy dew.

I believe in an afterlife, "Luce" Thayer solaced himself. If anything happens to me, I know Olivia and I will meet again.

"Bid" Biddle was too proud to pray. At the least, he

vowed, I shall shuffle off this mortal coil with style. A pity I haven't a grander theater.

They are only boys, Stanley Dinkle reminded himself, and any blood they shed will be on your gold bar. So if there's dirty work to do this morning, you do it.

"Ace" Carberry did not know who to blame for his fix: the Wright brothers or the simple-minded citizens of Delicias. Eh bien, he rationalized, if you're due for a nose dive, it might as well be for a dame in distress.

I'm too young to die, declared "Phew" Pugh. Besides, if I live, I know what I want to be. It's the Army for me. A career cavalry officer, galloping about in a Cadillac.

We must show what stuff we're made of, lads, exhorted "Lex" Phipps silently. Let's make Lieutenant Dinkle proud of us! Let's be true to the glorious traditions of the Philadelphia Light Horse!

I've led a life of sin, confessed "Freddy" Den Uyl. Tomorrow I turn over a new leaf. I shall eschew hooch, quit tomcatting, and spread alms amongst the poor like manure.

"Stew" Darlington shuddered. Some of us will die today. Because he's here, Grim Death, the old man who stole our Motometer. I can feel those awful eyes. He's here. He's waiting.

I'm going to save you, girl, promised Stanley Dinkle. Wait'll you see what's in my suitcase. Wait'll I pop the question. You're all I've got in this world, you and Hassan. I love you, Flossie Grebs.

He took off his necktie and folded it into a breeches pocket, and as he did so, the darkness before and below him seemed to dissolve almost chemically. Places and things became precipitates filtered out of night and hung suspended in a gray solution.

The line of soldiers squinted.

The ridge on which they lay was like a rib. In the hollow between it and the next rib was the estancia, a low building of adobe plastered with clay. It had one doorway, center, and two wide window openings.

At the east corner they could make out the curve of a corral at the rear, an enclosure of ocotillo withes.

Revolution had already been here. A section of roof was caved in and one wall of the ranch house had toppled.

They looked for signs of life, for laundry or cooking smoke or animals, but saw nothing. And then, as it grew lighter, each time the crow cawed they noted movement against the graying sky and presently knew themselves for chumps.

El Cuervo was a rickety wooden windmill beyond the corral—nothing more. As the fan turned in the wind, rusty pump rods were forced through rusty sockets, producing a sound remarkably imitative of the bird after which the estancia was named.

The CO was absorbed in tactics. Ten yards to the front of the ranch house, what had once been a stone fence was now separate piles of rubble. The distance down the ridge to the rubble was approximately a hundred yards. Suppose a man reached the stones, which would afford him cover. A final rush of thirty feet after that would have him down their gullets.

He moved. To one end of the line he crawled, then the other, whispering instructions. Fill shirt pockets with rifle and pistol clips for rapid reloading. Hold fire until he fired. Aim for the door and windows, throw a full clip into them, then do as he did—one man at a time, rise and run twenty yards down the ridge, fall and fire, run another twenty, fall and fire, then take cover behind the rubble and wait for orders. He didn't know whether Contreras was here or not, but they'd damned soon find out. They nodded and licked dry lips.

He crawled to Carberry, who admitted he had only thirteen shells for his cannon. Dinkle said to save 'em for close-in work. Carberry would have inquired the meaning of "close-in work," but the CO had crawled away.

Dinkle unholstered his .45 and slipped the safety. He looked up and down the line. They were in the prone position, elbows dug into the dirt, gun barrels depressed, sights raised.

The wind died. The crow ceased to caw.

Dinkle sighted on the doorway.

In the east, the sky blushed hot. The day would be a blinger.

He squeezed the trigger.

On either side of him the Springfields crashed.

He leaped up and ran down the ridge and threw himself onto chest and belly and fired again at the doorway and leaped up and ran signaling with an arm for the line to follow and as he fell a second time the doorway and two windows went off like angry beehives and he heard the sting of lead overhead.

Contreras was there.

He let go a round and dashed downhill bent almost double and after two more bursts and belly-whoppers neared a stone pile and tore for it on hands and knees the way a badger tears for a hole, tail down and digging. Rather than look behind him he reloaded and blazed away at door and windows to give the others as much protection as possible.

In a minute more, firing from the estancia stopped for good reason. The bandidos had no targets. The Tin Lizzie Troop was safely off the ridge and hidden. All seven of them hugged hard ground behind rubble, grim and breathing hard and hats blown off on the hillside and a long, long way from Philadelphia. But they had finally played with gunpowder and flirted for the first time with Miss Mortality—and they had survived. So far thank God so good.

They reloaded rifles and awaited his orders. His own hat, he found, was gone, and also found that Stanley Dinkle was disinclined to move. It had been exactly like this the morning the 14th Cavalry ringed the edge of the crater on the island of Sulu. Someone had to do something, and to Private Dinkle's amazement, since he had been as disinclined then as now, it had been Private Dinkle.

They were waiting orders.

Efficiently he removed the empty magazine from the butt of his automatic. Decisively he inserted a full one. Besides, he had sworn that if blood must be shed this day, it would be his.

They awaited orders.

He had a peek round the stone pile. The bandidos were conspicuous by their absence. The rancho was precisely where it had been. And it was still thirty feet to the nearest window, the lower sill of which was four feet above ground level. Traversing that much territory a man might suffer as many perforations as a sieve.

On his left, Thayer, Biddle, and Pugh were staring at him.

A mere thirty fateful feet separated Stanley Dinkle from Flossie Grebs.

On his right, Phipps, Den Uyl, Darlington, even Carberry, stared at him.

He crouched. He shouted. "Cover me!"

They nodded strenuously.

He wondered if, at this very moment, up in Wisconsin, Tipton was doing the milking.

Then as they waited, fingers on triggers, in the lull of battle, as they itched with impatience to extricate themselves, or to be extricated, from their predicament, his men heard from Stanley Dinkle a strange, unwarlike exclamation.

"Ouch!" he cried.

The source of pain was in his nether regions. He had been bitten by a flea, by Willie undoubtedly, the male sibling, for the nip was not so much one of adult encouragement as of boyish deviltry.

In any case, it was effective. For as the troopers watched, open-mouthed, something actuated Stanley Dinkle out of his crouch and around the stone pile into a sortie as athletic as it was intrepid.

He ran as if his life depended on it. And it did. Recollecting its duty, his command covered him wisely but too well. A fusillade rang out from the rubble as the doughty officer made for the estancia, bowlegs pumping. There was no resistance from his front, but from the friendly rear bullets buzzed his ears and smashed adobe shards out of walls and lent incentive to his boots.

Finally, in desperation, in simultaneous assault and escape, he propelled himself upward and forward, his body described an arc, and headfirst, full-length, pistol extended from an arm, he hurtled through the air and through the window into the lair of the enemy. The instant his trajectory carried him over the windowsill he commenced to fire with such rapidity that in the split second before return to earth he got off all seven rounds from his weapon in as many directions.

The ensuing several minutes were a period of utter hecticity.

Lieutenant Dinkle landed upon an object with an impact which knocked the wind out of him.

Rising to one knee, attempting to reload his automatic and regain his breath, he discovered that the object which had broken his fall was a wooden case of brand new Ingersoll watches.

Just as he recognized case and contents as having earlier been displayed on a counter in the general store at Edhogg, he was bowled over by a reinforcement.

Hearing the shots and believing his commander at bay inside the estancia, Corporal Phipps had dashed from the safety of the rubble and sailed valiantly through the window to the rescue.

Rising, Dinkle and Phipps were both battered to the earthen floor by still another savior. Following their example, the gallant Thayer, then Biddle, Carberry, Pugh, Den Uyl, and Darlington flung themselves one by one through the window into the fray, so that shortly the room was an unsoldierly melee of bodies, bruises, oaths, and Springfields.

When they were unraveled, a furious Dinkle shut them up by gesturing at the loot of watches and indicating the doorway to the adjoining room. Tiptoeing to it, he was about to reconnoiter when the impetuous Carberry pushed past him and sprayed four rounds from his relic six-shooter through the aperture.

Three chickens rocketed to the ceiling, unscathed but squawking terror.

Flushed by the fever of war, burning to close with the enemy in mortal throe, rifles and pistols at the ready, the Americans charged through a hail of feathers into the next room—and the next—and the next—to encounter only a scatter of cooking utensils, a litter of empty bottles, and the toppled wall at the other side of El Cuervo.

They halted, blowing hard, glaring questions at each other, completely consternated.

Where was the foe which but minutes before had delivered deadly volleys at them from these very rooms?

What had become of the unfortunate female in their clutches?

How could Contreras & Co. have flown the coop?

"The corral!" shouted the CO.

They followed him pell-mell up, then down the adobe debris and approaching the crude enclosure of cactus stopped short.

There, penned and in good condition, were the six Morgans stolen from them the night of the raid on Fort Dinkle, together with three piebald Mexican ponies. And there, ranged along the rim of the corral, were nine saddles.

A cheer started from the throats of the Philadelphians, only to die upon their lips.

For it was superseded by a sound incredible but unmistakable—the trumpeting of two brass-belled, hand-operated Klaxon horns.

The Tin Lizzie Troop needed no command. It raced en masse around the ranch house to stumble—to slow—to stand unhinged and undone by the sight upon the ridge.

"Nooooooo!" howled Stanley Dinkle.

It was an elemental howl, the natal protest uttered by every human infant welcomed into a barbarous world by a slap upon the buttocks.

Along the ridge toward the east sped two Model T's, spewing dust and honking. In each was a bevy of bandidos waving exuberant sombreros, while in the tonneau of "Olivia," the rear Ford, surrounded by her captors and clearly visible in the morning sunlight, was the figure of a woman. "Henrietta's" driver wore a checkered vest and a derby hat.

29

The Fate of Flossie Grebs

The Tin Lizzie Troop stood like louts. Had the motion picture genius D. W. Griffith, creator last year of *The Birth of a Nation,* appeared at that moment to swear that what they saw was not reality but a scene from one of his epic spectacles, a serving of celluloid applesauce, they could not have been consoled.

"I will be damned by God," whispered their commander, speaking for the lot of them.

I will resign my commission before they take it, decided Stanley Dinkle. I will take my Postal Savings and sail back to Zamboanga and lie in the shade of the ylang-ylang trees and smoke opium.

But first I have got to save dear Floss from those fiends.

"They won't get away with it!" he bellowed. "To the corral! Saddle up! We've got horses and we're U. S. Cavalry again and we're going after 'em!"

Around the corner of El Cuervo he headed, the others after him as fast as rage and disgrace would take them, snatching up blankets and bridles and Mexican saddles with high pommels and leather rosettes, and plunged into the corral to catch the six Morgans. The CO cut out one of the ruffians' piebalds for himself, saddled it, and noting "Ace" Carberry standing about as though waiting for a streetcar, ordered him to do likewise.

"Me? On a horse?" the pilot dissented. "Tell it to the Marines!"

"Shoe's on the other foot now, Carberry!" snapped his superior. "I need every gun I can get, so saddle up or we'll tie you on like a sack of wheat! Contact, God damn it, contact!"

Dinkle cut out another Mexicano, slapped on a saddle, and three men maneuvered the pilot onto the cayuse, which had a tendency to be fractious. Then, mounted and ready, they larruped out of the corral and up to the ridgeline, where Dinkle held them. Below and to the desolate east, the Fords were half a mile to the good, and kicking contemptuous dust.

"We've got 'em!" he exulted. "Now we settle the argument once for all—horse or flivver! I say those tin cans won't roll a mile before they fall apart!" He waved an arm. "Full gallop—forward!"

Away booted the Tin Lizzie Troop, down the ridge and onto the level, galloping eastward after Encarnacion Contreras, alias Angel Salcido, his bandidos, and their captive. It was not a particularly merry chase. Extended to their utmost, for half a mile the animals gained upon the autos until the interval between them narrowed to less than three hundred yards, until Biddle and Den Uyl and Thayer were encouraged to get off several potshots from their rifles at the fleeing Fords, taking several in exchange. But fire from a saddle or a tonneau under such conditions could not be effective, and soon the range increased again. After half a mile at top speed, the six Morgans and two Mexicanos had laid their resources upon the altar of duty, and Dinkle halted his troopers. They were bleareyed and grimy, their mounts were lathered, and they were about to lose Carberry. The intrepid aviator had given up any pretense at equitation, and clung to his nag with both arms about its neck and both long legs entwined beneath its belly. Dinkle hauled him upright.

"We can't catch 'em, we'll run these animals into the ground," he admitted angrily. "But those jitneys of yours are bound to bog down any minute, so we'll hang on their tails till they do. I promised you a fight and by Jehu, you'll have one. All right, at the trot—forward!"

They fanned out in line, eight abreast, hatless and relentless. They were more than a mile from El Cuervo, and seven miles out of Delicias, and headed across the state of Coahuila in the general direction of Portugal. Now it was to be a contest not of wits but of endurance, of bone and tendon against iron and rubber, of men versus the machines which man himself had devised. And now it was that the two touring cars exhibited a perversity, indeed a treachery, of which their youthful masters would not have believed them capable. For they did not break down. They ran like tops. Sisters under the skin, and heartless as only creatures of their sex could be, they carried foe as grandly as ever they had friend. And after minutes of swallowing their carbon monoxide the Philadelphians, who had rewarded the brutes with so much affection and repair in the past, began to shake fists and fire occasional imprecations after them.

"Damn you, Olivia!" yelled Pugh. "Boil over!"

But the Fords rambled in high gear and spirits over a smooth, trackless desert floor. Sunlight refracted from quartz and mica shale, sometimes blinding the pursuit.

"It's beyond me," Den Uyl puzzled. "We must have popped off a hundred rounds at the bounders this morning, and didn't hit a thing!"

"Well, neither did they," was Darlington's defense.

Through creosote bush and greasewood the horsemen kept pace, but could not close the gap.

"Spring a leak, Henrietta!" shouted Thayer.

Carberry stood up in the stirrups to relieve his coccyx of the motion of the beast under him. "I am a man of modern times," he groaned. "Day before yesterday I flew, last night I rode in an automobile—what in hell am I doing now?"

They buttoned collars against the dust and shielded eyes from the sun with their hands.

"Why, that blasted mechanic Salcido was actually Contreras!" exclaimed Phipps, just catching on. "We had him right in our laps!"

"You don't say," jeered Biddle, in as evil a temper as the rest. "Tell us another."

Suddenly the two vehicles disappeared, having dropped down into a dry wash along which grew a stand of paloverde trees. Sensing their opportunity, the Americans spurred into a gallop, but as they neared the wash, the flivvers bucketed up the far side and soon drew away, braying derisive horns.

"Up your exhaust pipes, you fickle bitches!" bawled Den Uyl.

Carberry caught up, still pondering his plight. "What am I doing hanging on to a horse? Mon Dieu, I'm going backward!"

Lieutenant Dinkle kept his own counsel, peering ahead to count noses and sombreros. By his dusty reckoning, Contreras had three men with him in the first auto, while four cutthroats kept watch over Flossie Grebs in the second. When it came to a fight, as he was sure it would sooner or later, it would be even-Stephen.

"But why would they want our cars?" demanded Pugh. "They don't even have garages in Mexico!"

"Worth their weight in gold down here, you boob," was Darlington's tart retort.

"Got 'em!" bugled the CO unexpectedly, applying the lash. "Charge!"

The bandits had vanished again into a dry wash, and whooping death and destruction the Americans put spurs to their mounts. When they had drawn nigh the prey by a hundred yards, however, out of the ravine emerged the shifty demoiselles from Detroit, and pulled away again.

"Damn the damned horse!" cursed "Ace" Carberry. "Damn the Nineteenth Century!"

Onward chugged the Fords. Onward trotted the Tin Lizzie Troop, so near and yet so far from the foe, so near and yet so far from the bloody crisis which must result in the salvation of a woman, the vindication of the Philadelphia Light Horse, the justification of the U. S. Cavalry, and the gratification of a nation. Onward they rode, one dogged mile, then two, until the Fords nosed into a third dry wash. This time a skeptical Dinkle gave no order to advance, preferring to spare the animals. But this time, when the flivvers debouched from the other side of the wash, "Olivia," in the rear, was observed to stop, and a despairing prayer of steam to issue from her radiator.

There was commotion in her tonneau. "Henrietta" backed up to her. Bandidos ran from her to the lead Ford and scrambled aboard and her gears clashed as Contreras got her under way once more, leaving "Olivia" behind.

No need for orders now! The Tin Lizzie Troop was already in motion, pounding headlong into the dry wash, across the gravel bottom, and over the far bank to pull up, animals rearing, beside the abandoned auto and its passenger.

"Flossie!" cried the CO. "I mean, Miss Grebs!"

But she did not seem to know her name.

She sat in the rear seat. Her feet were bare, but she wore the same patched pants and galluses and sleeveless shirt. Her long hair was disheveled. Her hands were not bound. Her homely face was expressionless. She sat stiffly, by no sign acknowledging the arrival of her samaritans. Beside her, on the floor, was the cardboard suitcase left there when the jitneys were parked behind the ridge above El Cuervo.

"I hope you're as glad to see us as we are to see you!" the CO continued, trying to bridle his voice.

She did not seem to hear. He dismounted slowly, stepped slowly to the touring car. "Miss Grebs," he said. "I'm Lieutenant Dinkle. Don't you remember me?"

The horses stomped and snuffed and "Olivia" sighed steam and those were the only sounds.

"Ahem," said the officer. "This is too bad."

Enlisted men and aviator looked the other way. "It's her mind, sir," blurted Thayer. "After all she's been through."

From a pocket Dinkle took his necktie, examined it briefly, then put it back.

"You go on after them," he said apologetically, speaking from the side of his face. "I'll stay here a few minutes and try to bring her to. Drive them up a hill if you can. These gas buggies get fuel by gravity, from tank to carburetor. Drive them up a steep hill and they'll stall. But if you manage it, don't attack. Wait for me." He ran a hand through his carrot hair. "Phipps, you're in charge. Is that all right, Carberry?"

The pilot nodded. "Sure is. Dink, I am sorry as hell about this."

"Thank you. Very well, Phipps."

"Yes, sir. They'll pay for this, sir. And, Lieutenant, we're sorry too."

"Thank you."

30

"Squad to the Pistol Attack!"

They set out at a fast trot—seven horsemen of some kind of apocalypse. If they were clad in olive drab, they were shrouded in horror. If they had been relentless before, they were obsessed now. If the expedition into Mexico had been a motorized monkeyshine until today, this turn of events made of it a deadly business. The game, and the party, were over at last. The seven were at war.

A quarter of a mile ahead, the Model T showed its heels, mocking them in and out of dry washes despite a load of eight bandidos and a bad conscience.

The Americans rode in silence except for the click of pebbles cast from hooves like dice and the sharp breathing of the animals. They would ride to the dreaded realms of Pluto, if need be, or to the Pearly Gates. They cared not a fig for courts-martial now, or the prospects of cavalry as a branch of service, nor even the approbation of their ancestors. They had seen a woman rendered speechless, perhaps mindless. And as they took up the pursuit across the burning plain, Thayer thought of his betrothed, Phipps of his wife, Carberry of the girls he'd found and fondled and forgotten, the others of their sisters, mothers, sweethearts.

The fate of Flossie Grebs stunned them much more than had the mutilated corpse of her father. She was their commander's intended. They recalled the almost adolescent shyness with which, in My Contented Heart the night before, in a last-straw effort to persuade the pilot to sacrifice his aeroplane, he had displayed the finery he'd bought for her in El Paso, and the reluctance with which he had confessed his love. They recalled with remorse their initial harassment of Stanley Steamer, with gratitude his arrival in Delicias to deliver them from their own incompetence, with pleasure the handshakes offered and accepted in tequila brotherhood, with wonder his projectile leadership at El Cuervo. In their estimation the worm had turned indeed. The tarantula had become a comrade-in-arms. Manly Stanley was a friend. And in their breasts the young men took a solemn pledge upon their manhood itself: that before the sun had reached its zenith on this day, they would avenge their friend.

"Look!" shouted Pugh.

Otherwise occupied, they had not noticed the terrain. Along their front, from horizon to horizon, reared a ridge similar to that along which they had waited above the estancia. The Ford began to climb it, and as they strained their eyes, slowed perceptibly—slowed and stalled.

Their hearts beat faster. A figure leaped from the flivver, ran to the radiator to crank, then scurried to a running board.

Again the auto essayed the incline, and promptly stalled again.

In the law of gravity, combined with the innocence of her fueling system, "Henrietta" had met her match. Encarnacion Contreras was hoist with his own mechanical petard.

"They're ours, Light Horse!" cried Biddle. "Let's go!"

They licked off into a gallop. It seemed too good to be true. From five to four to three hundred yards the range closed.

Bandidos piled out of the Model T and took defensive positions on either side of it, kneeling. Sunlight ricocheted from rifle barrels.

At two hundred yards the first shot was fired at the Americans. It cracked overhead, causing them to slow and mill and muddle in circles. Now that the hour was actually at hand, the moment, for the life of them they did not know what to do. They glared at Phipps.

"In line—in line!" he yelled, for lack of anything else, and they gigged into line abreast of each other.

"Lex" Phipps, aged twenty-four, mature and proud of

his maturity, responsible and overwhelmed by his responsibility, had not the slightest doubt what his decision must be. He must obey orders, which were, in the event Contreras was brought to bay, not to attack but to await his commanding officer. This is the Fourteenth day of May, he thought, in the year nineteen and sixteen.

"Squad to the Pistol Attack!"

He disbelieved his own voice.

"Draw pistols!"

They drew.

"Forward, charge!"

31

Stanley and Flossie

"Flossie?"

When she did not respond, he tied his Mexicano pony to "Olivia's" steering wheel.

"Flossie?" he tried again. "Don't you remember me? This is Stanley. Stanley Dinkle."

He walked twice around the car, pacing off the enormity of his problem as he might have the length and breadth of a barn. Finally he stepped again to the Ford, opened a rear door, took the woman by a hand, and, tugging, indicated his wish that she get out. She complied. He led her along the bank of the dry wash into the shade of a small paloverde tree and sat her down. Then he noticed that her hands and bare feet were dirty.

Returning to the auto, he opened the suitcase, found his shaving mug, raised one side of the hood, opened the petcock, filled the mug with hot water from the radiator, closed the petcock, and mug in one hand, suitcase in the other, walked to the tree and washed her face and feet. She let him like a weary child. He began to understand that this was what she had been reduced to.

"Well, well, this is a crime and a shame," he said, seating himself beside her. "We won't talk about what they did to you. It must've been pretty low-down. And they had no cause to. They could've let me have you the way you were. I don't have much else."

Since it was spring, there were yellow blossoms in the tree. Bees toiled at them.

He thought it best to change the subject. "But look what

I do have, Floss," he said, opening the suitcase and lifting out the dress. "Ain't this a peach? And look, a hat, too, a Gage, the best there is." He held up the fedora. "You wouldn't believe the trouble I got into in El Paso. I started with these and a gushy clerk got to selling me doodads and I went the whole hog. A hundred thirty-three dollars and some cents."

She stared at dress and hat but did not see them. In desperation he emptied the suitcase, ticking off the price of each item because, being a woman, he thought she'd be interested—hauling out corset and cotton vest and shoes and bloomers and making a heap of them in her lap. But when at last he understood that they meant nothing to her, that she recognized them neither as garments nor gifts, he shook his head. "Well, well," he said, and packed them away again in the case.

He drew up his knees and hugged them. Flossie Grebs was lost to him as surely as she was found. "It's her mind, sir," Thayer had blurted, but it was not that entirely. Animal men had robbed her of more than a mind. She had never really known a mother. With her father dead, and the mules, all she had to show for thirty-one years of drudge and dirt and tin cans and Sir Walter Scott was spunk and a raucous, shotgun chastity. She must have fought like a catamount to keep them, must have bitten and clawed and screamed, but when they were gone, when she was finally raped of spirit and old maidenhood, Flossie Grebs had pitiful little left but her homeliness.

After a time he hitched closer to her and took one of her sledgehammer hands in his. "Here's what we'll do, Floss," he said gently. "We'll take you home with us, to Fort Dinkle. And I'll tend you till you're well again." This was cartainly not the time to mention her lack of kinfolk. "Why, you'll be up on your hind legs again quicker than greased lightning, Floss. Same way with a good horse—use him too hard and he'll play out on you, he's only human. But rest him and feed him and in a day or two he's full of oats again. Well, you will be too, girl, I promise, because I'll take crackerjack care of you."

He squeezed her hand. "And now, Floss, the time's come to tell you the worst about me. The long and short of it is, I'm pretty poor pickings. I've been a second lieutenant eight years. I can't even control my own men—not these high-faluters anyway." He scowled. "Floss, there's naught to Stanley Dinkle but beans and dreams."

Above them, swarms of oblivious bees battened on the yellow blossoms.

"You think about it, girl," he said. "Because what I'm leading up to is—when you're sound again, and if you'll have me after what I've told you—well." He made himself smile. "I mean, I'd like us to get married."

He leaned forward and looked inquiringly into her face, at the mole on her big chin and the bent nose and finally into her green eyes. "Would you like that, Floss?" he whispered. "Would it make you happy to marry me?"

Gone were the glints of gold under the green. The ponds were stagnant. There was nothing in her eyes now. The proposal she had waited thirty-one years to hear she could not comprehend. And in his breast, something was crushed like a lump of ore.

He dropped her hand, sprang up, and jumping suddenly, caught hold of a tree branch, tore it free of the trunk, and began to lambaste the tree with it, thrashing blindly until the bees buzzed away and a gauze of blossoms floated down upon her. When grief was exorcised and fury spent, he leaned against the tree like a small boy lost and stricken.

"I wish I knew why this had to happen," he said brokenly, to the woman under the tree. "I never loved anybody before, but oh, dearie, how I do love you!"

Locating his handkerchief, Stanley Dinkle blew his nose. A little ashamed of himself, he took Flossie Grebs by the hand again and led her back to the Ford. He had just settled her in the rear seat and stowed the suitcase beside her when, from a distance, he heard a staccato of pistol fire.

"Oh my God," he said. Untying the pony from the steering wheel, he eased into the saddle so as not to alarm her. "You sit right here and rest, Floss," he soothed. "They've got themselves into trouble and I have to get 'em out. Everything's going to be all right. You sit here and wait till I come back, there's a good girl."

32

On a May Morning in Mexico

Thus, on a May morning in Mexico, the Tin Lizzie Troop undertook a Mounted Pistol Attack.

If it acted contrary to orders, let it be said in extenuation that it acted upon instinct. For these were National Guardsmen, after all, green as grass but called to duty in a national emergency. They were young. They were rendered rabid by tradition and noble intent. They foamed at the mouth with war. This was the maneuver in which they had been most thoroughly trained, moreover, and which they believed to be most effective, not to say dramatic. In any event, although there is evidence that the War Department was later at considerable pains to expunge every reference to it, however indirect, from official records, it was the first Mounted Pistol Attack ever executed by United States Cavalry against an armed enemy.

What they learned within yards was that the real run was more fun than the dry, even more tonguebiting, heartbursting, loinlocking than a gallop down a parade ground in Texas to spray blanks at targets tacked onto mesquite limbs.

So did the animals. Worn though they were, they fairly exploded up the ridge. Wind whistled from their nostrils. Their great wet rib cages ballooned and collapsed like bellows.

Up the ridge charged the line of troopers, leaning low and forward in the saddles, rein hands clamped on the horses' necks as they had been taught, right hands gripping the heavy automatics and extending over the horses' heads between the ears, the aviator with a fistful of mane and aping the others as best he could.

Suddenly they aimed at living men. They were fired upon by living men.

Over the trample of hooves they heard themselves halloo like women.

The .45's cracked.

The minds of few mortals can tolerate a collision between their small two-legged selves and the thundering apparatus that is cavalry. When the line was forty yards from the Ford and the foe, the eight bandidos could bear no more. They swayed to their feet and threw down rifles and raised arms high and from huge holes in their faces screamed surrender.

It was too late. It was too late by many a story, many a song, many a generation. No power here or in the heretofore could have checked the momentum of the Tin Lizzie Troop—neither command of superior nor intercession by grandfathers or great-grandfathers nor ordinance of the City of Brotherly Love.

As though they rode against the Hessians, they loomed upon the unarmed Mexicans and shot them down from the muzzle. An agile "Bid" Biddle shot one from one side and a second from the other. "Ace" Carberry put a round from his six-shooter into a forehead, the heavy ball striking with such impact that the skull was shattered and a glistening mass of exposed brain pulsed as the bandit fell. "Phew" Pugh and "Stew" Darlington killed men with gray hair and gray stubble on their cheeks. "Freddy" Den Uyl's target was a plug-ugly with a mustachio so thick and virile that it seemed artificial. The gallant "Luce" Thayer sent two rounds into the breast of a youth his own age. A boy of sixteen or so fell to his knees and turned his face upward to "Lex" Phipps, his mouth open wide in supplication, and Phipps fired into the open mouth. They passed then through hosts of dust and hauling leather, rearing the beasts upon their haunches, wheeled and leaned again and rode back, still firing, emptying the magazines of pistols into bodies writhing, bodies already lifeless, in a gluttony of slaughter feasting the need which peace starves and only war may feed.

33

"Give a Little Credit to Your Dead"

Lieutenant Stanley Dinkle arrived at the foot of the field of battle on the gallop, dismounted, tied his transportation to a cactus, and marched at a brisk pace, then slowly, then more slowly up the ridge. His shirt was dark. The heat and glare of sun were vicious now. Behind him, out on the desert, dust devils tottered along like old soldiers, senile, brown, and solemn. He first inspected his command. Not one of them could face him.

H. Horace Biddle and Frederick Den Uyl stood near the stalled "Henrietta," gripping pistols still, as though they could not let go. They stared westward from the ridge but saw nothing.

Alexander Phipps sat on a running board studying an empty .45 magazine.

William Pugh III held the reins of his Morgan and considered a lizard.

Lucien Thayer had removed his leather puttees. Now he strapped them on again.

Stewart Darlington knelt near a boulder, his eyes closed, his lips moving.

Edgar Carberry bent over a front fender of the Ford, vomiting quietly.

The CO looked them up and down and sideways for a full minute. "Well, well," he said. "If this ain't a fine gang of goo-goos."

He walked next to the fallen and examined each one, turning the corpses over when necessary. Encarnacion Contreras, the bandit jefe, and Angel Salcido, the self-styled "mecánico terrífico" who had restored the autos in Delicias with shoe leather, were indeed one and the same.

Salcido, Contreras, whatever his true name might be, had been shot through the heart, as well as elsewhere, and his checkered vest was bloody. His five-and-dime teeth protruded from his mouth. Three of the bandidos were husky villains in the prime of life and evil. Two were elderly peon types who, until the Revolution, had undoubtedly been content to plant corn and predict the weather. One was a youth as thin as a rail, whose shoulders, even in death, seemed to sag under a bandolier of ammunition. The last was a muchacho who couldn't have been more than sixteen if he was a day.

Dinkle mused alone. Every body was riddled, as full of holes as if used for target practice. He noticed, too, that none of them clutched weapons—that a motley of rifles lay in fact some distance from them, as though thrown.

He strode back to his troopers. None of them had moved a muscle. He ran fingers over his head, dislodging a paloverde blossom.

"I asked you not to attack," he said. "I told you to wait for me." He addressed his non-com. "Looking them over, Phipps, none of them has a weapon in his hands. Did they throw down weapons?"

The corporal remained on his running board.

"I asked you a question, Phipps. On your feet and speak up. Did they drop their guns?"

Phipps rose unsteadily. He was sunburned, but his pallor was that of the dead, and his eyes were blank. "Yes, sir, they did."

"In other words, they tried to surrender. Well, did they?"

"Yes, sir."

"And you shot them down. You butchered them."

There was no response. But something tortured in the officer's tone slapped Phipps out of his state of shock, and the others as well. Biddle and Den Uyl turned round. Pugh dropped his reins. Thayer came to a kind of attention. Darlington ceased to pray, Carberry to vomit. Moments ago they had been unable to face him. Now they could not unfasten their eyes. They watched his keg chest inflate, his shoulders thicken, his spine stretch and elevate him a full three inches. They did not know what he might do because he did not know himself. Stanley Dinkle was a man about to break.

He began to walk on bandy legs around and through and about them. He was stalking them, or himself. Suddenly, beside the Model T, he brought a fist down on its hood in a tremendous blow.

"Do your pizzles stand up straight with pleasure?" he shouted at them, his face contorted out of recognition. "Do your hearts swell with manly pride?"

He banged the hood again.

"Dear God Almighty, d'you think she wanted you to do this? D'you think I did?"

He stepped back, bent over, and scooping up two handsful of sand and stones, hurled them at his men.

"Piss-ants! Polo-players! Killers! What the hell's the difference—red blood or blue? You're as rotten as they are! You stink the way they stink!"

He swiveled and pounded on the automobile again with force enough to injure his hands, hammering at it as insanely as he had thrashed the tree over a Flossie Grebs who did not know him.

"You wanted war! You wanted war and now you've got it! I told you!" he yelled. "So smell it, God damn you! Smell it, taste it, roll in it! How d'you like it? Now you've killed—now you're soldiers—and how d'you like yourselves, gentlemen? Gentlemen! Gentle-men?"

His shouting stopped. So silent was it on the hillside that the entire Tin Lizzie Troop heard something else, or thought they did. They listened.

It was the terrible unison ticking, in the pockets of the dead, of eight Ingersoll watches.

34

The Philadelphia Light Horse Depart Fort Dinkle

In the early afternoon, when the last patrols along the U.S. side of the river had returned, they cleaned out the Sibley tent and loaded "Henrietta" and "Olivia" with everything but ivory, apes, and peacocks. After luggage carriers and tonneaus were chock-full, they brought their Morgans from the pecan grove and tied them behind the autos. Then they waited about like warts, passing diffident time until the CO dismissed them and bade them farewell. Their month in the field was up, they were due that day to rejoin their comrades at Camp Stewart, they tingled at the prospect of conjunction once more with their own kind, and the cultural pleasures of El Paso.

Lieutenant Dinkle, who had been observing this process from his purple headquarters, emerged from it, and Corporal Phipps lined them up and snapped them to. The officer gave them a cursory once-over—Phipps, Biddle, Den Uyl, Thayer, Pugh, and Darlington. They passed muster. Their custom-tailored uniforms were washed and pressed, their mustaches trimmed and romanticized again, although the gilt cords about their hats had assumed a veteran tarnish. On the whole they seemed an older, sadder, but much wiser bunch—which was exactly what duty in the field was intended to accomplish.

"At ease," he said. "Well, I hope you make it on those leather bearings."

"We will, sir," promised Pugh slyly. "They say a flivver never lets you down."

"So they say," replied the officer.

"Sir, we'd like to leave you a token of our appreciation," said Phipps. "For all you've done for us."

"Oh?"

Phipps and Den Uyl turned to one of the cars, and lifting out the Victrola and a stack of records, piled them in his arms.

"Well, well," he said, obviously touched. "Thank you very much."

"Could it be a wedding present, too, sir?" asked the gallant Thayer.

"Of course it could. Miss Grebs is going to be fine and dandy any day now." He had an idea. "Let me see. I'm sure she'd like to reciprocate and so would I. Just a minute. Put up a mallet while I'm gone, will you?"

He carried his gifts into the house, and when he came back they had lashed a polo mallet to one of "Henrietta's" windshield uprights.

"Here," he said, "you need a proper guidon." And to the mallet he tied a pair of pongee bloomers.

In the window of the purple adobe house, something moved. She was watching.

The Philadelphia Light Horse were heated with gratitude and chilled with guilt. Did she know, despite her condition of mind, what he had given them? Had they the right to accept a souvenir as personal as this? To evade the questions, they mumbled hasty thank-you's and good-by's and shook his hand, warmly, one by one, then cranked up the muddy but invincible Model T's, hustled aboard, and rattled away along the sand road, bloomers flapping, around the pecan grove and out of sight, wishing him good luck with an emotional salute from their Klaxons.

Stanley Dinkle went up to his porch, set the Victrola and records on the cot, removed boots and shirt since the day was hotter than a fiddler's bitch, and sat down to have still another go at his article for the *Cavalry Journal* entitled "Selecting the Service Mount." But he was unable to concentrate. Her presence beyond the door, inside the single room, laid heavy hand upon his spirit. The lave of the Rio Grande fifty yards from his door and the lament of leaves in the pecan trees were also melancholy reminders. Rather than good riddance to bad rubbish, to his surprise he was gripped with regret that the Philadelphians were gone.

I am lonesome already, admitted Stanley Dinkle. I am lonesomer than Billy Sunday in a brewery.

I wish I had Conchita here. Wouldn't I wind her up, poise my needle, find that groove, and play "The Stars and Stripes Forever!"

Forgive me, Flossie, dear.

When he had finished eating out their souls and asses after the carnage on the hillside in Coahuila, they started the stalled "Henrietta" and returned to "Olivia" and Flossie Grebs, who sat, in a state resembling rigor mortis, exactly where she had been left. "Olivia" being cooled off by now, they cranked her up and in the two touring cars, to which the Morgans were tied, retraced the route of the chase after Contreras & Co. They paused at El Cuervo only long enough to find their hats, then drove the additional six miles to Delicias like a cortege. What awaited them there, in the plaza, stopped the Tin Lizzie Troop as abruptly as a puncture. "Ace" Carberry soared to his cowboy boots in "Henrietta," a-gape. "What in the holy hell—" he demanded.

On the bandstand, her wings extended out two sides, her tail from a third, her Paragon propeller from the fourth, his Jenny, sole survivor of the 1st Aero Squadron, had been placed on public exhibition. But she was like no other Curtiss JN-3 on earth. The same simple, devout citizens who had denuded her of fabric had recovered her wings and fuselage in multicolored strips of this and patches of that, so that she was now a red-green-blue-orange-cerise-fuchsia phenomenon as reassuring and irrefutable as a rainbow.

Perfecto Lopez, the mayor, provided an explanation. "Joo see, señores," he told the soldiers, "thees ees why I wan' joor aeroplano. Delicias ees a poor place. For five years we are rob' by Rurales, Federales, Villistas, Maderistas, Obregonistas, Carranzistas, an' other bastardistas. An' we don' have too many turistas. But now we got sometheen' they don' have een Chihuahua or Sonora or een la

Ciudad de Mejico. We got an aeroplano. The *gente,* the people, they weel come from all roun' to see eet, they weel eat an' drink an' buy, we weel be reech. So we have change' our name. Thees town ees Delicias no más." He turned to the bandstand and removed his sombrero. The Americans took off their campaign hats. "Now," said he in grateful, reverent voice, "now we are Caballo del Dios. Now we are call' 'Horse of God.' "

Tugging on his boots, Stanley Dinkle banged out the screen door, strode to the picket line in the pecan grove, fed Hassan a handful of oats, scratched his ears, returned to the porch, and seated himself once more at his article, to no avail whatever.

I am going bughouse, he thought.

It's been five days now, and no change. She sits in there like a bump on a log. She hasn't made a sound, she still doesn't know me, I expect she don't even know herself. I feed her and wash her and would have to dress her if she didn't sleep in her clothes, but only the Good Lord can help her in the attic, which is where she needs it.

What'll I do with her if she stays this way? No father, no folks that I know of. I can't send her home to mine—they won't even have me. What'll become of her if I'm ever reassigned out of this place? Shall I leave her to starve? Shall I put her out of her misery in the river like a sack of kittens?

Oh, Floss, you are only six feet away from me on the other side of that wall, but you might as well be in Heaven tickling a harp for all the use we are to each other!

For her sake, I will quit thinking about sex.

The Tin Lizzie Troop covered the thirty-odd miles from Delicias back to the border in less than seven hours. Like hayburners heading for the stable after a hard day behind the plow, the Fords followed their noses gladly and efficiently, incurring only six boilovers, two clogged oil lines, and one recalcitrant timer. Over those thirty-odd miles Flossie Grebs did not utter a word. When they reached the river at dusk, the driving honors having been shared, the CO was behind the wheel of an impatient "Henrietta." Determined to display his prowess as a chauffeur, he ignored all suggestions that the animals be employed to tow them across the stream, and backing up to get a flying start in high gear, assaulted the Rio Grande at breakneck speed, only to have his jitney founder midway of the flood.

"Damnation," said Stanley Dinkle, pitching his pencil into a corner of the porch.

Sometimes, he confessed, I am glad my boys cut down those bastardistas. After what they did to my darling. An eye for an eye. Still, two wrongs don't make a right.

They were snobs and highbinders, but I miss 'em. But I miss my Flossie more, the way she was. My life is a grave now, and my heart lies a-moldering in it.

In the dawning after their arrival he left Phipps in charge of Patrol Post #2, asking him to keep watch over Miss Grebs as well, and lit out with Carberry for Edhogg, where he was informed by Harley and Mrs. Offus, who were rebuilding, that the telephone line to Marathon was still inoperable. Luckily a rancher happened by in a buckboard, and the two officers hitched a ride with him, Carberry to entrain for Columbus and his squadron, Dinkle to contact General Funston, who was waiting there with the 8th Cavalry and the gents of the press to dash south in pursuit of Contreras—and who, furthermore, must by then have been stark raving at the delay. But when they attained Marathon, to Dinkle's bafflement no Funston swatted flies, no 8th Cavalry champed at the bit, no pack of reporters growled over a bone of umbrage. He telephoned Fort Bliss, was put through to the Commanding General, Department of the Southwest, and at last—at long, long last—told his tale.

It was time then for cavalryman and airman to say their fare-thee-well's—an uncomfortable chore for both. Waiting on the platform of the El Paso & Southwestern R.R. station, Carberry stood on one boot, Dinkle on the other. For old times' sake, Carberry hooked thumbs in his gun belt and struck a Wild West pose.

"Guess this is aw revoor."

"Guess so."

"War's hell, Dink. But remember, women are like street-cars—always another one along."

It was a low blow, though unintentional, and Carberry disgusted himself. "Good thing my mouth's big enough to fit my foot." He shook his head. "Just between you and me and the lamppost, what're you gonna do with her, Dink?"

"I don't know. Marry her for sure, as soon as she's capable."

"Think she ever will be?"

"She'll be fine and dandy in a few days. I hope. Right now she just sits in that room with her hands in her lap. Now and then she'll get up and look out the window like she's expecting someone to come get her—Contreras, her pa, whoever. But she's got to come around. If she doesn't, I dunno. There's nobody to take her. I couldn't put her in an—institution. I just couldn't."

His fellow officer peered down the track. "Train's late. Say, while we're waiting, care to amble across the boulevard and wet the old whistle?"

"No, thanks."

"Shucks, come along. Misery loves company."

Dinkle gave in, and together they crossed the street and entered The Pray-For-Us, Marathon's most elegant and only saloon, which was being patronized that morning by two dogs, a one-armed barfly, and a woman with a long past and a short future. Carberry ordered a shot of imported rotgut, Dinkle a ginger beer.

"The fact is," admitted the former, tossing off his potion, "I hate to go back to the squadron. First Aero—that's a hot one. All we can put in the air is a good spit, thanks to me. I tell you, everytime I think of Jenny sitting on that bandstand, all dolled up and no place to go, it brings a tear to my eye."

Dinkle was reassuring. "Maybe you did her a kindness, Ace. If you'd flown 'er back, she might be in bits and pieces by now. This way, with the dry air down there, she might sit in that plaza for fifty years, and stay in fine shape."

One of the dogs slunk out the door.

"You reckon?" But the aviator was only slightly consoled. Ordering another shot, he arranged himself at a table and beckoned to his drinking companion. "Don't know what got into me, on that hill," he confided gloomily. " 'Thou shalt not kill,' the Good Book says, but there's blood on my hands now, and someday I'll pay for it."

"War's hell, Ace."

The other dog left the saloon.

The two lieutenants sat in sepulchral silence until, without prior notice, Edgar Carberry tore off his helmet and leaned over the table, hands twisting the orange silk of his now-dishonored plume. In his eyes was a foreboding and a terror his friend would never have predicted. "I know how I'll pay for it, Dink," groaned the daredevil pilot. "We'll be in the big fracas soon, as sure as we're sitting here—I'll be over there flying another Jenny—some Heinie will get me in his sights—I'll be out of ammo and signal him—but instead of being a gent and letting me go, he'll dive, Spandaus blazing—ah-ah-ah-ah-ah—he'll shoot me down the way I shot down that bandido—and that'll be Taps for Ace Carberry. I dream about it, I wake up with the cold sweats. That's the price, Dink. I'm going to die for what I've done—die—and I don't want to. Dink, I'm scared stiff. What'll I do?"

Dinkle was touched. He searched for words, letting his look linger on the barfly, whose right, or drinking, arm was missing. "I'm sorry," he said. "But you're not alone, Ace. We've all come out of Mexico different men than we went in. Maybe we can try to make amends. I mean, try to be better from now on, to do better—"

Just then, across the street, the El Paso express clanged into the station. He rose, expecting Carberry to do likewise, but the aviator remained seated, tossed off his shot, and ordered a third.

"But that's your train!" remonstrated Dinkle.

"You said it."

"What're you going to do?"

"Sit here and get spifflicated."

"Oh." Dinkle nodded, as though that explained everything. "Well, I've got to be up and at 'em, Ace. Happy landings."

They shook hands.

"Toodle-oo, mon ami. See you in church."

The pilot bit his lip. "Goddammit, good-by and good luck to you and her and congratulations I hope."

On the way out of The Pray-For-Us, the officer paused at the bar, where the unfortunate female had fallen into a stupor. "Conchita?"

She raised her head. Her features, such as they were, set themselves in a concrete, commercial smile.

"Thas' me, sport," said she.

"I knew it," said the cavalryman darkly, and quick-stepped out the door to the stable, where he reunited himself with a fat and sassy Hassan. Together they hit the trail back to Edhogg. The CO had learned from bitter experience not to absent himself from his command any longer than friends and necessity dictated.

"Damnation," said Stanley Dinkle, and gave up his article for the day. He heard her moving about inside the house. Hauling on his boots again he went outdoors and wandered his acreage, among the pecans, over the parade ground with its targets tacked to mesquite limbs, past the yellow pyramidal tent, and through the stand of river cane, where, accommodating habit to convenience, he lowered his breeches and seated himself in the pink pagoda. Here, hidden from the world, he could think clearly. Here, in sylvan, Sears, Roebuck refuge, was surcease from his cares.

The telephone conversation with Frederick Funston had been a shocker. The expedition into Coahuila was an almost unqualified success, he told the general. Contreras & Co. had been wiped out to the last bandit and the American woman salvaged, with the loss of only one aeroplane. The raid on Edhogg was revenged, the Fords were out of Mexico and sight, cavalry dash and initiative had won the day again, and the mission given Lt. Stanley Dinkle had therefore been completed. Capital, approved the general. However, the heroics would have to be hushd up, he regretted to say, for neither he nor the Army dared risk a line in the papers which might put some damned newshawk on the scent of any damned Tin Lizzies. He had no intention of giving Henry Ford an advertising advantage over his competitors. And besides, the Edhogg ruckus had blown over by now, John J. Pershing was making the headlines down in Chihuahua, where he'd had a couple of bang-up fights with Villa's bullyboys. No, he was sorry, but he, Dinkle, would have to take solace in his, Funston's, personal but unofficial commendation. Sic, sighed the second lieutenant, hanging the receiver on the hook, transit gloria.

Hoisting his breeches, buttoning up en route, Stanley Dinkle stumped through the cane to the porch of his HQ. There, spying the Vic on his cot, he wound it up, took the top record from the stack, placed it on the turntable, and angling the horn, noticing the bullet hole through it, poised the needle, found the grove, and treated himself to a tenor's lachrymose version of the popular "When the Black Sheep Returns to the Fold." During the second chorus, however, he chanced to turn—and almost jumped out of his boots. She stood in the doorway. It was the first time she had set foot or face outside the cell into which shock had locked her. She stared wide-eyed at the instrument. Flossie Grebs had never before seen or heard a talking machine.

35

Music Hath Charms to Soothe the Babylonians

He waited till the music stopped, then lifted the needle and shut off the Vic. She remained in the doorway.

"Well, well, Flossie girl," he said gently. "If you aren't a sight for sore eyes. Do you know what this is? It's called a talking machine, or phonograph. This one's called a Victrola."

He waited again. "Would you like to see how it works?" he coaxed. "Come here and I'll show you."

But she wouldn't budge. Her expression was one of awe rather than curiosity, something like that, he imagined, on the faces of aboriginals given their initial gander at glass beads or the effects of gunpowder—but it was at least an expression, the first she had managed. It gave him an idea. Take toys to a child and it would play. Or, as the poet says, music hath charms, etc.

He picked up the machine. "I know what, Floss—let's take it inside. Then you can learn to run it and play music all day long—wouldn't that be nice?"

He started for the door, and she fled at once. He persisted, carrying the phonograph into the house and placing it on the table among some unwashed dishes, then wound it up, brought the stack of records, and put another on the turntable. She had retreated to a corner.

"Now," he smiled. "Let me show you how to wind it up. See this crank?"

She was not persuaded.

"Please, Floss," he begged. "It won't hurt you. Once

you learn how, you can play pretty music to your heart's content—it'll keep you company in here. Please?"

He might as well have been talking goo-goo. Her hair hadn't been combed for days, her patched pants and shirt were food-stained, a torn suspender strap was fastened with a safety pin. He sat wearily down on the chair.

"This is a sad state of affairs," he said. "Girl, what am I ever, ever going to do with you?" He reflected. "Maybe if I went up to Marathon and they had *Ivanhoe* in the library I could read it to you. But I can't leave you alone. And they probably don't have a library in Marathon anyway."

He brooded upon the room he'd taken for granted when he was its occupant—at the greasy pot and pan and kerosene stove and sooty lamp and cases of ammunition and canned rations and the nails in the walls on which were hung his spare shirts and breeches and, on one, the glamorous getup he'd bought for her in El Paso. To be penned in such quartermaster squalor might be preferable to being chained to a bed in an asylum, but that was all you could say for it.

He started the Vic and sat there listening to a snappy orchestral rendition of "Give a Little Credit to Your Dad." She started at the sound, and then, attracted as though by a bauble she was too feminine to resist, edged toward the phonograph. He did not move. She watched the turntable revolve. She bent her head to the horn, listening. Her body began to spasm, almost to sway, to the rhythm of the number.

The record ended, and she shrank again to the far side of the room. "You like that, huh, Floss?" he asked. "Shall I give 'er another spin?"

He rose, rewound the machine, placed the needle, and continued to stand, his back to her, humming. After a few bars he turned.

"Flossie!"

He did a frantic, flabbergasted about-face.

"Flossie, no, please, you mustn't," he choked. He stood at attention, his back to her like a barracks wall. "Flossie, please, it isn't ladylike!"

She was taking off her clothes!

He didn't want to see what or how many. He closed his eyes and petitioned the Almighty. He could cope, he declared, with burned-out bearings, murders, saddle sores, warped props, Conchitas, drunkards, and similar adjuncts of war, but at the present moment, and in his situation, love-sick and a bachelor, he couldn't be expected to cope with the attractions of a female in the Altogether. He asked for strength and purity of mind and body in order not to take advantage. He asked further that Flossie Grebs be forgiven, since she was but a blameless victim of that carnality before which all men bow down now and then. And besides, it was plain that she was nutty as a fruitcake. Amen.

"Flossie, I'm going to turn around now," he told her hoarsely. "I hope you have come to your senses and covered yourself, there's a good girl."

He turned. He stopped turning.

His expression was one of awe rather than curiosity, something like that on her face when she had first seen the miracle of a talking machine, and like that on the faces of simple-minded citizens of Delicias when they had knelt before the miracle of an aeroplane.

Stanley Dinkle witnessed another now. While his back was to her, Flossie Grebs had donned the black velvet fedora with pink ostrich feather, the pink velvet dress with muttonchop sleeves and lace "Bertha," and the Selby high-lace shoes with pointed toes and Cuban heels. Corset, vest, and taffeta petticoats still hung against the wall, while pongee bloomers were on their way to El Paso, but they were superfluous to the tableau.

"Well, well," he said, his tongue thick. "You told me you might be beautiful and you are. You know, the nicest thing anybody ever said to me was what General Scott said in the Philippines. 'Dinkle,' he said, 'I like your style.' Well, Floss, I like yours."

The record ended, the needle scratched.

Swallowing the lump of love in his throat, he rewound the Vic and restarted the music.

He bowed low. "Miss Grebs," he said, "may I have the honor of this dance?"

He came to her with great dignity, and she did not shrink from him. He placed her hand upon his shoulder, put his arm delicately about her waist, and took her other hand. Then, maneuvering his bowlegs and boots to the best of his ability, he instructed her in the rudiments of the foxtrot. No matter that they both seemed to have as many feet as a Ford had pedals. No matter that she was a head taller and had never danced a lick in her life and he was clumsy as a traveling salesman with a pitchfork and reversed her into the table and her fedora fell off. Stanley Dinkle held Flossie Grebs in his arms and there, in his humble purple house, he in BVD top and breeches, she in a trousseau purchased out of Postal Savings, they danced.

The record ended, the needle scratched.

"Floss," he murmured, still holding her, "can you say my name? Please try. It's Stanley. Stan-ley. Can you say it? Stan-ley?"

She tensed. He could not look up at her. She trembled. And then he heard issue from her lips, as from a child's, two sweet, nonsensical syllables:

"Stan. Leee."

His arms entwined about her in gratitude—to science, to modern dance, and to the Philadelphia Light Horse, who had made him a wedding gift indeed. This was the sign he had pined for. Talking machine and foxtrot had planted the seed. The very Twentieth Century he had damned would eventually bless him with her flowering—that and the fertilizer of his love. She might not have all her marbles yet, but she would have soon, this proved it, and that would be the last, best miracle of all.

His eyes were level with the mole on her chin. He dropped them and glimpsed, marvelous 'neath the bodice of her dress, that additional wonder of the world, her Hanging Gardens of Babylon. He felt his expectations rising.

"Oh, dearie," he swore into her neck, "we will fight this out together. You're a miner's daughter and I'm a brave man and we will fight together and win and tie the knot and be snug as two bugs in a rug!"

But then, despite the scratching of the needle, his ears alerted him. "Oh, no," he groaned, hugging his Flossie even tighter. "Not now, not now—"

Someone or something was coming down the sand road from Edhogg. Peeling himself from her, he stepped to the porch to see who or what.

36

The Duquesne Dragoons Report to Fort Dinkle

"Thunder and damnation!" said Stanley Dinkle.

Round the pecan trees chugged two virgin Model T touring cars. Wheel spokes twinkled, sunlight spangled off brass head lamps and radiators, and each auto trailed a string of three pedigreed polo ponies. The tops were down, as were the Fords themselves, almost to their axles, under a ton of baggage and a complement of three military dilettantes. These the officer pegged with one disgusted glance—more silk purses out of which he would be expected to make sows' ears.

He yanked on a clean shirt, looped and tied a necktie. He pinned a gold bar on his collar, dusted his boots with a dirty shirt, clapped on his hat, trimmed it, opened the porch door and marched, box-shouldered and iron-spined, to welcome his new command.

The engines were shut off, but the newcomers continued to sit in their equipages, struck dumb by the beauties of the scene to which Dame Fortune had dispatched them for a month.

"Any non-coms here?" the officer inquired.

"Right you are." One chap lazed over the side and strolled to report, smiling, a lanquid hand extended. "I'm Corporal Cadwalader."

"Corporal. Cadwalader. Sir."

The smile congealed, the hand was withdrawn.

"Sir."

"That's better. Now, you get your men out of those cast-iron butter churns and into formation chop-chop," the

CO proceeded calmly, "or I'll have the hide off you and tanned and cut into a saddle and ride it till you rot."

He waited, whistling an indifferent tune, and when he confronted them again the six were in line and at such stove-poker attention he could hear their sacroiliacs. This time he didn't bother to gauge their green or estimate their height advantage or scorn their haberdashery or critique the sculptures on their upper lips. He merely cleared his throat.

"Ahem. Orders?"

Cadwalader gave him a folded sheet. "Sir."

They were troopers of the Duquesne Dragoons, ostensibly a National Guard outfit from Pittsburgh but actually a society as select and clubby as the Philadelphia Light Horse before them and the Keystone Lancers before them.

"I will call the roll," he said. "Charles T. M. Cadwalader."

"Here, sir."

"Marcus G. Taggart, Jr."

"Here."

"Sir."

"Sir."

"Orlando F. Ewing."

"Here, sir."

"Anthony St. John Smith."

"Here, sir."

"J. Conyngham Hamilton."

"Here, sir."

"Peters D. Dillon IV."

"Here, sir."

He folded away the orders. "Very well." He'd be damned if he'd put them at ease for a while. "My name is Lieutenant Dinkle and I'll be your CO. Our duty here is to defend the United States. We patrol twenty miles of the border and we train. Training will start in the morning." A thought struck him. "I suppose, on your way in from Marathon, you met the Philadelphia Light Horse coming out."

No one let out a peep. "Well, did you?"

"Yes, sir," admitted Cadwalader.

"I thought so. Then I can suppose some other things. That you were informed this place is often referred to as 'Fort Dinkle.' That I am known behind my back as 'Stanley Steamer.' That the Mounted Pistol Attack is more fun than a picnic. And that you also heard a very funny story about my sawing a man in half in the Philippines to get a commission." He paused for effect. "But I'll bet my bottom dollar there's one item they didn't mention. The other morning on a hill down in Coahuila. Well, I won't mention it either. I'm an officer and a gentleman. By act of Congress."

Their eyes wavered. They had seen someone at the window behind him, in the house. They must have heard about her, too. He squinted at the blue, untenanted sky of Texas and pretended not to notice. Folding hands behind him, he began to pace the line, addressing his remarks to a series of smooth, Episcopalian chins.

"You'd better assume I know considerable about you, too. That you've toted along a Victrola, for instance, and your shiny little sabers. That you like to stand Retreat. And that you hate like sin to be stuck in this Godforsaken place when you'd rather be across the Big Pond winning medals and fighting a real war."

He stepped front and center again, facing them. He pulled down his hat brim. "Well, let me tell you something else, gentlemen. Let me stick it so far down your gold-plated gullets you choke on it. You don't know what discipline means. In the next month I intend to teach you. More important, you don't know one dirty, damned thing about war. What it can do to you. What it can cost you. In the next month, maybe—"

He choked. He could not continue. They could not understand why. But how were they to suspect that at this point in his peroration he had suddenly become, under the bland exterior of his breeches, the subject of a flea's attentions? He had utterly forgotten the family which shared with him the abode of his flesh, and he was not so much injured as surprised. For what he felt was a caress rather than a chew, a felicity of female lips in his most erogenous zone. Father, mother, and brother had earlier identified themselves. This was Ethel, the small sister, reminding him by means of her bicuspids.

Of his bride of silence, who must be saved a second time. Of boys upon a hillside sickened by their deeds, and of the boys they would themselves beget, who would one day ask forgiveness after other battles. And finally of all mankind, lorn and bestial, hands red with blood, faces lifted to the stars, begging bread and love and peace and a more merciful God. Suffer the little children to come unto to me, and I will make them soldiers.

A terrible minute of silence ticked away. Then the Duquesne Dragoons dared to sneak stares in his direction. Under the hat brim his face worked in agony. But the six young men before him were as embarrassed as they were amazed. Stanley Homer Dinkle wept.